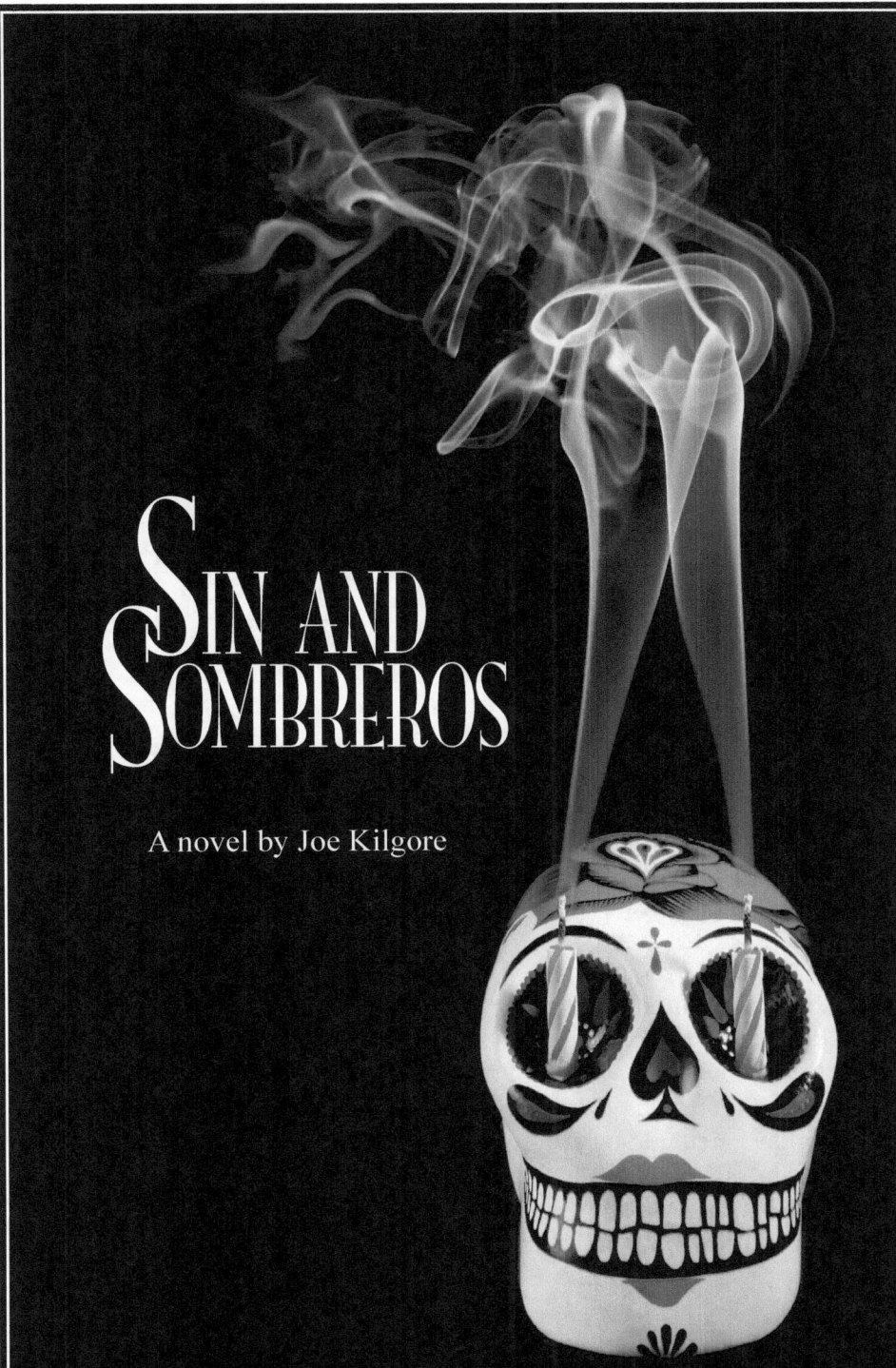

SIN AND SOMBREROS

A novel by Joe Kilgore

Sin And Sombreros
Presented by Jezebel Publishing

ISBN-13: 978-0692275542
ISBN-10: 0692275541

Dedicated to the three amigos:
Heather, Sean, and Lauren.

If you're smart,
there are some jobs you don't take.
Of course, if you're smart,
you're in another line of work.

CHAPTER 1

Ellis woke to a gunmetal morning. You know the kind. A fog shrouded sunrise that begs you to stay in bed. He didn't. That was his first mistake.

Driving to work, he noticed the charcoal skies and wet streets hadn't dampened the entrepreneurial spirit of the rush hour hookers. The ones who saw opportunity in early risers. Pun intended. They worked both sides of the street he always took to his office. Different blocks of course. There's something to be said for professional courtesy.

Ahead, to his right, he noticed a short red Ford engaged in conversation with a tall black stop sign. As he rolled by, her eyes looked toward him to make sure the merger she was negotiating wasn't about to be interrupted. Once they stop they're easy money, and she didn't want anything interfering with a quick fifty bucks. Who does?

Ellis didn't recognize this particular businesswoman. She wasn't one of the two or three regulars he always noticed but never did business with. The stringy-haired, strawberry blonde with the pierced navel and sad eyes. The plump Latina with shorts that ended mid-cheek and a chest that put him in mind of the Grand Tetons. The beehive brunette with the crooked teeth. Guess competition never really lets up, he mused.

Dank days have a way of making you focus on the negative. At least that's how they affected Ellis. So the more he drove, the more he felt that cheating husbands, and wives who gave a damn, were becoming endangered species. Couples were taking longer to panic over teenagers who hadn't come home overnight. Even guys who were convinced their partners were skimming didn't care enough to hire someone to prove it. Apathy was becoming the national pastime. Or, so it seemed. Maybe it was just the lousy weather.

Ellis pulled into the basement garage and found a space close to the elevator. It was easy this time of day. The sedans and the SUV's and the mini-vans didn't get in until much later. They had papers to read and eggs to fry and kids to drop off before making their way to this particular cement cavern. It wasn't that Ellis was a workaholic. He didn't have anyone to impress by getting in early. He just never slept very well. And he didn't have the predisposition or the patience to simply lie in bed staring at the back of his eyelids.

Turning off the engine he looked around and muttered "*Christ*," as he thought about what kind of skills it didn't take to design parking lots. Gray walls, gray ceiling. Concrete floor, which just happens to be gray. People didn't ask much of parking lots, or the people who design them. Function over form. Substance over style. Be adequate but don't be noticed. It didn't slip past him that he could have been talking about himself.

The elevator was small and the ride up interminable, even though it was only a few floors. He didn't like cramped spaces. Never had. And today this one put him in mind of a casket on a hydraulic lift being slowly raised to heaven. No, he thought, with him inside it would surely be going in the other direction. Then, oddly enough, after climbing a couple of floors, the damned thing dropped like a stone.

CHAPTER 2

It's a bitch to start the day with your stomach coming through your windpipe. Not that the experience was totally foreign to Ellis. Actually, it was pretty similar to when he used to jump out of airplanes or heave up that excess Jack Daniels. But in both of those cases he knew it was coming. He could prepare for it. This morning was a bit of a shocker. Especially when his knees got even with his eyeballs as the floor of the elevator hit bottom a good half-second before he did. Which was immediately followed by Ellis going ass over elbows, corkscrewing himself into the corner.

The good news was...there wasn't any intense pain. No hot, knifepoint wake up call to let him know he'd just broken a bone. He did lie there for a second though. Just to make sure the flimsy box he was encased in had reached its maximum depth. Satisfied it wasn't about to drop any further, at least for the moment, he struggled to his feet and rechecked himself to make sure every body part he had walked into the elevator with was still reasonably functional. That seemed to be the case, so he took a quick moment to glance up and say a silent thanks to whomever or whatever was responsible for him still being in once piece. This was a habit he had gotten into some time ago. Usually when he was able to stand up after completing a thousand foot plunge from a plane or a chopper that had left the drop zone long before its human cargo got there.

He reached over and started to hit the button to see if the doors would open. Of course, he hesitated a second before actually doing it. This elevator, like most others, didn't go out of its way to make it apparent which button opened the doors and which button closed them. But he made the right choice and even though he wasn't expecting it, the doors opened. For a moment he wished they hadn't. There's something disconcerting about doors sliding open to reveal a solid brick wall staring you in the face. Sort of put Ellis in mind of Poe's *Cask of Amontillado*, from a vantage point he never had any desire to see. So he quickly pushed the button that closed the doors. The elevator was not equipped with a phone or speaker system for reporting emergencies. That was the sort of thing you had in classy buildings with granite walls and monitoring systems. His building was a rehab owned by the kind of guy who knows enough people at city hall to constantly be granted grandfather clauses that get around the kind of safety upgrades which would really come in handy for times like these. But since no such amenities were available, and the idea of sitting there, waiting to be rescued, was simply not in Ellis's DNA, a degree of trial and error was called for.

Yelling is always a good first step he thought. The thing made a hell of a noise when it hit. Maybe someone heard that. Then he remembered that he usually arrived before most of the other tenants in the building. But even so, he figured he had little to lose and decided to give it a go. "Hey!" He shouted. "Anyone out there? Can anyone hear me?" The lack of response spoke for itself. Okay, he said to himself, so much for whining. Time to try something else.

Luckily, the elevator did have a wooden railing about waist high that ran around all three sides. With his hands against the walls to use as a brace, he stepped up on the railing. From that height he was able to easily reach up and see if the ceiling panels were moveable. They were. So he pushed one, two, then the third one out and he was able to see exactly where he was. The elevator had dropped a few feet below the garage level where he left his car a few minutes earlier. He knew that because there were only two levels of parking, and since he had been staring at brick wall when he opened the doors, it meant he must be between the basement floor and the ground floor where he had parked.

It looked as if he could climb up on top of the elevator, then make his way along the wall with one hand on the cable until he came to the opening on the floor above him. Of course there was always the possibility of the elevator dropping the rest of the way to the bottom while he was still scrambling around on top of it. But hell, he thought, you can get run down by a bus just crossing the street. And because his patience was about as short as his close-cropped hair, he climbed atop the vertical casket and started making his way slowly up the shaft wall. One leg and arm against the wall, his parallel appendages against the cable. He looked like one of those Circ de Soleil acrobats. Except no one was paying to watch this performance.

When he got a foot or two below the ground floor doors, it occurred to him that in his haste to secure his freedom, there was one scenario he had overlooked. The elevator rising instead of falling. He didn't have this insight entirely on his own. It quickly popped into his brain when he felt a shake on the cable, then heard something not unlike a metallic groan. Quickly looking down, he saw the last thing he wanted to see. The elevator on its way up to meet him. As most people do in supremely stressful situations, he chose the universal articulation of shock and dismay. "Shit," he said. Now there was no time to think about alternatives. He had to get to the doorway and hope there was enough room between him and the doors to let the elevator pass. Harnessing all the speed and might he could muster, he scrambled the last couple of feet, let go of the cable, grabbed the ledge of the doorway with both hands and pulled himself up to his elbows. With the elevator now rising faster, he took one last breath and managed to haul himself upright and stand flat against the door. But while his body managed to squeeze within the protected confines of the doorframe, his feet didn't. His heels were still dangling off the edge and smack dab in the way of the oncoming elevator, which was now only a few feet away. A grimace and a fatalistic *fuck* was all he uttered milliseconds before the doors opened, spilling him into the ground floor garage at the feet of Harley, the building security guard.

CHAPTER 3

Harley, whose seventy plus years had seen all kinds of bizarre starts to lots of strange days, simply looked down and said, "Is that you, Mr. Ellis?"

For the second time that morning Brig Ellis was picking himself up and checking to make sure he was in one piece. And he hadn't even had his coffee yet.

"Yes, Harley, it's me. What the hell's going on with this elevator?"

Harley had scant knowledge of elevators. In fact, the old fellow had taken this job precisely because it promised little or no need to increase his acumen about such things. Harley reasoned that being a septuagenarian entitled him to limit his learning so he could concentrate on more important things, such as the Field & Stream magazines he kept underneath the building security manual he had yet to actually read.

"I wish I knew, Mr. Ellis. I heard this loud bang a few minutes ago and I started looking around to see what it was. Didn't occur to me for a little while that it might have been the elevator. You sure you're okay?"

"Yes, I'm okay. But you better have someone over here pronto to look into that death trap before the rest of the tenants start to arrive."

"I'll do that Mr. Ellis. But first I'll put up some Out of Order signs so nobody'll get into the fix you did. They might not be so lucky." Harley may not have been bucking for employee of the month, but he definitely took his responsibilities seriously. Well, some of them.

"Good thinking, Harley."

On his way up four flights of stairs to his office, Ellis felt a little twitch in his back and a bit of stiffness in his shoulder. But all things considered, he felt he was pretty lucky to be walking away with just a few bumps and bruises. Stepping out into the hallway on the fourth floor he headed straight for the men's room. There wasn't one in his office. But the Gents was only three doors down. He didn't realize until he saw himself in the mirror that he had grease and dirt all over his hands and a few smudges on his face as well. It was a well-worn face. A face that had seen its share of scrapes. But it wasn't a hard face. The kind you turn away from. All things considered, it was a good, honest face. Strong chin. Straight nose. Green eyes that sometimes drew women's attention when the mouth south of them widened into a smile. Which wasn't all that often. And certainly not at the moment.

It took a dozen or more mini-squirts from the soap machine to remove the smudges from his face and hands. Then, using wet paper towels, he set about getting the scruff off his jacket and pants as well. They'd have time to dry later. Best to get this crud off now, he thought. For just a second he entertained the idea of hitting the building management up for a new suit, maybe even threatening to sue in the process. But unless he was pretty banged up, which he wasn't, he never really gave it more than just a passing thought. There are more than enough jerks out there with bogus beefs taking up the courts' time and making attorneys rich in the process. He didn't fancy lumping himself in with any type who spilled hot coffee in his crotch and then expected some company to pay for individual clumsiness or sheer stupidity.

A few hours later Ellis had started to stiffen up. He knew he wasn't hurt that badly so he chalked it up to the unfortunate but inevitable mileage and wear and tear his body had taken over the years. His morning free fall was simply the latest installment. It was a little earlier than he usually took lunch but he decided it would do him good to get some fresh air and sunshine. What started as an overcast, gloomy day had reversed itself. It often did this time of year in San Diego.

Tramping down the stairs on the way to his car, he realized it had been months, maybe even years since he had used the stairwell in his building twice in one day. How easy it is to fall into routines, he thought. The same patterns over and over again. Maybe it takes some kind of jolt to the system, like having an elevator fall out from under you, to make you realize you're in a rut. Walking to his car, he noticed two uniformed patrolmen talking to Harley. One was leaning into the elevator shaft pointing up at something, while the other took notes. Knowing that he would get held up for half an hour or more answering questions, Ellis decided not to join the conversation. Plenty of time for that later, he thought. Now he needed something to eat and maybe something a little medicinal to wash it down.

The morning fog had burned off, so turning from the parking entrance onto Ash Street, he got one or two head swivels. He usually did when he had the top down. He liked to think it was him, but he knew it was the car. She was forty years old but still had a way of attracting attention. Small, sturdy, white. Big, teardrop headlights. From a distance she looked pretty damn good. Up close it was a little different story. Kind of like him, Ellis mused. He had run across the little Mercedes 230 SL skimming through the classifieds one day. A buddy had given him a lift to take a look at it. And while he had yet to meet a woman that produced anything near love at first sight, that little German roadster nailed him. Over the next year or so he spent some money fixing her up. Seats stuffed and upholstered. New floor mats. A bit of touchup paint here and there. The wooden molding rimming the windshield and the top of the dashboard had cracked. He wanted to take care of that. Seemed like he just never got around to it though. There was always something else to spend money on. In fact, he was beginning to wonder if he wasn't becoming the sole support of his mechanic, Lothar, who ran a little shop that was unashamedly called Deutschland Motors. It was the essence of what was often referred to as a shade-tree operation. There was even a big oak on one side of Lothar's steel-framed, tin-covered bays that allowed him to work on or house three cars at the same time. Why did one of them always have to be mine, Ellis wondered, as he cruised down Harbor Drive on his way to Benny's.

CHAPTER 4

Benny's was a seaside eyesore that served shrimp and salvation. The shrimp was spiced right and priced reasonably. The salvation was on the house. Or on the boat, you might say, because that's really what you thought Benny's was the first time you saw it. It looked like an old wooden-framed fishing trawler that had beached itself and been left on the shore by one hellatious tide. Inside, a bruised and battered mahogany bar made a semicircle in the middle of a wide, open room. There were tables rimming the outside of the inside so you could look at the ocean while you ate. Or look at the parking lot if you didn't get there early enough. And there were stools bolted to the floor that ran the course of the bar. They were the perfect height for a pair of tired elbows.

To get salvation at Benny's all you had to do was tell your troubles to Grif behind the bar. Grif was a long, tall, black purveyor of booze and bullshit who had perfected an uncanny ability to listen to anyone's sob story and immediately respond with both sympathy and something not unlike penance. Grif had perfected his bar tending skills and his mood-altering advice over years and years of daily conversations with people who were buying drinks but paying for friendship.

Most people thought Grif was the owner, which he was. But most people didn't know this was only recently the case. Grif had stumbled into Benny's almost two decades ago looking for any kind of work he could find. He quickly found the business end of a mop and broom and all the industrial strength Liquid Plumber he could handle. But Grif wasn't one to let a good thing go by. He realized that Mr. Benny, as Grif always called him, was a decent man who was willing to help someone in need. And you didn't find those kinds of white folks just anywhere. So Grif started out in the restrooms but soon found his way to the kitchen and then to waiting tables and eventually behind the bar itself. One morning Grif came to work, opened the door and found Mr. Benny leaning back in his seat at one of the ocean-view tables with his hand clutching a half-finished bottle of 21 year old Scotch, his mouth wide open and his soul somewhere other than a rundown bar on the beach. The paramedics came, pronounced him dead of a heart attack, and suggested it was probably quick and relatively painless due to the

Glenfiddich overture. A week later when the old gentleman's will - was found, then read, Grif learned that Mr. Benny had left the place to him. Somehow it didn't seem right to change the name. So yeah, it was Grif's place. But it was still Benny's.

"Well Brig Ellis, as I live and breathe, haven't seen you for...how long has it been?"

"Oh, I'd say at least a day or two, huh," Ellis replied, as Grif chuckled at his own joke.

"You must have found someplace more to your likin'. Looks like you slept in them clothes."

"I was on my back in these clothes this morning, but sleeping had nothing to do with it."

"Decide to patronize one of the working ladies, did you?"

"Give me a Bloody Mary and maybe I'll tell you about it."

"I'll sell you a Bloody Mary and you will tell me about it."

Grif didn't have to ask Ellis how he wanted his drink. The first time he asked Grif for a Bloody Mary, he simply added, "Short glass. No vegetables." That was all it took. Grif had a knack for remembering how certain customers preferred certain drinks. Especially the customers he liked. And Ellis was one of those.

After a few minutes Ellis had pretty much brought Grif up to speed on his less than stellar morning.

"Well I can definitely see why you're in here an hour or so earlier than usual," Grif sympathized. "The kind of morning you've had deserves one on the house. Can I freshen that up for you?"

"Now there's an idea I won't say no to," Ellis replied. "And why don't you have cook put together a shrimp salad to go with it."

Grif came back with a smile, "Yeah, that's makin' my cash register ring." He turned and shouted toward the kitchen, "Hey Nunez, one shrimp salad...and put some fucking shrimp in it this time. This ain't no tourist out here. We got ourselves a regular who's had a shitty mornin'."

By the time Ellis had finished his salad and his second Bloody Mary, he was feeling considerably better than when he had walked in earlier. The lunch crowd had started to show up and Grif had gotten pretty busy making drinks and taking orders. So Ellis decided to get his coffee to go. Maybe drive a few miles up the coast before heading back. He had already used his cell phone to check his office messages and there were none. So another half hour or so driving along the beach made a lot more sense to him than rushing back to kill time sitting around waiting for the phone to ring.

As he was pulling the money out of his pocket to pay his tab, Ellis heard Grif say, "Hey man, listen, I was goin' to mention this earlier but things got a little busy in here. I need a few minutes of your time, you know. I mean I got somethin' that I need to talk to you about. Kind of a business thing. Well, sort of business."

Ellis could tell that something was up. He had been coming into Benny's and shooting the shit with Grif for years, and the conversations had always been on a pretty uncomplicated basis. Typical barkeep, customer chatter. But this seemed more than that.

"I was just going to take a little spin up the road before heading back into town. Want to ride and talk? I've got to turn around eventually and come back by here anyway."

"Yeah. That's a good idea. Let me get Irma to cover the bar 'til I get back. I'll meet you out in the parking lot," Grif said.

There's something spiritual about the sun on your face after a couple of drinks. You feel the heat etching into your skin. It feels redemptive. That's what Ellis was thinking as he and Grif rolled down the coast road. After a few minutes he turned to Grif and said, "Well, what was it you wanted to jaw about?"

"Look man," Grif began, "I know a little about you. I know you're ex-military and all that stuff. I know you do things for people every now and then."

Ellis could tell his passenger wasn't sure how to begin. He felt he should set things straight quickly. "Look, Grif, I investigate things for people. I do a little security now and then. It's all very straightforward, you know. Whatever you may have heard from anyone else, take with a grain of salt. I'm just a working stiff like everyone else. But you didn't leave your place of business in the middle of lunch to talk about me. Why are we really having this little chat?"

"Look man, I didn't mean nothin' by it. It's just that I had a little trouble the other day and I'm not sure what to do about it. Or whether I need to do anything about it. Or whatever."

Ellis cut in, "Just lay it out for me. I'm not the judgmental type. And you don't have to worry about me passing anything on. In my line of work, the one thing I have to be is confidential."

"Sure, sure. I understand. It's just that I ain't used to goin' to anybody else with my problems, you know. But anyway, here's the deal. After I closed up the other night, I was heading' back into the city. I live just on the other side of the bridge. Well, anyway, just as I was comin' off it, I guess I was dozen' a bit cause I had a pop or two before I left. I must have slipped off for a second you know...then damn if I didn't ram into the back of a car."

"You didn't leave the scene?" Ellis questioned.

"No. But I wonder if maybe that would have been better."

"Believe me, it wouldn't. Go on," Ellis encouraged him.

"Well, I guess I popped that car pretty hard because it sure seemed to be jumping off my bumper as my eyes opened up. Then it swerved to the right and kinda' banged up against the guard rail."

"Don't tell me it went over the side."

"No man," Grif came back quickly, "it just sort of eventually skidded to a stop on the side of the highway. I could tell there was a woman driving. She got jerked pretty hard. Least that's the way it looked. So I pulled up behind her. I was about to get out and walk up to the car and make sure she was okay. It was late you know. Nobody around. And I started thinking, wait a minute here. I'm about to walk up to this woman's car at three in the morning...after just banging into her. She's gonna' look up and see some big black guy coming toward her...man, no telling what she's gonna' do."

"But you said you didn't leave the scene," Ellis broke in.

"I didn't man. I was about to. I admit it. Then I saw her bring her hands up to her head, and I thought, shit! What if she really is hurt? So I cut the engine on my car and walked up to where she was. Real slow like' you know, so I wouldn't scare her or nothin'. I kept sayin', are you okay, mam, are you okay? I didn't want her to think I was out to hurt her. I also didn't want her to reach in her purse and pull out a piece and open up on me. I mean you just never know what women are carrying around these days. Specially late at night."

"So far, so good," Ellis replied. "You're doing what you should. So what went wrong?"

"Nothin' really. I mean she said she thought she was okay. And she didn't want to stay out there on a dark road with some idiot who had just clipped her. So she got me to give her my name and address...gave me her name and a phone number. Didn't want to give me her address. Said her insurance company would give me a call. Then she took off."

"Well, Grif, that's an interesting story. But if it doesn't have some kicker on the end of it, I'm not sure why you're telling me about it. Sounds like you did everything right. What's the problem?"

"I was kind of shook-up too you know. I wasn't thinkin' real clear myself. So I didn't give her my home address. I gave her the cafe address you know, Benny's. And it's been over a week since it happened. I expected to hear from her the next day. But nothing in a week. So now I'm really startin' to worry. I'm thinkin' to myself, she's been by here you know. Or she's sent her insurance people. And they've seen Benny's. Probably looked up the ownership. There's public records on that kind of stuff. And I bet they're getting' ready to shaft me, man. I bet they're getting ready to take me to the cleaners. That's what I'm thinking'. Mostly that's what I'm thinking'. Then I start to think maybe it's even worse, man. What if she got home and died in her goddamn garage? What if she's still sitting in her car getting really ripe in the garage, man. It's been a week. Why haven't I heard somethin'?"

"You've got her number. Why don't you call and find out. Beats worrying yourself silly about it, right?"

"I don't want to do that. I don't want them to think that I think she might really be hurt.

They might use that against me. They might say I knew she was hurt and I let her drive off anyway. Then they'd really fuck me, man. Then I'd really be fucked."

"You know," Ellis said, "there could be all sorts of reasons no one's gotten back to you."

"Yeah, and all those reasons are bad. Look, can you just call her? You know, maybe call and go see her. Try to find out if she knows I own my own establishment. I do drive a Lincoln. I bet she saw that too. I bet they're plannin' to hit me big time. Man, I can't afford to get ripped off like that."

Ellis had pulled over to the shoulder of the road and put his emergency lights on. He looked at Grif and said, "You've' got car insurance, right?"

Grif was in no hurry to get logical. He had been obsessing over this for seven days.

"Sure, I got insurance, but I know how these things go. They wind up taken' a guy for everything he's got. This is just the wrong time for this sort of thing to be hapnin'. Things have been slower than you think at the cafe. And I've got other expenses, man. You can help me find out what the deal is, can't you Ellis? I can pay you for your time."

"So, you assume my time's worth a lot less than what you might be out in insurance, huh?"

"It ain't that man. It's just that I know you won't shaft me. I don't know about them."

"You got the number on you?" Ellis knew the answer.

Grif reached in his shirt pocket and pulled it out. "Yeah. Here, man. I just gotta' know what the deal is. You know how to look into these things real quiet like, right? It ain't right. I dozed off. Could have happened to anyone, you know. I wasn't drunk or nothin'. You don't think she smelled liquor on my breath and they're gonna' try to say I was drunk do you? Man tries to do the right thing and look what it gets him."

"Look," Ellis said, "I need to get you back. I bet it's no big deal. I'll check it out tomorrow and let you know what I learn. It's probably going to cost you whatever it takes to repair her car. Her insurance company is probably looking into that now. Once they know what that will be, they'll probably get back to you." Ellis couldn't help himself. He went on. "Unless of course you're right. If her ride's become a mausoleum and she's stinking up the place, you could be in a world of shit."

"Don't even joke about that, man. That just ain't funny at all. I ain't done nothin' but worry for the last week now. Hey, listen, you're not gonna' charge me a lot for this are you? I mean business ain't been all that good lately, you know."

"Why don't we just say we'll run me a tab at Benny's until we find out what the deal is. If it looks like it's going take more time than I think, I'll let you know. "We'll work something out."

Back at Benny's parking lot, he let Grif out and headed toward the city. Ellis noticed that his back and shoulder were getting tighter and even sorer. "Fuck it," he said. Meaning he had no intention of returning to his office. The route would be straight to his apartment for a long shower and a short evening. Sometimes it makes a lot more sense to just put the day behind you, he thought. Before it gets any worse.

CHAPTER 5

By the time the morning sun was starting to show itself, Ellis was half way through his run. He wasn't a fanatic about it, but he found that if he ran four or five days out of every seven, he managed to keep himself in reasonable shape. Balboa Park was close to where he lived and it was a pleasant enough place to put in four miles. Headphones to keep up with the news or listen to some music made it more bearable. Running was discipline to him, not fun. He had never really understood those fanatics who would go on and on about runner's high and what a cleansing thing it was. Shit, he thought, it was a way to keep fit. Probably the easiest way. But he'd be damned if he had to enjoy it.

Unlocking the door to his apartment, he was met immediately by his roommate, Osgood. Osgood was a fourteen-inch high, fifty-pound pot roast with a face. At least that's the way Ellis thought of his English bulldog. White as a snow-covered fire hydrant, except for his black nose of course, Osgood always liked to nuzzle and lick Ellis's sweaty shins when he came back from running. The salty taste was very much to Osgood's liking. As was what always followed. Most dogs are pretty much anti-bath. But Osgood had become accustomed to stepping inside the shower with Ellis when his master returned from his jogs through the park. He would stand there stoically, as if on guard at Buckingham Palace, and let the water spray and bounce off him. That was one of the things Ellis liked about Osgood. The way he maintained his dignity regardless of the situation. It was a sort of grace under fire thing that Ellis felt a kinship with.

Ellis had won Osgood in a poker game. The proud pooch was the result of four tens that beat a kings over jacks full house. Ordinarily Ellis wouldn't have let a poker opponent wager an animal in lieu of a raise that couldn't be met, but the loser was an odious jerk who didn't deserve the noble canine. At least that's the way Ellis saw it. And frankly, Osgood agreed.

Most people don't think much about a shower when they're taking one. But Ellis always thought about what an overlooked and under appreciated invention the shower was. All that hot, steamy water flowing over your body. Seemingly no end to it. The ability to make it last as long as you wanted. It's often the ordinary things that can mean the most to you, he thought. Especially when you don't have them. Of course the majority of people hadn't gone days, or sometimes weeks without a shower. Or a bed. Or a toilet. Or hearing another human voice. Or seeing another face. A face that if it was unlucky enough to see yours, wouldn't be seeing anything ever again.

Ellis didn't think about those faces all that much. He had worked hard at putting them out of his mind. The way he saw it, the last day he took off his fatigues was the first day of his new life. At least that had been the plan. But plans change. Or get changed. Sometimes by forces beyond your control. So Brig Ellis did everything he possibly could to stay in control. Bad things happen when you don't, he reflected. Occasionally very bad things.

He pulled a green suit out of his closet. Nothing fancy. No designer label. White shirt, open at the neck, to go with it. It's what he wore every day. Suit, no tie. Of course he had ties. He kept one folded and in the right breast pocket of each suit. There was even one or two in the glove compartment of his car. Ellis believed a tie was a good thing to have handy, but he didn't like wearing one unless he had to. The passing psychologist or psychoanalyst would have a field day with all this Ellis said to himself. I can hear the psychobabble now. "Mr. Ellis, you've just traded one kind of uniform for another. The contents of your closet and dresser most closely resemble that of a footlocker. You body may be out of the service but your mind is having problems disengaging." What a crock, thought Ellis. Some people actually pay money to have eggheads tell them crap like that. Navel gazing is about as productive as feeling sorry for yourself. All it does is slow you down. And life does enough of that on its own.

Like most men, Ellis had a regimen for getting dressed in the morning. But unlike most men his regimen included a shoulder holster with a Glock 19 caliber. He was partial to Glocks. The polymer frame made them lighter than most. Even with a twenty-round clip. An absence of any external safety levers, hammers, or other operational controls that had to be deactivated prior to firing was an advantage as well. Just pull, point and shoot. When it really mattered, there was little time for anything else. He had always liked the Austrian weapon. It gave him a lot of firepower plus fast reloading. Though these days he seldom found it necessary to carry more than one clip. Those days were behind him, he hoped. However, he still finished dressing by strapping his Glock field knife to his right calf. Outside his sock, inside his pant leg. Not only was the blade tough enough to bust open an ammunition box, it was also perfectly balanced for throwing. And if he really found himself in a jam, the crossbar hand-protector could be used as a bottle-opener.

CHAPTER 6

About a twenty-minute ride from where Ellis was going through his morning ritual, Laney Wilson was sunning herself by the apartment pool. It was anyone's guess how many lonely eyes were peering from behind closed drapes at the leggy blonde. Laney was not one to be overly concerned about how many men, or women, might be regretting their marital status as they took in the morning's view. In her business, you couldn't afford to get caught up in that. She got paid to have people look at her. Modeling is not a job for the squeamish, she thought. But anyway, there was nothing improper going on. She was wearing her swimsuit. What there was of the two tiny pieces that covered enough to keep her out of jail.

Her chair was tilted back. A towel had been strategically placed to keep the straps from leaving indent marks on her back or legs. Beside her on the small round table with the glass top was a tall glass of orange juice and her cell phone. She seldom strayed very far from that. It was too important. There were jobs on the other end of it. When it rang. Which frankly, wasn't as often as it used to. At thirty, most were out of the business. Or at least making the transition to agent, or wife or whatever it is that polite society calls those women who seem to have no visible means of support yet always turn up on the arm of graying gentlemen at restaurants or cocktail parties. But Laney hadn't chucked it in yet. And even though she was getting a lot more car shows and conventions than fashion spreads, she still felt she had some time left before she had to make any real decisions about her life. So when the phone started to emit an electronic version of Hail, Hail, The Gangs All Here, Laney just naturally assumed there was a job on the other end of the satellite's coordinates.

"Hello."

"Hello. Is this Laney Wilson?"

Laney didn't recognize the voice. "Who is calling, please?"

"This is Lieutenant Brig Ellis, I'm with the police."

"The police?"

"Yes. Am I speaking to Laney Wilson?"

"Ah, yes officer. I'm Laney Wilson. Is there some kind of problem? No one's been hurt have they?"

"Well, that's one of the things I'm trying to find out, Ms.

Wilson. We're looking into a traffic accident that may have occurred about a week ago...and there's some question as to whether or not one or more of the parties may have left the scene."

The last thing Laney had expected was a call from the police. She stumbled to say, "I was kind of in an accident...I've been a little shaken up and I haven't ...well I haven't had time--"

Ellis cut in quickly. "Look, Ms. Wilson, we should really talk about this in person. I can come by your place in about two hours, say noon. I'm sure we can clear this up very quickly and then you won't need to be bothered again."

"Well, all right. Noon you said?"

"Yes. Noon. Are you still living at the same address that's on your vehicle registration?"

"Oh gosh, I really can't remember if I was here when I bought--"

"Just give me your current address, please."

"It's 521 Kettner Boulevard. Apartment 3B."

"Yep. That's what we have on the registration. I'll see you about noon. Thanks."

"Ah, okay, Thanks officer...what did you say your name--"

The click on the other end of the phone kept her from finishing her question. The police, *Jesus*, Laney thought, why are the police involved in this? She had wanted to get a lot more sun this morning, but her plans obviously had to change. She picked up the glass of orange juice and emptied it on the grass near her chair. Then she put it back on the table by the cell phone and wrapped the towel she had been lying on around her waist. Scooping up the glass and the cell phone, she turned and walked away from the pool to the chagrin of those who had been spending the last few minutes watching her from the anonymity of their apartments.

Back in her own place, Laney's mind was racing. How did the police find out about this? She certainly didn't remember seeing any police that night. Damn, she thought, there's never a cop around when you really need one and now this. She started to light a cigarette, then stopped. No, she reasoned, I'm not going to let this get me started again. It's probably no big deal, she went on to herself. Maybe someone just saw the cars on the side of the road and assumed something happened and called the cops. Maybe that was it. Damned busybodies. Why can't people mind their own business? That must be all there is to it. Must be. Couldn't be anything else. Could there? What if...what if someone was maybe walking on the side of the road that night...maybe they saw something. Maybe even...no, God no. What if someone was walking that neither of us saw? What if that someone was hit by one of the cars? No. No. That's crazy thinking. No way.

There couldn't have been anyone there. The policeman would have said something. Something would have been on the news. Sure. If there had been some sort of accident that the police thought was a hit and run, then it would have been on the news. And I would have seen it. Surely I would have seen it. But I haven't. So that must not be it. And if that's not it, then it can't be that bad, right? Right. Maybe it's the guy who was driving the other car. Maybe it's him. Maybe there's something that the cops have on him. I could be getting all worked up over nothing. I'll have another orange juice. Better yet, I'll make that a screwdriver. Still plenty of time to have a drink and a shower before that cop, that...what did he say his name was? Well, anyway, plenty of time before he shows up.

Laney finished her screwdriver slowly. She didn't normally drink this early in the day but the phone call had really unsettled her. It wasn't something she was expecting. And she wasn't a big fan of the unexpected. After finishing her drink, she put her glass in the sink and on the way to the bathroom she started the stereo. The music would help keep her in a somewhat calmer state. She chose the soundtrack from Midnight In The Garden of Good & Evil. It had all those great standards in it. Nothing too raucous. Nothing too jarring. Certainly nothing as jarring as the ringing doorbell that made her jump.

Who could that be at this time of the morning? Surely not the cop. It had only been about thirty minutes since he called. And he said noon anyway.

But there was the doorbell again. And this time it was followed by a voice that said. "Ms. Wilson? This is Ellis. Brig Ellis. I called you on the phone a little earlier."

"Shit!" Laney whispered. The guy said he was coming at noon. What's he doing here now?

"Ms. Wilson? My other appointment got canceled. I was in the area so I came on over."

"Just a second," Laney called back. She ran to the bedroom, tossed the towel on the floor and quickly pulled on some blue jeans. She was about to grab a sweatshirt out of the closet when she caught sight of herself in the mirror and made another decision.

Ellis heard the deadbolt lock being turned just before the door started to open. That's good, he thought. She takes care of herself. He found out just how well she took care of herself when the door swung all the way open.

Laney was standing there barefoot, in jeans that looked like a pair of denim leotards. And the only things above her waist were her white bikini top and a Cervmax patented T-back neck brace.

CHAPTER 7

"Sorry for the way I look, "Laney started, "I was out by the pool getting some sun when you called. And I didn't expect you for another hour and a half."

"Oh no, please don't apologize," Ellis replied, "it's me that's here a lot sooner than I said I'd be and you look...well, believe me there's nothing wrong with the way you look."

"Officer I have to admit I've forgotten your name."

"Ms. Wilson my name is Ellis, Brig Ellis. And you don't have to call me officer because the truth of the matter is...I'm not with the police."

"What? But you said..."

"I lied. I didn't think you'd talk to me if I didn't."

"Well you were right about that. And if you don't leave right now, I'm going to..." but she stopped in mid sentence quickly remembering the reason he gave for the call.

"Look," Ellis began, "don't be alarmed. I'm not some moke who's here to scare you or hurt you or anything like that. If I was I'd be inside your apartment already. I'm just here to talk with you about the accident. We can leave the door wide open if you like."

"Yeah. Let's do that," Laney said as she stepped aside and let Ellis in. "And I've got neighbors on both sides of me, you know. They don't work and if you start something they'll be here in a minute and..."

"Okay, okay, that's fine," Ellis said. "Don't worry. I don't plan to start anything."

"Go ahead and sit down," Laney said as she motioned toward the couch. She took the straight back chair opposite him. "I can't believe I fell for that bit over the phone. *Jeeze*, I even gave you my address, didn't I? You didn't have it, right?"

"Right. I didn't have it. But don't beat yourself up. Most people react the same way to authority figures."

"But what if I hadn't?" Laney questioned. "What if I didn't give you my address and open my door to you like some idiot?"

"Nothing ventured, nothing gained," Ellis admitted.

"And you showed up here an hour and a half early...on purpose. You never planned to get here at noon, did you?"

"If I had gotten here when I said I was going to get here,

you'd be showing me what you wanted me to see. Not necessarily the truth."

That got Laney's Irish up. "The truth. You're one to be talking about the truth. You've done nothing but lie since I first heard your voice."

"Not exactly," Ellis countered. "I haven't done anything to scare you, or hurt you. Now have I?"

"So what am I supposed to do, thank you for that? Jesus. So who the hell are you anyway?"

"I wasn't lying when I said my name was Brig Ellis. I'm an acquaintance of the fellow you had the vehicular altercation with the other night."

"You mean the guy who hit me. Let's keep that in perspective. He ran into me. But are you his lawyer or...just why are you here?"

As he spoke, Ellis reached into the outside right pocket of his suit and handed Laney a business card. "I told the individual...the gentleman you say hit you...I told him I'd look into the matter."

Laney looked at his business card, which read, Brig Ellis, Investigations, Security, Confidential Matters. "So, which is it?"

"I'm sorry?" Ellis replied, leaning forward.

"Is this an investigation, a security thing, or...Laney glanced back and read from the card..."a confidential matter?"

"That's one of the things I'm here to determine."

"Look, I don't have to talk to you. If the guy was so concerned, why didn't he just call me himself?"

"Actually, he was wondering why you hadn't called him. It has been over a week since the event. He informed you that he had insurance. He expected to hear from you or your insurance agency right away. When he didn't, he got a bit concerned. So he asked me to look into it for him."

"Well", Laney said, "as you can plainly see, I've been out of sorts. I didn't have to wear this thing before the other night."

"The bathing suit?" Ellis quipped.

"Don't be an ass" Laney retorted as the sides of her mouth turned up.

"See, you can smile," said Ellis. "Look Ms. Wilson, you strike me as a lovely young woman..."

Hmm, Laney thought, at least he got young in there. Most

guys don't use that unless they're twenty years older than me. And that's certainly not the case with this guy. Five years older, maybe. Maybe eight. Hell, maybe even ten, but certainly no more than that. Then Laney picked up on the rest of what he was saying.

"...and I've had occasion to look into insurance scams in the past. That sort of thing can lead to all types of problems and--."

"Insurance scams?" Laney bristled. "Look, I haven't been feeling well, as you can see. It's taking my car insurance longer than I thought it would so I just haven't gotten back to...to...what's his name. Anyway, look Mr. Ellis, my neck's starting to hurt me and I really don't feel like talking anymore and--"

"Let me suggest this," Ellis cut in, why don't I go now and we can get back together on this later. You probably don't have all the paper work close by regarding your insurance company and the doctor you've been seeing and the pain medicine that's been proscribed and all that sort of thing. So, you have my card. Why don't you just call me tomorrow and I can get all the information from you and we can go from there."

At this point, Laney really wanted, and needed, some time to think for herself. "Okay. I'll call you tomorrow."

As he was getting up and heading toward the door, Ellis said, "I apologize again for the deception. And I do look forward to speaking with you again and trying to get this worked out to everyone's mutual satisfaction as soon as possible."

As Laney was closing the door, she leaned against it and said, "Mr. Ellis, there's nothing I'd like better. Good-bye."

Ellis tried to say Good-bye, but the door was closed after his first syllable.

As he walked back to his car he felt satisfied. If there was an insurance scam on the way, he had let her know it wasn't going to be easy. He could go back and let Grif know the woman he ran into was alive and the police wouldn't be visiting his beachside establishment, at least in regard to this, any time soon. And he had spent the morning conversing with a member of the opposite sex who made him glad she was a member of the opposite sex. Truth is she looks better than some of those models you see in magazines, Ellis thought. If the neck brace was just a prop, he had to admit it made an interesting accessory to blue jeans and a bikini top.

CHAPTER 8

Returning from his meeting with Laney Wilson, Ellis ran into Harley in the lobby of his building. Before he could say hello, the ineffectual but affable security guard said, "Mr. Ellis, how are you, sir? Are you feeling okay?"

"I'm fine Harley. How are you doing?"

"Well I'm doing okay, but I wasn't the one who rode a rocket down the elevator shaft."

"That's true Harley. And I'm glad for your sake it was me. But I'm fine, thanks for asking."

As Ellis started to walk away, Harley kept talking because lack of interest on the part of his listeners never seemed to dissuade Harley. "I don't know if you heard, Mr. Ellis, but the police are pretty convinced that the elevator was tampered with. You know, like, on purpose. You don't think it was terrorists, do you?"

"What do you mean tampered with, Harley?"

"Well sir, they didn't go into detail with me. But they did say they didn't think that elevator dropped because of some mechanical or electrical malfunction. And they asked me if I had seen any suspicious looking characters around here."

"Harley, everybody who works in this building looks a little suspicious to me, " Ellis joked.

"Well Mr. Ellis, you got a point there. But look," he said, reaching into his pocket and holding out a card, "the officer said I should give you this and you should call and talk to him so they can follow up, you know?"

Taking the card, Ellis said, "Thanks Harley. I'll do that."

"You do that Mr. Ellis, cause if it ain't terrorists, (Harley was a diligent antiterrorist, at least in his own mind) well it might be somebody out to do you harm."

In spit of himself Ellis liked the old guy and didn't want to be rude. "You think so, Harley?"

"Well," Harley went on, "if that elevator was rigged to fall, chances are it was rigged late at night. Maybe it was someone who knew that you're usually the first one in every morning. Except this morning of course."

"Now just wait a minute Harley, you're making yourself the prime suspect."

The frail-framed senior draped in the floppy, ill-fitting uniform got a bit flustered. "Don't even joke about that, Mr. Ellis. You know I'd never..."

Ellis cut in, "Of course I know it Harley. I was just kidding you. And anyway, there's probably some reasonable explanation to the whole thing. Cops have got to find bad actors behind everything. It's the way they keep their jobs."

"You just keep an eye out for yourself, Mr. Ellis. And I'll keep my eyes open for any suspicious looking terrorist types."

"Will do," Ellis said, walking away a second time and once again taking the stairs up to his office.

As he was entering, he heard his phone ringing. Going directly to his desk he picked up the receiver and answered with his usual response. "Ellis here."

The voice on the other end was male. To a degree. It was the kind of voice a lot of people affect when they're making a joke about gays, Ellis thought.

"Oh, Mr. Ellis, I'm so glad I was able to reach you. I've been at my wit's end for sometime now and I didn't really know who to call or contact, and then today, out of the blue really, I stop in for a little sea air and a little sunshine and maybe a toddy or two and get into this conversation with the most remarkable fellow who suggests I give you a call and I do give you a call and you answer, and well I'm just so glad I was able to reach you and..."

Ellis jumped in at the first available pause. "Yes. You said that already. But you haven't said who you are."

"Oh you're absolutely right. Please forgive me. It's just that I'm so distraught really, and well, I just forgot my manners, and I've never really done this sort of thing before so..."

"Your name?" Ellis interjected.

"Oh yes. I'm so sorry. My name is Terrance Whitfield. I'll go very slowly. I'm Terrance Whitfield and I want to discuss a confidential matter with you. A matter where I may need to employ you to help me."

"And how did you come to contact me specifically, Mr. Whitfield?"

"Well, it's amazing really, I was just sitting here at the bar in this beach side bistro and I began to talk with the bartender. And the more we talked...well the more I unburdened myself I guess, and as I did, the bartender was kind enough to suggest that you might be able to help me."

"Let me guess," said Ellis, "tall, black fellow, asked you to call him Grif?"

"Why, yes. How did you know?"

Ellis replied, "Just a lucky guess. He doesn't happen to be standing there, does he? If so, put him on the line."

Ellis heard Whitfield turn from the receiver and say, "He wants to talk to you."

"Hey Ellis," Grif said after grabbing the phone, "maybe you can give me a break on my rate since I've found you a new customer."

"Look, what the hell's going on here? Who is this guy?"

"He's a guy who needs someone like you, man. He's got a problem you can help him with and he said he's willin' to pay for the help. Why don't you come out here, grab some lunch, talk to the guy and decide for yourself. Maybe you can even tell me if you've found out anything about that little matter we discussed too."

"Yeah, I can give you some insight into that," Ellis said. "But if this guy is as loony as he sounds and I drive out there for nothing, then--"

"It won't be for nothing, believe me. And I want to hear what you found out. So are you on your way?"

"Okay, I'm coming out. Are you sure he'll be there when I get there?"

"Oh yeah," Grif replied, "I'll give him a primo table by the window."

"All right. See you in a bit," Ellis said.

As he turned onto Harbor Drive and started toward Benny's, the things on his mind were of more interest to him than the Sinatra version of Witchcraft on the tape in his car. And that was odd. Normally, when he was driving, he could lose himself for a few minutes in the tunes that were already old when he was a kid. He didn't care much for current music and he cared even less for people telling him that he ought to keep up more.

In fact, Ellis had a problem in general with people telling him what to do. That type of life had been all right once. When he was a kid, he determined it was the best thing for him. That's why he joined the army. But he had put in his time taking orders that made little or no sense and going on missions whose outcomes often left a bad taste in his mouth even when they were successful. So the day his twenty years were up, he walked away from answering to others for good. With a reasonable pension to put in the bank, he didn't have to take the first thing that came along. And so far things had worked out okay. He wasn't getting rich but he wasn't going broke either. Sure, he worked for other people, but he did the work on his own terms. If they didn't like that, they could hire someone else. And sometimes they did.

His shoulder was still a bit sore and what the hell was that Harley had been saying? The cops think the elevator was messed with. Who would want to do that? And why? He didn't have any pissed off husbands or irate clients or homicidal elevator repairmen who were after him. As far as he knew. I guess I should give the police a call, he said to himself, knowing he really had no intention of doing so. Come to think of it, he wasn't exactly sure what he had done with the card Harley gave him. Maybe he put it in his pocket. Maybe he left it on the desk. For whatever reason it didn't seem that important to him. The cops were probably wrong anyway. The building management was likely encouraging them to think it was foul play so they wouldn't have to be bothered with potential litigation. Whatever.

None of that seemed to be occupying as much space in his head though, as the blonde in the blue jeans and white bikini top. Yes, Ms. Laney Wilson was definitely a looker. Even with that damned neck brace between her head and shoulders. I wonder if she really needs it, he pondered. Wonder if she's on the square or running a con? Good looking lady like that...surely not. Wishful thinking, he realized. Got to check it out. Let it play and see what develops. It will be interesting to see if she's got those doctor bills and prescriptions and whether or not she's with a reputable insurance company. Don't want Grif to get screwed. Grif. Damn. Just can't keep from talking to his customers and trying to fix their lives while he fills their glasses. Now he's even hustling up business for me, Ellis reflected. Well, we'll see. That guy sounded pretty flamboyant over the phone. But money from guys who are light in the loafers is as good as any. At least that's what Ellis was thinking as he pulled into Benny's.

Grif was drying off some wine glasses he had just finished

washing and had his back to the bar. Ellis came in and took a stool directly behind him. "Well, you don't have to worry about any manslaughter charges," Ellis said.

Grif recognized the voice and turned as he heard it. "Then she's still alive, huh?"

"Oh, she's definitely alive," Ellis replied. "Why didn't you tell me she was a knockout?"

"It was dark out there, man. I didn't get that good a look at her. But she's okay, right? I mean she seems to be fine?"

"Oh she's fine all right. Except for that neck brace."

"Neck brace? *Motherfuck!* I knew that bitch was trying to nail me."

"Now don't jump to conclusions," Ellis responded. "It's still too soon to tell. She could be on the up and up. She seemed to get pretty pissed off when I suggested I had some experience with insurance scams."

"Oh good, man. You put the fear of God into her, huh?"

"She didn't seem all that frightened to me. Just mad. But she knows we know she could be faking it. And, if she is, now she knows it's not going to be that easy. Sometimes that's all it takes to make someone look for a new mark."

"I knew you could help me man. I really do 'preciate it," Grif said.

Ellis countered, "Well, you're not out of the woods yet, Grif. She could be telling the truth you know. And if she is, your insurance company is going to be on the hook for car repairs and probably some medical bills."

"Yeah, well, I can handle that," Grif replied. "I just wanted to make sure they weren't out to take me to the cleaners. Maybe even take my place away. Good thing it was just a neck brace and not a damn wheelchair, huh Ellis?"

"Well, you know, I threw her a curve by getting to her place early. Maybe she didn't have time to get the wheelchair out of the closet."

"What?"

"Just a joke, man. Just a joke. I'll know more in a couple of days," Ellis assured him. "Now where's that new business you seem to have drummed up for me?"

"Over there by the window," Grif motioned.

"You're kidding, " Ellis said. "By that voice over the phone I was expecting something a lot more...well, over the top. He looks like your average yuppie type."

"Yeah, he looks like a yuppie-puppy, but he sounds like a beautician, baby."

"So, what's his story?" Ellis asked Grif.

"He has a sister who's apparently got herself lost or hooked up with some dudes down in Mexico. Anyway, he'll tell you about it. That is if he's still making sense. He's on his fourth Mai Tai."

"Well, give me a Bloody Mary, then. A drink makes anyone's story a lot more interesting."

Ellis got his drink and walked to where Whitfield sat looking out the window. He was a slight man in his late twenties or early thirties, Ellis guessed. He was wearing one of those designer polo shirts and a pair of khakis. Naturally, the belt and shoes matched. Ellis introduced himself, sat down and tried to put his potential client at ease. "Mr. Whitfield, whatever your problem is, it's probably one that I've heard before, so just lay it out as straight and as clear as you can for me...okay?"

"Yes. Absolutely. I'll do that. It's my sister, Rena. She's very young. Just out of college. And you know how people are at that age. Or at least how some people can be. Idealistic, you know? Incredibly idealistic. They seem to think they can solve the world's problems. And it's always the big problems, isn't it? It's always the problems of class struggle and the downtrodden and all the inequity in the world. And who can really ever do anything about that?"

"Mr. Whitfield, can you..." But Ellis didn't have time to finish his question.

"Yes, yes. I'm sorry. Get to the point, right?"

Whitfield went on. "Well you see Rena went down to Mexico. She saw some photographs on the Internet. Some photographs showing these cave children. Indians. I think they're called the Tarahumaran. Well, they're incredibly poverty stricken, you know, and according to Rena their children have the highest mortality rate in the country. And well, if you knew Rena at all, you'd know that she would feel personally compelled to try and reverse what I'm sure is centuries of this sort of situation. I'm not even sure what she intended to do down there initially, she just knew that she wanted to try to help so she went down with one of those humanitarian aid groups. They bring them things. Food and medicines and toys and things like that."

"Sounds like a very laudable thing to do." Ellis said.

"Yes. It does, doesn't it?" Whitfield replied. "But do you know who doesn't think it's particularly laudable? The Mexican officials, that's who. They confiscated all the supplies and goods that the group wanted to bring in. They wouldn't allow them to be delivered. Said it was illegal to bring in food and medicine. Might not meet their standards. Is that a hoot or what? Might not meet their standards. As if they had any to begin with!"

Ellis interjected, "Mexico is like a lot of countries. The local authorities pretty much rule the roost. They can be pretty autocratic and sometimes corrupt. Chances are the local authorities will keep the supplies for themselves. Either to dole out to their family and friends, or more likely, to sell. Was the group even allowed in?"

"Oh yes. Once they had nothing to bring these poor Indians, the despots were more than happy to let them in. They even let them keep a few trinkets to take along. Can you imagine that? These poor little Indian children are living off virtually nothing...and when Rena and her group arrive, all they have to share is junk like paper crowns and bubble bottles."

"Bubble bottles?"

"You know, those plastic bottles filled with soapy water that have this ring you blow and it forms bubbles. Is that pathetic or what?"

"Yes. It's a shame, Mr. Whitfield. But you still haven't told me what, exactly, is the problem."

"Oh yes. Well, you see, the aid group came back. But Rena didn't. She told them she was going to stay another week or so and see if there was anything else she could do to help."

"Well a week or two is not that big a deal," Ellis began, but didn't get to finish his thought.

"She's been gone almost three months," Whitfield cut in. "And just yesterday I received this letter from her," he said, as he pulled the folded papers from his pocket and slid them across the table to Ellis.

Ellis unfolded the papers and began to read the handwritten letter. It was a letter that seemed to rush headlong, as if the writer wasn't even stopping to take a breath.

Dear Terry,

I'm sorry I haven't written sooner, but I really haven't had the chance. I know you must be worried about me, but please believe I'm fine. I'm really fine. My life has been so amazing the past few weeks, and I guess by now, months. I came to Mexico to see what I could do to help. But I was woefully naive. I didn't have a clue as to what these people really needed. I thought I could just get together with some liberal friends, put some supplies together, bring them down and distribute them and then go back to my safe, cozy life in the states. Well, you already know what happened to the supplies. But you don't know what happened to me. I couldn't just walk away from these people, Terry. I couldn't just go back to the kind of life I was living before and not help. And these people need help Terry. They need it desperately. They have nothing when so many so near to them have everything. Their children are dying of malnutrition. Little babies, Terry. Dying because they don't have enough food, or medicine. Dying because the government is deaf to their cries for help. Dying because the local authorities (what a ridiculous name for them) are only out to help themselves and keep the Tarahumaran basically a slave labor force. I tried talking to the government. That was fruitless. I even tried talking to the American Embassy in Mexico City. They said lots of sympathetic things of course. But in the end they would do nothing. Saying it's not their country. They can't intervene. They certainly seemed to have intervened a lot of other places. But they won't do it here. Well, to hell with them if they won't help. I've found people who are helping. People who are aren't afraid of the local thugs or the government or anyone else. People who are not afraid because they have nothing to lose, Terry. They're in almost as bad a shape as the Tarahumaran, but still they persist. Maybe that's what it takes. Maybe you have to have nothing and no hope for anything in the future. Isn't that what they say about alcoholics, Terry? Isn't that what they say? That you have to hit rock bottom before you can start clawing your way back to the top. Well, these people have hit rock bottom Terry. And they're clawing their way back. Bit by bit. Sometimes it seems like inch by inch. And I'm with them Terry. I've become one of them. This is a way I can help. This is a way I can do something. This is a way to give meaning to life, Terry. My life anyway. Everyone is different. I guess we both know that, don't we? But I'm helping

Terry. I really am. And now I need your help. We need your help.
We need it very badly Terry. I want you to meet me. I want you to
come to Mexico and meet me. I'll make it easy for you. We'll meet
in a nice place. A place the tourists go. I'm going to ask a favor of
you, Terry. A favor that you can do. One favor for me. To help
these people, Terry. People who need more help than you or I will
ever be able to imagine. I've told the people I've joined that I can
do this. I've told them that you will help me do this. You can't let
me down, Terry. I know you won't let me down. Please. Help me.
All you have to do is come to San Miguel de Allende. Be there the
evening of April 15. The Plaza Allende. By 9 p.m. You need not
look for me. I will find you. Please be there, Terry. Please be there
for me. But don't look for me. It's important. Don't try to find me.
Just be in the plaza at 9 p.m. I'll find you. And we'll talk. And I
know you'll help me, Terry. I know you'll help these people. I've
told them you would. Terry, you're my big brother and I've always
loved you. But I've never asked anything of you. I'm asking you
now. Please be there, Terry. Be there for me. Be there for people
who need us so. And be there for the people... the Zapatistas...who
really are helping. Please, be there.
> *Love, Rena.*

When Ellis put the letter back on the table, Whitfield spoke.

"You saw that last line. Zapatistas! She's joined some rebel group, right?"

"Well, it would seem so, Mr. Whitfield," Ellis replied.

"Oh god. I knew it. I just knew it. What are they? These Zapatistas. Do you know?"

Ellis's military background, and his penchant for keeping up with hot spots around the world, enabled him to answer quickly. "Zapatista means Indian warrior. It's what the peasants were called during the revolutionary days of Pancho Villa and Zapata. Today, the Zapatistas are causing all kinds of trouble for the Mexican government. They've kidnapped people. Beaten others. In southern Mexico. Threatened to take over ranches owned by foreigners. For them, it's all about land redistribution. Same as when the revolution was going on there. Some think the revolution has never really stopped. They believe the land rightfully belongs to them. So, in some places, they're actually taking it back. As long as it's a little trouble here, a little trouble there, and it stays in the remote areas, the government's in no big hurry to get in the middle of it. Though it sounds like your sister already has."

"She's just so idealistic. So idealistic and so very naive. You don't think they'd hurt her, do you?"

"Well, look Mr. Whitfield, from reading her letter, she sounds okay. But these guys aren't just messing around. A lot of people have been beaten. A lot of people hurt. Some have even been killed. This is not the sort of group a young American college girl ought to be involved with."

"She left me no other way to contact her. I've got to go down there. I've got to make sure she's okay. But I can't go alone. I just can't. I'd be just too frightened. I need someone to go with me. Someone to accompany me. That's why I contacted you Mr. Ellis. That's what I want you to do. Will you go down there with me? San Miguel's safe, isn't it?"

"Yeah, it's in central Mexico. Like she says, tourists go there. But look, in the letter, Rena says she needs to ask something of you. Do you have any idea what that is?"

"No," Whitfield murmured. "No I don't. I just know that she's my little sister and she's gotten herself into this mess and I need to see if I can help."

Later on, no one would say they saw her come in the door. But by the time she was passing the bar on the way to the table Whitfield and Ellis were sharing, everyone heard her yell "You candy-ass, two-timing son of a bitch!"

When Ellis turned he saw a striking redhead in a tight black dress making a beeline for their table. When Whitfield turned, he said "Oh my God. Oh my God." And started to stand up as he was saying, "It's not what you think, this is just…" But that's all he had time to get out before the redhead kicked one of the empty chairs at their table squarely into Whitfield's crotch. The force knocked him back into the chair he had been attempting to vacate.

"Look Miss," Ellis began, already on his feet, "Mr. Whitfield and I were just talking."

"Oh really," she spit back, "well why don't you take your tight ass over to the bar for a minute while Mr. Whitfield and *I* talk?"

"Please," Whitfield said, visibly shaken, "do give us a minute will you…it won't take very long."

"You got that right, honey. It won't take very long at all," the redhead retorted. Then she plopped her butt down on the table in front of Whitfield and raised her leg up on the edge of the seat Whitfield was occupying.

"It's okay." Whitfield said to Ellis. Obviously embarrassed.

"I'll just be over at the bar," Ellis said.

"Well you're taking your fucking time getting there," the redhead shot back.

Ellis gave them both a quick glance, then turned his back and started walking toward the bar. He never got there. Just as he was about to straddle one of the stools he saw Grif's face grimace in horror as he said, "Jesus!"

Ellis whirled around. What Grif had seen and he hadn't, had been the redhead pulling a straight razor from her purse and slashing it across Whitfield's throat. Now Ellis was looking at Whitfield, still seemingly stuck to his chair clutching his gullet while blood seeped through his fingers and down onto his shirt, and the redhead, holding a chair in one hand and the red-tinged razor in the other, was already starting toward the bar.

Some things are instinctual. They're so ingrained they don't require thought, just reflexes. Ellis's right hand came up in one quick motion disappearing into his jacket for less than a second and coming back out with the Glock already pointed at the still approaching redhead.

"Drop the razor, now!" Ellis bellowed. The tone of his voice and the gun at the end of his hand sent the few patrons, as well as the proprietor of Benny's, scurrying to take cover behind the bar, or under their tables, or racing for the exits. It seemed to have no affect whatsoever on the redhead who was now close enough to Ellis to launch the chair straight into his gun hand. Ellis didn't shoot for fear the chair might cause his shot to go somewhere other than where he intended. In the millisecond it took for him to recover from brushing the airborne chair aside with his arm, the redhead had already begun a swipe at him with the bloodstained steel. Once again his instincts reacted before his brain told him what to do. His gun came up and blocked the razor, but the defensive maneuver wasn't enough to jar it from her grip. Then both his feet left the floor and shot out at the middle of his assailant. He could feel his heels pushing deep into her stomach. She was catapulted onto her back as he too hit the floor.

Scrambling up, Ellis stole a quick glance over at Whitfield who was still sitting in his chair, blood now covering the entire front of his shirt. That made the decision for him. When he turned and saw the redhead again rising, he cupped his left hand under his right to steady his aim. Undeterred, she rushed at him again until the bullet from the 19-millimeter entered her heart, sending her straight to the floor. And straight to hell as far as Ellis was concerned.

He immediately pulled two cloth napkins from the tables in front of him as he raced over to start applying pressure to Whitfield's throat, and began barking orders just as quickly.

"Call an ambulance. Get me some more napkins. No. Something bigger. A tablecloth. And get that ambulance. Quick."

The redhead lay dead where the bullet dropped her. Blood now making the black dress even darker just to the left of her cleavage. As she had fallen, the side of her dress had hooked on a chair hiking the already short hemline up nearly to her waist.

Ellis was so involved with trying to make sure Whitfield was still alive, he would later say he didn't hear Grif, who had walked over to make sure the redhead wasn't going to get up again. But everyone else left in the bar had no trouble hearing the black man exclaim, "Goddamn…she's got a dick!"

CHAPTER 9

The flight to Leon wasn't as crowded as he thought it might be. In fact, Ellis had a row to himself. San Miguel was too small to fly to directly. The choice was either a flight to Mexico City and a three-hour drive to the village nestled at the foot of the Guanajuato Mountains, or fly to the industrial city of Leon, and drive for an hour. That wasn't a difficult decision. Ellis knew he'd have to add even two more hours to the trip if he flew into Mexico City. An hour to rent a car. An hour or more just to get out of the city. If he was lucky. Traffic in Mexico City was some of the worst in the world. It was to be avoided if at all possible. So Ellis avoided it.

As he flew through a particularly blue sky with cotton ball clouds, Ellis smiled. He always enjoyed flying commercial. Others on the plane might worry about the weather, or the occasional bump in the sky, but Ellis always thought of himself as lucky. Any flight that allowed him to land with the plane, rather than before it, was a good flight.

The trip was too short for any real sack time. But it was long enough for him to think back on the week that had unfolded prior to his getting on board. He had probably already made the decision to go to Mexico before Whitfield got his windpipe opened by a jealous transvestite hell-bent on mayhem. But seeing the poor guy laid up in the hospital with a pathetic pulse and just enough energy to say "Please go to Mexico and find Rena for me" sealed the deal.

Some additional checking turned up the fact that Whitfield was part owner of Butterfly's, a club in the city that offered music, dance and floor shows with an emphasis on bizarre performers. Business was fat, as was Whitfield's bank account and he was more than happy to pay for a month's worth of Ellis's services in advance. What else could he do? He had more gauze around his neck than a mummy and he wasn't going to be leaving the hospital anytime soon. So Whitfield had one of the girls, well, Ellis assumed it was a girl, but he sure as hell wasn't positive anymore, retrieve a picture from his office and deliver it to Ellis. It was a picture of Whitfield and his sister Rena, taken less than a year ago when they were enjoying a drink and better times at some resort near her school. The picture showed two people laughing and having a good time together. A small-framed, happy guy who didn't as yet have an eight inch scar running from one side of his neck to the other. And a young, pretty dark-haired girl with a grin on her face and the sparkle of wonder in her eyes that reality hadn't yet had time to dim. Though Ellis wondered by now if perhaps it had.

He also spent some time wondering about another woman. Not the redhead, if woman was the right word for her. Frankly, Ellis put her out of his mind as quickly as he put her out of this world. She had tried to kill Whitfield and she was trying very hard to do the same to him. He assumed God only knew whether or not she had already done the same to anyone else. But whether she had or whether she hadn't, she obviously wasn't going to try it again. The police had been satisfied to wrap it up quickly as self-defense. Particularly when they found out that Ellis had a license to carry the Glock he dispatched her with, and that all of the patrons of Benny's, including Grif and Whitfield, backed up Ellis's version of how the events transpired. There was probably someone somewhere who mourned the passing of that particular red-haired, green-eyed shemale, but it wasn't the loner sitting by the window in seat 8A on his way to Mexico.

No, for the moment, Ellis had his mind on a blonde named Laney. Even though he had taken on the Whitfield case, Ellis hadn't forgotten that he told Grif he'd try to help him. So before he headed south of the border he made plans to get back to Ms. Laney Wilson. As he mulled over their meeting just the day before his getting on the plane, Ellis put his elbows on the armrests, brought his hands together, fingers extended, and rested them against his lips. The casual observer might have wondered if this guy sitting by himself was praying for an uneventful flight. He wasn't. He was thinking about the pleasant evening that proceeded it.

Ellis hadn't had to call the blonde with the neck brace as he thought he would. She had called him. She even suggested that they get together for a drink at the end of the day at Greystone in the Gas Lamp District. Ellis was aware of it. It was a little more upscale than he usually went in for, but remembering the bare feet and the blue jeans and the bikini top, he decided to take her up on her offer. When Ellis arrived he didn't have any trouble spotting her. She was sitting at the bar dressed again in blue jeans. But this time she also had on a blue blazer, red high-heeled shoes and a red turtleneck sweater. From a distance, he couldn't quite tell if she still had the neck brace. As he got closer, he realized she didn't.

"Ms. Wilson," Ellis said as he walked up to her, "I almost didn't recognize you without...(she assumed he was going to say your neck brace)...your shoes off."

"Really?" she said. "You look remarkably similar."

"That's probably because I'm so predictable," Ellis countered. "I've got a green suit, a gray suit, a brown suit, a black suit, and, oh yeah, a blue suit. They all pretty much look the same."

"I like a man with simple tastes," she said. "But as for being predictable, if that were the case, you would have been here before me, waiting for me to arrive...to see if I was still wearing that damn brace or whether I was just going to put it on before I came in."

"How do you know I wasn't?" Ellis asked with a smile.

"Touché," she responded. "I guess you're always one step ahead, right Mr. Ellis?"

"Please, no need for formality. Just call me Ellis. Can I get you another wine?"

"Why don't I just finish this one while I give you a chance to catch up. Wouldn't want to get ahead of you, you know? That might give you an edge."

"Ah, good thinking," Ellis replied. "I'll do the right thing and catch up." Turning to the man behind the bar, he said, "Bartender, give me what the lady's having."

They talked around things for a while, avoiding the reason they were both there. Usually this would have put Ellis off and he would have cut to the heart of the matter right away. But there was something rather easy about talking to this woman. The typical tripe about the weather and the wine and the world at large was actually kind of fun when batted back and forth with this blonde who was obviously much more at ease than in their first meeting. And why shouldn't she be. She had called him. She had picked the time and place. Ellis realized he was playing in her ballpark, and for a few minutes anyway, by her rules. But he didn't mind. He was actually enjoying himself.

"Okay, he said, downing the last of his wine, "that makes us even. One to one. Shall we have another?"

"Sure," she said confidently, "but why don't we take it with us to a table. Maybe follow it with something to eat. If you have time, of course."

"It just so happens there's a hole in my social calendar this evening, " Ellis replied. "And dinner would fill it quite nicely."

After they got their second glass of wine they asked for a table and were seated near the back as the restaurant began to fill. As they drank and spoke and ordered dinner, they continued to find ways to talk about things other than accidents and insurance. It was almost as if addressing the issue that had brought them together would signal an end to a rather pleasant interlude. And neither one of them wanted that. So, over his swordfish and her sea bass, they filled each other in with parts of their lives they felt comfortable revealing. He learned that she was a model and had done a lot of things in a lot of places that sound glamorous and intriguing. But she tended to talk more about the tedium of it all and how that sort of life wasn't nearly as exciting as magazines and gossip shows made it out to be. She did enjoy the travel, she said. To keep the conversation from being totally one-sided, Ellis let her know that he had joined the military at a young age and made a career of it by following orders well and keeping his head down. While he did share a number of places in the world where the military had sent him, he avoided entirely indicating the kinds of things he was doing in those places. As well as who he was doing them for, and whom he was doing them to. He also enjoyed the travel, he told her.

They both passed on coffee and desert, opting instead for an after-dinner drink to top off the third glass of wine they had each had with their meal. As the waiter went to retrieve the drinks it was now more than obvious that one of them would have to address what had brought them together in the first place. Ellis sensed the beginning of an embarrassing lull in what up until then had been a full tilt running conversation, so he figured he might as well jump in. Laney beat him to it.

"Is this crazy or what?" Laney said rhetorically. "We've been here for almost an hour and a half and neither one of us has brought up why we were getting together in the first place."

"Well, as long as we're here." Ellis said. She had initiated the meet, so he expected her to begin.

"Look, I just recently got this new agent. And he's pretty good at what he does. I mean he gets me lots of gigs, you know. But he's not the nicest guy in the world. And frankly, he's not beyond trying to get everything he can out of every situation that comes along. Well, the next day...when he found out I had been in an accident, and when I told him that the guy who hit me had given me his name and the name of this bar or something...well he said he'd look into it for me. He said he had this specialist he wanted me to see and that he'd just take care of the whole thing."

"And did you see this...specialist?" Ellis asked.

"Yes, I did and I told him I wasn't feeling all that badly, but he insisted I take x-rays, and he gave me that neck brace to wear and all. I didn't really think I needed it, but he insisted that I wear it whenever I was...well...out in public."

"Must be a special neck brace," Ellis joked, "it's only beneficial when there are other people around. Can't say as I've heard of that particular model."

"Look, I know this must sound horrible, but Riley, that's my agent, well he said it's not really about the guy that hit me, you know. He said it was really the insurance company that would be taking care of everything anyway...and that there might be some compensation in it for me...not from your friend, but from the insurance company. And they have all those unconscionable profits, don't they?"

"Insurance companies do okay for themselves. But why do you think the rates are always going up?

"I know. I know. Listen, we're here, aren't we? We're talking about this thing. I mean I probably wouldn't have gone through with it anyway. I've never done anything remotely like this before. It's just that I sure could use some money to put away. I'm not necessarily at the top of my profession, you know. I'm fast reaching the point where there are going to be fewer and fewer jobs and more time in-between them."

"Don't sell yourself short," Ellis said. "You're a very attractive woman. And people are going to enjoy looking at you for quite some time. But tell me this. Where did you leave things with this Riley fellow? Does he know about our meeting the other day?"

"Yes." Laney said softly. Followed by a rather telling pause.

"Okay. Does he know about tonight's little sit down?"

"His idea," Laney said.

"Really?"

"But he wanted me to do it with the neck brace. And maybe just a slight limp." She barely got the last word out of her mouth before she started giggling. And Ellis couldn't help it. Maybe it was the alcohol, maybe it was the fact that she was so damned good looking, but he was chuckling right along with her.

"Well, unless you've got it underneath that turtle neck, I don't seem to see any neck brace. And if there was a limp, it must have been slight because I missed it altogether."

"I said I was a model. I never said I was an actress."

"I believe you," Ellis said. "You're not an actress and you're not a criminal. And hopefully that's why we've had a rather pleasant evening."

"Oh, I noticed the past tense there. I guess I'm not as high as I thought I was," Laney quipped.

"It's just that I've got a plane to catch early in the morning and I haven't packed yet. I'll be out of town for just a few days. And I wasn't necessarily calling a halt to the evening. In fact, I was wondering if perhaps you wanted me...or you and me, to go see your Mr. Riley."

"Oh no. No, that won't be necessary," Laney replied. "I'm perfectly capable of letting Riley know that he'll have to look elsewhere to pursue his business interests other than representing extremely talented but somewhat maturing models. And I'll get the insurance adjusters, the real insurance adjusters, to touch base with your friend right away."

"You sure there wont be a problem with Riley?" Ellis asked.

"Well, something tells me I'll be needing another agent soon. But at least I won't be needing a defense attorney."

They both smiled. Ellis found it particularly easy to smile with this woman.

When the bill came they quibbled a bit about the check, but Ellis wound up convincing her that he should pay as a reward for her decision to take the straight and narrow path. A few minutes later as they were outside waiting for the valet to bring Laney's car, Ellis said, "Perhaps when I'm back from out of town, I can give you a call. I had a great time tonight. I got the feeling you did too."

"Well, you're pretty sure of yourself, aren't you?"

"Not really," Ellis replied. "Just thought it was worth the potential humiliation."

Just then the car arrived. The valet hopped out, opened the door for Laney, took the tip and the exit cue from Ellis, then left as

Ellis closed the door once Laney was inside. "Well, Mr. Ellis," Laney said, with a smile in her voice, "I would not mind terribly if you gave me a call. I might even answer it. And I might even suggest we get together for another evening not unlike this one."

"Consider it done," Ellis said. "And if there's even a hint of a problem with Riley, call me."

"There won't be a problem," Laney said. "He'll just move on to his next sleazy idea. I'm sure he's got a number of them. And he can be persuasive you know. In fact, it wasn't until I pulled in the parking lot, when I got here earlier this evening, that I decided not to wear this," Laney said laughingly as she tossed the neck brace to Ellis and drove away.

Before he went to bed that night, Ellis called Grif and filled him in on his conversation. Assuming he would be just something shy of jubilant, Ellis felt a bit odd when Grif took the information in a rather low-key way. Something was obviously distracting him but Ellis didn't have time to plumb the depths of Grif's psyche. He had a plane to catch the next morning.

The following day Ellis dropped off Osgood at the kennel and drove his car to Deutschland Motors. It had been sputtering a bit lately. Ellis didn't know what was wrong with it, but he knew Lothar would. He took a cab to the airport from there.

And now as the plane began its descent, Ellis thoughts turned back to the mission at hand. Odd he thought, the fact that he continued to refer to his assignments as missions. If only to himself. Old habits do indeed die hard.

CHAPTER 10

Outside the window, Ellis could see the bajio below. The Mexican heartland. Mountains and valleys that, from this distance, resembled the western United States. He had been in Mexico before. Most often as a tourist. Usually in the coastal enclaves of Puerto Vallarta or Acapulco or Mazatlan. Once in Mexico City. And once had been enough. There he hadn't been a tourist. And he hadn't stayed very long. Just long enough to oversee the dispatch of a rather nasty drug lord who had run afoul of the U. S. government for getting too much of his product onto too many military installations. He hadn't had to do the work himself. Just make sure it was done. Then leave a few non-stenciled dog tags behind to let the dead man's successor know that it might be wiser to pursue his business somewhere other than Uncle Sam's bases.

The locals he had contracted made rather sloppy work of the job. They were probably quickly rounded up by the drug lord's henchmen and made to pay a price far greater than Ellis had given them. But he lost no sleep over that either. In their own way, they were probably just as bad as the asshole they left in a Mexico City gutter. They probably had aspirations of taking his place with the money they got for their wet work. Ambition is a bitch, Ellis reflected. Especially if you're only doing something for ambition's sake. Better to have some sort of moral imperative. Even if it's as misguided as the next guy's. At least that way there's some sense of completion. Ambition is insatiable. No plateau is ever high enough. It was probably the driving force that took that particular Mexican kingpin from a blood soaked birth in a dusty rural village to a blood soaked death in a grimy urban gutter. Surely there were some highs along the way Ellis thought, but the guy's exit was not that different from his entry into this world. Maybe nobody's is.

Leon was as sun splashed as most of the Mexican cities Ellis had visited. He made his way down the ramp and across the tarmac to the airport terminal. But being in the central highlands, at a higher altitude, it didn't seem as hot as Ellis remembered Mexico. Customs took more time than it should have. This was always a gringo's reminder that things move considerably slower south of the border than in the states. Which is not a bad thing, Ellis thought. It just always took some getting used to.

The car he rented was no prize. But it would do. A brown Nissan sedan at least eight to ten years old. No power steering. No power windows. It did have an air conditioner. Of course the air conditioner didn't work. Not at all the sort of thing one would expect from a rental car company in the states. But in Mexico you adjust your expectations just as you adjust your personal metronome. Ellis was used to adapting to whatever situation he found himself in. Adaptation was often the difference between survival and something much more unpleasant.

The drive from Leon to San Miguel de Allende was relatively easy. Once outside Leon there were few cars on the highway, which was in good condition. The two-lane snaked its way around hills and boulders running right down to the pavement. Cactus, sand and rock formed a landscape most would find unappealing. But once the road straightened out into the plain, Ellis appreciated the barrenness of it. Its unapologetic sterility appealed to him.

Like most other parts of the car, the radio didn't work either, but Ellis didn't mind. He listened to the wind whipping his shirtsleeve as his arm rested on the flat of the doorframe--the window having been rolled down beneath it. As he drove he thought about his assignment, Rena Whitfield. She had certainly been moving around a lot. Her involvement with the Indians, the Tarahumaran, had been in the Chihuahua province in the north. But the Zapatistas rebellion was based in their home of Chiapas, in southern Mexico. And now, here Ellis was, driving through the central highlands for a potential meet in almost the geographic center of this sprawling country. Well, he thought to himself, she had been here for three months according to her brother. Enough time to do some traveling. For pleasure? He thought not. The tone of Rena's letter led him to believe this young American was doing more than sightseeing. He hoped he would soon know for sure.

A few miles from his destination he caught his first glimpse of San Miguel sitting at the foot of the Guanajuato Mountains. White, brown and gray buildings dotted the landscape of what had once been a simple frontier post in colonial times. Today it was a popular destination for tourists and expats who sought out a bit of Mexico with enough of an American influence to be comfortable, but not a place so totally overrun with theme bars and Yankee hotels as to make it little more than a border town transplanted to the middle of the country. From where he was, he could easily make out the spire of the Parroquia de San Miguel Arcangel, the parish church that towered over the jardin, or main square. It was in that square that he would look for Rena as she looked for her brother.

Following road signs and using the church steeple as a landmark, he eventually made his way into the old part of the city. Cobblestone streets with holes and craters that served as natural speed bumps had slowed his entry to a virtual crawl. So much so that a young boy, who appeared to be no more than ten or eleven years old, had begun to walk along beside his car as he crept along. The boy was grinning and staring at Ellis intently. Ellis was a bit concerned that the youngster might hurt himself in the street.

"Precaucion!" Ellis said. Then, in English, "Be careful."

"No peligro." the boy replied.

Not dangerous? Depends on your point of view. Of course, he's probably done this a thousand times with a thousand tourists who had no idea where they were, but some idea of where they wanted to be, Ellis reasoned.

"Plaza Allende?" Ellis questioned.

"Si. Con permiso?" the boy replied. Then he quickly ran behind Ellis's car and coming up from the other side, opened the passenger door, jumped in and slammed the door shut.

"Izquierda, izquierda," the boy said frantically as he pointed to his left.

Ellis, who was already halfway through the intersection, made a quick check of his rear view mirror, and finding no one directly behind him, turned hard to the left, his right front wheel going over the curb but sending him in the direction his young friend had advised. Habit made him glance around quickly to make sure no police were watching his bumper-car maneuver as he headed up a steep cobblestone hill that lead to a left or right decision.

"Plaza Allende?" Ellis said again as he reached the point where he could no longer go forward.

"Derecha", derecha," the boy exclaimed as he gestured excitedly to the right.

Ellis let off the clutch slowly and turned to the right. He had gone no more than thirty yards down another pock-marked street before it opened into a wide square as the boy yelled, "Plaza Allende...Plaza Allende."

Ellis couldn't help but laugh to himself that he had been only a block and a half away when his young pathfinder had volunteered to help.

"Gracias, mi amigo," Ellis said as he reached into his pocket and handed the boy a dollar bill.

"De nada," the young one replied as he snatched the dollar from Ellis's hand, opened the door and was out on the street looking for his next gringo as he politely called back, "Buenos tardes."

And a good afternoon to you, Ellis reflected as he smiled at his own vulnerability and this enterprising young man's bravado.

Sitting in his car at the corner, making sure he wasn't blocking anyone behind him, Ellis surveyed the plaza where the next night he would be trying to find out just what this young American girl wanted from her brother, who wanted very badly to have her back safely in the states. The square was big and open with a large wooden gazebo in the center rimmed by trees and benches and shrubs and sidewalks. Surrounding the square were cafes and tourist information centers, the Parroquia de San Miguel Arcangel that Ellis had seen prior to entering the center of the city, and one or two large buildings that Ellis assumed housed the policia or some other governmental organization. Time enough to find out later, he thought. For now, he would get a hotel room and do as much reconnaissance as he could before the next night's rendezvous. As usual, Ellis had arranged to be where he needed to be a number of hours in advance of when he needed to be there. It had been drilled into him. Along with a couple of other mandates. If you agree to be somewhere, be there in advance. Have at least two ways out of anyplace there's only one way into. And don't leave things to chance. Chance is for gamblers. Gamblers who lose more often than they win.

CHAPTER 11

Ellis secured a room in a hotel just two blocks from the Plaza Allende. The street entrance was unmarked. If you weren't going there on purpose, you'd never know it was there. And he made sure no one other than himself knew he was going to be there. He had made his plans before he left the states. Plans made with nothing more than a street map in a Fodor's Guide to Mexico. But he hadn't shared those plans with anyone. Not even the man who was paying him. It wasn't that he didn't trust Whitfield. He did. But he had often discovered the more people you involve in something, the more you increase the chances of something going wrong. Loyalties change. Motivations adjust. Circumstances switch at the last minute and things can go wrong. People can get hurt. The fewer people who know exactly what's going on, the better it is for everyone involved. So Ellis kept his hotel room and his time schedule and whatever other plans he had to himself.

The hotel he chose, aside from having a relatively blind entrance off the street, opened into a high-walled courtyard. To the immediate right sat the hotel office. The ground floor consisted of the restaurant and six other guest rooms. The second and third floors were all guest rooms. Ellis selected one in the center that gave him a panoramic view of the courtyard. On his way to the room he made note of where the stairways were and how difficult it would or wouldn't be if he had to leave from some non-traditional exit like the roof. It didn't appear to be that difficult. Especially since so many of the buildings in the old part of the city were close together and shared common containing walls.

Having arrived a day and a half ahead of when the Whitfield siblings were to link up, Ellis had given himself some time to relax and to casually reconnoiter the surrounding area. Once he had stowed the contents of the small overnight bag he had brought with him, he left his jacket in his room and decided to take a turn around the neighborhood. He first went back to the square and spotted a large patio that was part of a restaurant just across the street from the side of the cathedral. It seemed that Catholicism and commerce had found the need over the centuries to combine their appeals to both locals and tourists alike. Giving thanks to a merciful God or sightseeing at a seventeenth century chapel was always more likely to occur if one could find a cold cervesa just a few steps away.

As he sat in the shade and drank his beer slowly, Ellis looked into the afternoon sun and wondered how full the plaza would be the following evening. How hard would it be to identify the pretty young brunette? From which corner of the square would she emerge? Would she be alone? Unlikely. Of course, she'd be looking for her brother and therefore might not feel the need to have her new compatriots with her. But they may not feel the same way. Maybe they'd be with her regardless of her predisposition. Maybe she didn't have a choice in the matter. Sure, her letter sounded as if she was doing all this voluntarily. But what if she wasn't? What if all of this was just a ploy to extort money from some gullible gringo? Or what if they had plans to kidnap the brother as well as the sister? All speculation, Ellis realized. The letter seemed real enough. Whitfield had planned to come to Mexico. He just didn't want to come alone. But now Ellis was alone. And he had no way of knowing precisely what he was getting into. That's why he was sitting there in Plaza Allende a day before he needed to be there. That's why he was running the options and the exits and escape routes over in his mind. That's why he pulled a small notepad and a pen from his shirt pocket and sketched the layout of the square with the precise number of buildings, alleys and streets that could take him away from the plaza if he had to get out of there in a hurry.

After finishing his beer, and his sketch, Ellis decided to take a stroll around the blocks that surrounded the square. Needless to say, he had been unable to bring a weapon with him on the plane, and even though he wasn't at all sure that he'd need one, he was sure that he'd rather have one and not need it than vice versa. Trying to locate a pistol or firearm from legitimate sources, or their opposite in this small town, would bring more attention to him than he really wanted to engender, so Ellis kept his eye open for any place that might supply some measure of defense, or even offense if necessary. He hadn't had to stroll very far before he came upon a silver shop that among bracelets, ear rings and belt buckles, he also found three or four hunting knives. The edge was sharp enough on each, but it was really the overall strength of the blade that Ellis was most concerned with. While the proprietor, an old man with hair as silver as his wares and skin more wrinkled than any of his leather goods, extolled the virtues of the ivory handles and the polished knobs and the innately hand-carved craftsmanship, Ellis pressed on the blades with the heel of his hand to see which might be the least likely to snap at the most inopportune time.

Having selected a skinning knife with a six-inch blade that the shop owner obviously considered the runt of the litter, Ellis asked "Cuanto?"

"Quinientos pesos," the proprietor quickly replied, accepting the fact that Ellis wasn't going to go for one of the gaudier ones he had been pushing. Then adding in broken English, "This is a...how you say....muy study knife."

Ellis realized what he was trying to say and added cordially, "Yes. It's a very sturdy knife."

"Si, sturrrdy...es very sturrrdy."

Ellis didn't mind paying a bit more than it was worth. Especially after he talked the shop owner into including the scabbard that held it for no extra cost. At the end of their negotiations both parted satisfied. Ellis had a bit of defense he hoped he wouldn't need and the old man had more pesos than before Ellis came in.

He ate dinner earlier than usual that evening. Carne asados zamora at the restaurant where he had a beer earlier in the day. He wanted to get there early enough so he could see how the square filled up in the evening. Which streets brought in the most people. How they gathered. What they did. He took up a position at a small table with a view of the square, intent upon making his meal long and leisurely. Which isn't hard to do in Mexico. A drink or two before dinner. An appetizer. The meal itself. An after dinner drink. He could take in a lot over that time. And if he indulged a little more than he should, well, this was the night to do it. He could sleep in tomorrow morning. It was tomorrow night when he really had to be on his game.

By the time Ellis was finishing his dinner, Plaza Allende was overflowing. Street vendors pushed their carts and hawked their wares to sunburned tourists. An elderly couple, obviously Anglo, but just as obviously familiar with their surroundings, sat on a bench and watched the others around them. Kids running and chasing each other. Lovers, or more likely would-be lovers, strolling hand and hand until a prime spot on the knee-high stonewall encircling the fountain was vacated by two teenage boys who had finished their cigarettes. Policemen in brown uniforms, two-man patrols taking a turn through the plaza about every half hour. Then returning to the dark three-story building up and to the left of where Ellis sat and watched and made mental notes to himself.

Ellis finished paying for his meal and planned to take a stroll through the plaza himself. He was in the process of putting his linen napkin on the table and pushing away from it when he heard a commotion near the center of the square. A small crowd had gathered and was bunched together looking at something that Ellis couldn't see from his particular vantage point. Voices were raised. Most in Spanish. And while Ellis was familiar with many words in the language, he couldn't tell what the exact hubbub was about. So he made his way down the steps of the restaurant entrance and was about to cross the street that separated him from the area he had been watching when two policemen emerged from the gaggle of bodies that had been the latest focus of his interest. They seemed to be holding someone between them who was squirming and kicking and entreating the crowd from which they had just emerged for help. But it was obvious the crowd was not in a hurry to follow the two uniformed men, preferring instead to shout after them and converse with others around them.

After waiting for a couple of cars to pass, Ellis crossed the street and headed for the center of the plaza, but continued to watch the policemen head toward the building where their compatriots had been entering and exiting all evening. As they got to the entrance, one policeman removed his grip from what Ellis now saw was a small boy, who was yelling and kicking and still trying to break free. As that policeman reached out to open the door, the boy made one last attempt to escape. He twisted round quickly and as he did the other policeman swung his arm under the youngster's neck just in time to pull him off his feet and back into his grasp. But not in time to keep Ellis from seeing that it was the same dark haired urchin who had bounded into his car that morning and directed him to the Plaza Allende.

The two patrolmen hustled the kid into the police station disappearing into the massive doorway that was the entrance to the building.

"Please, Henry, let's go home now," Ellis heard from just behind him. He turned and saw the elderly couple he had noticed earlier in the park.

"Pardon me," Ellis said, "but do you know what was going on there?"

The couple stopped as they heard his question. "We don't really know," the woman said. "Something about a possible theft."

"Theft my eye!" Her octogenarian partner replied. "It's those damned corrupt cops. If I were back in Seattle I'd give them a piece of my mind, I would."

"What do you mean?" Ellis questioned.

The old man continued, obviously grateful to be able to converse in English with a fellow statesider. "It's a rip-off, that's what it is. A rip-off. Those policia, they wander through the plaza and look for young ones like that to shake down. They know those kids have been out all day...doing things to make money. So they grab one and take him back to the police station and take the few pesos the kid has been able to earn for himself. They tell all the people in the plaza that they caught the kid trying to steal some tourist's purse. So they wind up looking like they're doing their job when they're really just ripping these poor little kids off. Can you believe those bastards?"

"Henry, please, your blood pressure. Just calm down and lets go," his wife urged.

"Yes, I'm sorry, "Ellis said, "I didn't mean to upset you. I heard the noise and I was just curious."

"God damned corrupt bastards", Henry kept muttering as his wife took his arm and they turned to walk away from the plaza. "Why don't they pick on somebody their own size?"

This was not what Ellis wanted. He had planned to keep a very low profile. And he knew it wasn't really any of his business. Especially if it had been going on for a while as the old guy said. But the kid had done him a favor that morning. Plus he looked scared as hell and was doing everything in his power to keep from being dragged in there. And even though Ellis told himself he was not one of these people who had to right every wrong he came upon, he still found himself walking across the plaza and making his way up the short steps leading to that massive doorway.

CHAPTER 12

Inside Ellis found himself in a square room that apparently served as the processing area for the building. There were a couple of offices on the left. Doors closed to both. As he walked further into the room he passed a long hallway on his right, which seemed to branch off right and left at its end. At the back wall of the entrance, a uniformed man sat at a gunboat-gray metal desk. His head was down and his hand was moving slowly. Making notes on the stacks of papers in front of him, he seemed unaware of Ellis's entry into the room.

"Habla Ingles?" Ellis asked.

The man at the desk looked up at Ellis now standing before him. He neither smiled nor frowned, but simply looked directly into Ellis's eyes and said, "Si. Habla Ingles."

"A few minutes ago a boy was brought in here", Ellis began, "I think I know him. I was wondering if I could see him. To make sure it's the boy I think it might be."

"Ju wait." the man said in a heavy accent as he pointed toward the one chair in the room next to the long hallway Ellis had seen as he entered. Ellis glanced at the chair and as the man rose from his desk, Ellis walked over and took a seat. The man then knocked on the door of the nearest office. A muffled "Si" came from inside. Then the man opened the door and walked in, closing it behind him.

As Ellis sat there waiting, he kept thinking to himself that he shouldn't be there at all. What difference did it make about the kid anyway? So the boy had helped him. So what? Ellis knew the kid only helped him because he assumed there'd be money in it. And it could get complicated if the police wanted information Ellis wasn't in a hurry to share. Like where he was staying or why he was in Mexico in the first place. But he also thought about what the old man had said. And how scared the kid looked when he was dragged into the building. He didn't have time to think much beyond that because just then the office door opened. The man Ellis had spoken to walked out and gestured for him to come. As Ellis rose and walked over, the man held the door open for him.

The greeting Ellis received was similar to the one he had gotten earlier. A man behind a desk, more interested in the papers in front of him than the gringo standing before him. But this was a very different man from the one Ellis had encountered first, the man now leaving the office and closing the door behind him. That man had been in uniform, but obviously under duress. His shirt collar was open and he wore no tie. His shoes were not shined. His hair was unruly. This sloppy appearance indicated to Ellis that the man was probably sloppy at his job as well. But there was nothing unruly or sloppy about the man behind the desk Ellis stood in front of now. The man who said to Ellis without looking up, "Take a seat, Senor."

As he selected one of the two chairs in front of the desk, Ellis took stock of the office around him. Papers in neat stacks. Books straight and tall in the bookcase. If a wastepaper basket was there, it was hidden. There were no pictures on the desk or wall. Nothing of a personal nature whatsoever. Ellis had seen and felt this aura before. The vibe was far more military than civil servant. As was the man who sat before him. His uniform was highly starched. A tie at his neck came down and disappeared between the first and second buttons of his shirtfront. No jewelry adorned his wrists or his fingers. Fingers that seemed inordinately long with nails precisely trimmed though not manicured. The pen clasped between his thumb and forefinger was definitely not government issue though. It was silver at the head and at the tip. The clip as well. In between, black with silver latticework gave the impression of a complex web. An appropriate accessory, Ellis would later concede.

"I am Capitan Morales," the uniformed man said without looking up. "Your name and passport."

Ellis answered quickly, but he was in no hurry to hand over his passport. "Ellis. My name is Brig Ellis. I'm here…"

"Your passport, senor." Morales said for the second time, still not looking up at the man sitting across from him. And again, a statement rather than a question.

Ellis reached into his pants pocket, pulled out his passport and put it on top of the papers the man was writing on. This had the desired effect. The man stopped writing and looked up.

For a moment, there was only silence. Neither man wanted to look away first. Neither was in a hurry to speak. Ellis saw a penetrating pair of brown eyes looking directly into his. But there was nothing else to read there. Morales was making a point of not revealing any particular emotion. Not interest. Not annoyance.

Certainly not friendliness. Ellis gave as good as he got. He felt he was, at least momentarily, in the driver's seat. He had both answered the captain's question and provided what was asked of him. It was now Morales's turn to respond. But Morales was in no hurry to do so. He continued to stare into Ellis' face. Not looking down at the passport. Not even blinking. But after a few seconds he realized the man across the table from him was not going to flinch. So he sat his pen down with one hand and picked up the passport with the other. Still staring at Ellis.

"I am surrounded by tedium." Morales said. "Are you a momentary diversion?"

"I would have thought that young boy they brought in here a little while ago, kicking and screaming, might have alleviated the monotony."

"You are particularly interested in young boys...are you, Mr. Ellis?" Morales asked, finally looking at the passport and thereby not giving Ellis the opportunity to see if the question was as odiously delivered as it was received.

Ellis had no desire to be baited though, so he simply replied, "Just this one. He helped me out earlier today."

"Are you a man who frequently needs help from young boys, Mr. Ellis?"

Closer to the line, Ellis thought. But he'd continue to play dumb. At least for now.

"I just thought there might have been some confusion, and if there was, I wanted to see if I could help in some way. Perhaps vouch for the boy."

"Do I look confused to you, Mr. Ellis? Do I look like I do not know what I am doing?" As he asked the second question he rose, and Ellis was struck by the fact that his legs, like his fingers, just seemed to keep going and going. A quick guess by Ellis put him at six feet, eight or nine inches. Yet still, almost frighteningly thin. He moved around the desk to the side where Ellis sat and waited for him to reply.

Ellis paused for a moment before saying anything. He understood what was going on. The small office. The strangely oversized man. The move around the desk to loom over him. These were techniques that Ellis had both encountered and practiced. So Ellis continued to keep it civil.

"Not at all, Captain Morales. In fact, quite the opposite", Ellis said. "You strike me as a man who knows exactly what he is doing."

Morales, still holding the passport in his hand, sat on the corner of the desk. His feet still easily planted firmly on the floor. "Such flattery is acceptable. Sometimes even appreciated, Mr. Ellis. As long as it is not...condescendencia?

"Condescension? Absolutely not Captain."

"Yes, condescension. Speaking down...as if to one beneath you. You would not do such a thing, would you, Mr. Ellis?"

"Oh, like most, I've probably been condescending before. But I certainly had no intention of being condescending with you Captain. If that's how you took my remarks, then I apologize."

"I take no offense," Mr. Ellis. "Occasionally I take recourse. But never offense."

Ellis was momentarily silent, feeling the Captain obviously enjoyed talking about himself.

"A joke, Mr. Ellis. Do not Americans enjoy a good joke?" Morales asked with something approaching a smile. Though hardly a sincere one.

"Indeed we do," Ellis replied. "Without a sense of humor, where are we?"

"Perhaps we are here, in San Miguel, Mr. Ellis. Here in my office." As Morales glanced at the passport he continued to stride around the office that was much too small for him. "Where a thirty-six year old American seems to have a morbid fascination with a young Mexican male child."

Ellis couldn't help himself, "You know, I let that slide before. Not just once, but twice."

Morales raised his hand to his lips as if to say...what, me give offense...never. But what he actually said was, "But what is one to think, Mr. Ellis? You have already said to me that you do not think I am confused. You do not think I am someone who is unsure of what he is doing. If that is the case, then your continued concern about this young boy...who was brought in here...and is therefore now under my control...is hard to understand, Mr. Ellis. Are you afraid he might tell us something that you would rather we not hear?"

The Captain's belabored retort had given Ellis time to regain his composure. "Look, as I said before, I was simply concerned about the boy. I was thinking that the officers might have gotten him confused with someone else. He seemed like a really nice kid and I just wanted to see if there was anything I could do."

"The young grow up very fast these days, Mr. Ellis. They do things they should not do and they get into trouble. This is because they are undisciplined. They are not used to authority. They are not accustomed to doing the things they should do and answering to the people they should answer to. Often this is because their parents do not oversee them like they should. When that happens, we have to oversee them. We have to keep our streets friendly and safe and pleasant for wealthy American tourists, like you, to stroll through. Do we not, Mr. Ellis?"

By now Ellis felt there was nothing to be gained by engaging Morales in dueling repartee. He probably was a diversion for the Capitan. And playing the nice guy card didn't seem to be getting anywhere anyway.

"Perhaps I could see the boy?" Ellis queried. "Maybe help with a fine if there is one."

"Ah, you wish to be helpful. Yes. You would like to help with a fine. What exactly does that mean, Mr. Ellis?"

"It just means that if there is some fine...for something he's done...maybe I could pay it and the kid could be on his way."

"How noble of you, Mr. Ellis. You would do this for a boy you hardly know. How very American. Come, Mr. Ellis. Let us go see if perhaps we can help...you and I. I had asked that the child be prepared for interrogation before you came in. He is probably ready by now. Let us go see. Perhaps there is something you can do."

CHAPTER 13

The walk down the long hallway was traversed in silence. Ellis followed a step behind Morales. From that vantage point he was again struck by the length of the Captain's arms and legs coupled with the decided lack of meat on his bones. Yet his uniform fit like a glove. There was no way standard issue would look so sharp on such a nonstandard frame, Ellis thought. The towering policeman obviously had his uniforms tailored. Nothing really out of the ordinary about that, Ellis said to himself. He had known officers and even some noncoms in his previous life that had a bit of needlework done. It was a way to dress for success, even if you were wearing the same thing as every other inhabitant of your particular universe.

At the end of the hallway they turned left and that's when Ellis started to hear both the laughter and the whimpering. It was very faint at first. Ellis wondered if it might be coming from one of the cells they were passing. But the farther they walked the more it became apparent that the pitiful pleas of "No! Por favor!" and the snickering laughter that followed were coming from the area beyond the doorway now directly in front of them. The one just above the frame with the chipped paint that spelled out the word, bano.

As they entered the bathroom, the stench was enough to force an involuntary recoil in most. But Ellis wasn't like most. And from what he could see, neither was Morales. Neither man raised the back of a hand to cover the offense as they passed through the entryway and entered the toilet area, which was indeed the place from where the entreaties had emanated.

"No. No. Por favor, no!" Ellis heard the boy cry again. And now he could see why.

The kid was upside down in midair, hanging from a rope tied round his ankles that had been thrown over an open pipe that ran the length of the room. The other end of the rope had been looped around a radiator and was now being held by one of two jackasses Ellis had heard braying as he and Morales had approached. The boy's hands were also tied behind his back so that his head would be the initial point of contact in the reeking toilet bowl jackass one was slowly lowering him toward.

"Don't do this," Ellis said directly to Morales.

Morales replied, "Is this the boy you were looking for?"

"Yes, it is. Now tell that cretin to stop."

"Lentamente," Morales said, and the man slowed the boy's descent, but he did not stop.

"Look," Ellis said, you don't need to do this." Reaching into his pocket he pulled out a role of cash. Peeling off five hundred-peso notes, he said, "Here. I'll pay his fine."

"Cesar." the captain said. And the idiot who had been slowly letting the rope slide through his fingers now gripped it tight and smiled at Ellis revealing a mouth that would be a challenge to even the most skilled oral surgeon.

"This young one, Mr. Ellis, that you are so eager to help, is a thief. We have caught him many times taking valuables from tourists, just like you. We told him that the next time he was caught, he would regret it. Do you think he regrets it, Mr. Ellis?"

Tears had reversed their normal flow pattern, and were now running down the lad's temples as he looked at Ellis from his topsy-turvy position and moaned, "Aoudad, senor...ayudar."

Ellis's first inclination was to walk over and grab the boy, but he wasn't sure he could get there in time if the numbskull holding the rope got the order from Morales to let go. Ellis had also noticed that the dullard's compatriot had taken up a position behind him when the conversation started.

"Yes. I'm sure he regrets it. I'm sure he'll never do it again. Just let me take him out of here, now," Ellis said, as he started to move toward the boy.

"One second, please." Morales quickly intoned. And the rope-holder gave a quick jerk on the line just slightly raising the boy, then just as suddenly letting him drop back to his original position, now less than a foot above the fetid toilet.

"This young one's fine is fifteen hundred pesos, Mr. Ellis. For fifteen hundred pesos we can release this young man into your custody."

"Done," said Ellis. He immediately reeled off more notes and handed the remainder of the pesos to Morales. Then he quickly stepped over and cradled the boy; turning him upright again while saying to the man holding the rope, "Let it go, I've got him."

The man looked over at Morales and as the captain nodded, the policeman let the rest of the rope run through his hands. Ellis pulled the young boy down and began untying his feet and hands. As he did, the captain spoke.

"You realize, Mr. Ellis, that we will however need to keep your passport here, just to make sure that the young one will appear for his court proceeding."

There was no way Ellis wanted to walk out of that police station without his passport. "Well, is there anyway I can save the court some time...my schedule may not permit me to be here very long," Ellis began.

"Let us discuss this in a more appropriate place," Captain Morales said as he turned and headed back into the hallway, "my office."

Fifteen minutes later Ellis was standing outside the police station on the sidewalk. Darkness had fallen and lights lit up the plaza and it's surrounding shops and cafes. He held his passport in one hand, and the hand of the boy in the other. It had cost him another fifteen hundred pesos to do so. The little one wrapped himself around Ellis's leg. He squeezed tightly and just kept saying, "Gracias...gracias...gracias."

Ellis bent down and looked into the boy's eyes and said, "It's okay." He wasn't sure why, but for some reason he reached into his pocket and gave the boy a twenty-peso note. He didn't know if the boy was a thief or not. He didn't really want to know. He just knew he couldn't let those sick bastards enjoy themselves at the kid's expense. But he also knew he couldn't keep having run-ins with the locals if he was going to do what he had come to Mexico to do. And there was no way he could do that watching over some street urchin at the same time. He didn't have to worry about that for long though. With the money stuffed in his shirt pocket and one last, "Gracias senor, gracias," on his lips, the boy ran down the street, around the corner and disappeared into the night.

Under his breath, Ellis mumbled, "Big heart, small brain, dumb ass. Get with the program." He was talking to himself.

CHAPTER 14

The next day began ominously. Clouds sat atop the city like a clinging hangover. Soon the rain would start. But Ellis knew that wasn't the important thing. The important thing was when the rain would end. Hopefully before that night. If it was raining that evening, everyone would be covered up in hats, umbrellas, ponchos and rain gear. It would be a hell of a lot harder to spot a dark-haired American girl among the crowd in the plaza if headgear was the appropriate attire.

By mid morning the rain had begun. Slowly at first. Just a few drops that gave no warning of what was to follow. But as the skies darkened and the thunder seemed to rumble down from the mountains surrounding San Miguel, the drops began to splatter as they hit the cobblestone streets. Those who had ventured out earlier looked for shelter in whatever kind of establishment the closest open door might offer.

Ellis found himself standing in the entrance of a leather shop. Hurraches and hats, belts and bags hung on the wall of what was no more than a ten foot wide by twenty foot deep adobe enclosure dedicated to providing tourists with a way to wear their memories home. Ellis's only reason for dropping in had been the downpour. But now that he was there, it occurred to him that it might make sense to pick up a little something for Ms. Laney Wilson. She had stayed somewhere in the back of his mind since he left her outside Greystone. A smile crossed his lips as his eyes happened to land on a pair of beaded moccasins. "That'll work," he said as he thought about the first time he saw Laney sans shirt and shoes. He could tell her that now she didn't have to walk around her place barefoot anymore. It didn't really matter whether the moccasins fit or not. They'd be a good conversation starter. And it would let her know he was thinking about her. Maybe there was something worthwhile about this rain after all.

Even after he bought his gift and had it put in a plastic bag, he continued to stand in the doorway and gaze at what a few moments ago was only a street. Now it had also become a stream as water at least ankle-high gushed rapidly across the cobblestones and down the hill. Well, Ellis thought to himself, he could either stand there and continue to wait, or he could roll up his pant legs, drop his own shoes and socks into the bag with the moccasins and just go for it. Less that a minute later, after receiving another plastic bag for his head from the friendly shopkeeper who realized what he was about to do, Ellis was making his way back to his hotel via the rain swelled streets and cracked sidewalks that were not easy to manipulate even in good weather. He managed not to slip, but he didn't manage to avoid getting soaked. So, once back, he took his shirt, pants and underwear and hung them over the shower rod to dry as he stretched out on the bed for a quick forty winks. He wasn't sure how long a night it was going to be, but he was sure he wanted to be as awake and alert as possible. A quick nap would help assure that.

By mid-afternoon the weather had broken. All that remained were puddles children kicked as they tried, often successfully, to splash their playmates. The rains had left it muggy. But that didn't bother Ellis. People wouldn't be covering up, he thought. She'll be easier to spot. He debated with himself about the best time to go to the plaza. Not too early he reasoned. No sense taking more of a chance than was absolutely necessary of running into Morales or one of this goons. But on the other hand, not to late either. There would be a better opportunity of locating her if he could watch the plaza fill up rather than finding it that way when he arrived.

Ellis hoped Rena hadn't done anything to dramatically alter her appearance, like cutting her hair. She had long hair in the photo with her brother. Long, thick, black hair that probably made her stand out in California, but would have just the opposite effect here. He had looked at the picture a lot over the last couple of days. It would allow him to get close to her, he hoped. And he felt certain now that she wouldn't be alone. She had made too many references in her letter to we this and we that. When the time came, Ellis planned to just walk up to her, call her by name and tell her that her brother had sent him. He wasn't going to be specific about why her brother couldn't come himself. He'd simply say a traffic accident has him hospitalized. There was little to be gained, Ellis thought, by recounting the sordid details. Just get to the meat of the thing. What did she want to ask of her brother? And would she be willing to go back to the states? He feared he knew the answer to the second question already.

Rena had requested that her brother be in Plaza Allende by nine that evening. So Ellis left his hotel and headed toward the plaza by seven. He would once again have dinner where he was afforded an unencumbered view of the area. And he would be sure to finish his dinner early so he'd have time to take a leisurely stroll around the square by eight-thirty. Timing had always been a priority with Ellis. He had seen too many things go wrong when timing was off. And tonight there was only one chance for things to go right.

Later, as he sat on the patio eating dinner, he continually scanned the steadily growing crowd in the plaza. Not unlike the night before, the same types started showing up. Tourists. Young Mexican couples. Street vendors setting up shop on the corners or in the square. He even spied the same elderly couple he had spoken with about the police. They had taken up a spot on the very bench they had occupied the night before. Must be a daily ritual, Ellis thought to himself. A routine they obviously both enjoyed. He could see it on their faces as they talked and pointed at different people they saw wandering through Plaza Allende. Ellis bet they made a game of it. Probably making up stories about the lives of the people who mingled there. What would they peg him for, Ellis wondered. Just another tourist? A businessman on holiday? Or something more sinister? He hoped he wouldn't have a chance to find out. He hoped he wouldn't have to deal with anyone he knew that night except for the dark haired girl who seemed to have gotten herself mixed up with a rowdy bunch of would-be revolutionaries intent on righting old wrongs and taking back what they felt was theirs in the first place. Beware of zealots, Ellis thought. They're guided more by passion than reason. Such people often inflict a great deal of harm. Not necessarily on their enemies. Often on those they are trying to help, and sometimes, on themselves as well.

By eight fifteen Ellis was wrapping up his meal and paying the check. The sun was almost gone now and he felt he needed to take another angle on the procession playing out in front of him. Putting his napkin on the table and rising, something seemed to catch his eye on the right. Entering the plaza via the sidewalk beside the Parroquia de San Miguel were four individuals. They were dressed heavier than the weather dictated. Jackets and hats on three of the four. The fourth wore a red headband that circled the forehead and wrapped around a thick black mane. But as the four walked halfway up the stairs of the cathedral and turned to look out over the crowd in the plaza, two things were obvious to Ellis. The one wearing the headband was a woman. And the woman was Rena Whitfield.

Ellis paused for a moment, still under the canopy of the patio cafe. He watched as the foursome talked among themselves and started pointing and looking more intensely at the heart of the plaza. Rena pulled the dark glasses from her face and seemed to squint a bit as she perused the square's inhabitants. A few more hand gestures seemed to indicate they were going to split up and go in different directions. But only one of the group turned and started walking toward the far end of the plaza as Rena and the two remaining men began to descend the stairs and head into the heart of the crowd.

Ellis followed the trio. As he weaved his way through melon salesmen and teenagers and vacationers burned lobster-red in tank tops and khaki shorts, he kept his eye on the prize. He was close enough now to see she was decidedly smaller than her two compatriots. They kept her between them, seemingly more preoccupied with protecting her than looking for her brother. But she was looking. Looking hard. When the three reached the center of the square, she stood up on the flat cement edge of the fountain to get a better look. The she started to walk slowly around the structure to take a virtual three hundred and sixty degree scan of the people in the plaza.

This was it, Ellis thought. Better to do it with lots of people around than to wait until it was just him, her and two potentially unfriendly bodyguards. So Ellis walked around the fountain in the opposite direction. As he approached her, he could see that one of the two protectors was now looking at him and about to move toward him. Now, only a few paces from directly beneath her, Ellis looked up and said, "Rena? Rena Whitfield? Your brother sent me."

She paused for a minute, not saying anything. Both of the men that were with her stepped between Rena and Ellis. "Esta bein." she said. And as quickly as they had stepped in front of her, they parted to let her step down from the fountain rim. Looking Ellis directly in the eyes, she said, "Where is Terry?"

"He was in an accident," Ellis began. "An automobile accident. He's okay. But he's in the hospital for a few days. My name's Ellis, Brig Ellis," he said as he handed her his card.

"Your brother asked me to come in his place."

Looking back from the card to Ellis, Rena said, "But how

does he know you? Have you worked for him before?"

"No, " Ellis replied, "we met through a mutual friend."

"And he sent you down here to find me? Just like that. That's hard to believe."

"He was planning on coming. He just wanted me to accompany him. But then there was...well, he had this accident and he couldn't make it, so he asked me to come."

"Well what happened to him? How badly was he hurt?"

"Someone ran a stop sign and hit him," Ellis said, making it up as he went. "He got a fractured collar bone and he's going to be laid up in the hospital for a while. But he'll be okay."

"And how did you know who I was?"

"He gave me this picture of you," Ellis answered, as he took the snapshot from his shirt pocket and handed it to her.

She looked at it and smiled. "That was taken one afternoon on Coronado Island. It was a fun day Terry and I had."

Since Rena and Ellis began talking the two men had constantly been looking around as if to see whether anyone was planning to encroach on the conversation. Ellis couldn't help but notice their nervousness.

"Look, why don't we sit down and have something to drink," Ellis said to Rena, as he pointed toward a table for four near a lemon aid vendor not far from where they were standing. She accepted without saying anything and started toward the table, her two guardians still flanking her. Ellis walked over and bought four lemon aids from the Indian who was selling them and brought the drinks to the table. Neither of the two Mexicans who now sat on either side of Rena made any move to drink what Ellis had just put in front of them. Rena was still looking at the picture of herself and her brother and smiling. So Ellis began.

"He's very worried about you, you know. He has been for some time. And when he received your letter..."

Her eyes came up to meet his quickly, "He showed you the letter?"

"Yes. He did. I think he felt I might not take his request seriously unless I saw it."

"And have you talked to anyone about it," Rena questioned. "Anyone in the states, or anyone here?"

"No, I haven't," Ellis said. "You might have noticed that on

71

my card it says Confidential Matters. And it means what it says."

"All right. I guess I'll have to trust you. I mean if Terry did, I guess I can."

"You can Ms. Whitfield," Ellis said earnestly.

Since the two bodyguards, if that was indeed what they were, had made no move whatsoever to join the conversation up to this point, Ellis felt no need to start including them now. He continued to talk directly to Rena as if they weren't even there. "In your letter, you said you were going to ask a favor of your brother?"

Rena looked at him intently now. And for the first time Ellis noticed how very brown her eyes were. Almost black like her hair. He had noted from the photograph that her eyes were dark, but he hadn't noticed the depth of color, and he certainly hadn't noticed the intensity that was in them now.

"Mr. Ellis," Rena began, "we don't have much time. So, please listen and remember what I'm going to say to you. Please tell Terry that in two and a half weeks from tonight... nineteen days to be exact...on May 5, he needs to meet me in Guanajuato at the El Jardin de la Union...can you remember that?"

"Yes, I can remember it," Ellis said. The historical significance of the date did not escape him. "Cinco de Mayo. Guanajuato. The El Jardin de la Union. "But frankly Ms. Whitfield, I'm not sure that he'll be up and about and feel like traveling by..."

"If he's not up to it, I'm sure you are Mr. Ellis. I assume he's paying you for this trip which means he can pay you for one more."

"Look, Ms. Whitfield, I'm sure that whatever you're doing...well, I'm sure that you think it's the right thing to do. But this country has had all kinds of problems for some time and those problems are not going to be solved any time soon. Your brother had seriously hoped you would consider returning to the United States with me. That way you and he could talk about things. You could always come back to Mexico if that's what you wished. But sometimes it's good to get away from things for a while and get some perspective, you know?" Ellis had purposefully kept his gaze on Rena the whole time he was talking. He wasn't sure how much English the two silent ones understood. And, if it wasn't a lot, he didn't want his demeanor to give away his suggestion that she might want to separate from her current mates. On the other hand, if they did understand English, well, to hell with them.

"I would have hoped that Terry could tell from my letter that this is a very serious situation. I've made a commitment. I know that doesn't mean a lot to anyone in the affluent world many people in the states live in, but it means something to me. And it means an enormous amount to the people here."

"Your brother accepts the fact that you are very serious. That's why he wants you to come back to the states and talk to him about all this."

"Mr. Ellis, in the next few minutes I think you'll see why I can't go back to the states and talk to Terry or anyone else about any of this."

For some inexplicable reason, upon hearing what Rena said, Ellis began to wonder about the other man he had seen standing with these three on the steps of the Parroquia de San Miguel Arcangel.

"How much do you know of this city, this area, Mr. Ellis?"

"Not much. No more than the average tourist."

"Mexico is not a tourist attraction, Mr. Ellis. It's not Disney World or Epcot Center. This land...the central highland, is the cradle of the revolution. It was here, from the pews of a parish church, that Ignacio de Allende and Peter Hidalgo declared independence from the Spanish. Their fight wasn't a show for the tourists, Mr. Ellis. It cost them their heads, which were hung up in cages in the fortress of Alhondiga de Granaditas."

Ellis, mildly annoyed at a history lesson from a young woman whom he was sure got all her experience out of text books, said "I'm sure you know your revolutionary history very well, Ms. Whitfield, it's just that..."

"There's no more time." Rena said, cutting him off as the silent duo was growing appreciably more agitated. They continued to scan the square keeping an eye out for who knew what. "May 5. Guanajuato. The El Jardin de la Union. Same time, 9 p.m. You or my brother, it doesn't matter. Bring an overnight bag. Or two if it takes two. But no more than two bags. That should be all it takes."

"All it takes for what?" Ellis asked.

"For the two million dollars, Mr. Ellis. You or my brother and two million dollars for the Zapatista cause."

"Rena, look," Ellis decided that such a request granted him some degree of familiarity, "are you sure your brother can come up with that kind of money?"

"He knows where to get it. He knows who to get it from. Just give him the message and give him this." She reached behind her neck and unfastened a gold chain that had been hidden under her shirt. At the end of the chain were her initials, RW, also in gold, but set in a pearl obelisk.

"You give him this. Then you or my brother comes back with the money."

Ellis took the necklace and put it into his pocket as he said, "But even if he can get his hands on the money, what makes you think he would?"

"Because if he does," Rena said haltingly, "I'll come back. I'll come back to the states if he helps me help these people."

Ellis would think later that there are indeed some things you never get used to. Like being in the general vicinity of the shock waves generated from a C-4 blast. Depending on where you are, the impact and the sound reach you virtually simultaneously. When it happened this time, the proximity of their table to the blast's origin was such that they all were sent sprawling over adjoining chairs, tables, patrons and passersby. Ellis, being on the side of the table closest to the explosion was thrown the farthest and slammed his head into the wheel of the lemon aid vendor's cart. He wasn't sure at first whether the salty taste in his mouth was blood or lemon aid. It turned out to be the former. His three tablemates were knocked to the ground as well. But their swift recovery and exit would later lead Ellis to assume they must have known what was on its way.

Everyone checked to see if they were missing anything like arms or legs or various other body parts. Then they were turning to those around them who were crying or moaning or just continuing to sit stunned wherever the blast had deposited them. As Ellis brought himself slowly to his feet, he turned in a circle looking for some sign of the three he had been sitting with. Amid the smoke and debris he was sure he saw what appeared to be three jacketed forms, one small and two larger, turning the corner and disappearing around the side of the cathedral where he had seen them appear. There was no chance to catch them. He knew this because seconds after he stood and started to look around, dizziness overtook him and he had to brace himself against a tree to keep from tumbling over. Resting there for what seemed a long time, but in reality, was actually less than a minute, the dizziness faded and he saw ahead of him what surely had been ground zero, the Police Station. He headed that way and saw that all the windows and part of the front wall had been blown away. The massive doors that marked the center of the building were nowhere to be seen as black smoke billowed from what now looked more like the entrance to a cave. As the smoke continued to tumble out, the strangest thing started to emerge from the gaping wound. It moved slowly, on all fours, its appendages reaching out in long clawing motions taking it out of the smoke and closer to the curb. Blackened head to foot except for the red raw meatless indentions in it's body, it stopped at the sidewalk's edge and resting on its hands and knees, seemed to push up and down as if trying to regain whatever was left of it's capacity to breathe. Then slowly but surely, it curled its ridiculously long legs up under it and began to try to stand. Inch by inch it pushed itself up and then let its arms, crooked as tree branches, dangle and float awkwardly. Once upright, even with its bloody, soot-covered head cocked unstably to one side, Ellis could tell the resurrection from hell was none other than Captain Morales.

In no mood to help or hinder the captain, Ellis turned left and started to make his way out of the square in the opposite direction. As he got to the corner that would lead him toward his hotel, he came upon those massive wooden doors he had passed through the evening before. At least part of them. The part that had splintered into jagged spears, and as if fired from cannons, were now imbedded in the corpses of the elderly couple who would never again share a bench and a sunset and a guessing game together.

CHAPTER 15

Two days later the sun rose in San Diego and Ellis rose with it. He had slept soundly the night before. Which hadn't been the case in Mexico. He never seemed to sleep well in unfamiliar hotels. And a swollen scrape the size of a fountain pen along the side of his head hadn't done a lot for his nocturnal bliss the evening before he left San Miguel. But he awoke from his first night back in the states feeling reasonably well for someone who had been seated in close proximity to a plastics explosive detonation.

After getting dressed he telephoned for a cab that would take him to Deutschland Motors so he could pick up his car and swing by the kennel to retrieve Osgood. Arriving at the curb in front of the shop, Ellis gave the cabbie a sawbuck and told him to keep the change. Then, as he was walking across the gravel and grass that led to the shed where the cars were usually kept, Lothar appeared from beneath the bonnet of a Jaguar sedan.

Lothar was a tall, sun-tanned German who dyed his hair black. He did this so he wouldn't have to wear a wig at the Elvis-impersonator contests he was frequently entering. To Lothar, Elvis was America. The icon was the reason he had immigrated to the states. Lothar figured if an uneducated truck driver from Mississippi could become the world's greatest rock and roller, then the USA was the place for him. He had started out as just another foreign car mechanic upon his arrival. But he was as frugal as Gandhi was thin, and his savings soon gave him the opportunity to open his own shop. Even though he was an independent businessman now, he'd still close early on Friday nights so he could go home, shave, shower and put on his white, rhinestone-festooned jumpsuit. Then he'd drive to whatever club was having an Elvis contest that night. "Viva Las Vegas" was his signature number. And regardless of whether the club goers hooted and hollered or simply sat on their hands and sucked their rum and Cokes, whenever he started to sing "Bright light city gonna' set my soul...gonna set my soul on fire"...he knew in his bones what it felt like to be the king of rock and roll.

"Hello, my friend," Lothar began. Then he saw the side of Ellis's face. "Ugh. That looks like it hurts. What happened? Did you run into those guys?"

"What guys?" Ellis questioned.

"The guys who were here looking for your car."

"My car. What guys are you talking about?"

"Those two bruisers who came here and smashed the car all to shit."

"What?" Ellis bleated. "Smashed the car. You've got to be kidding."

"Why would I kid about such a thing? They took baseball bats and hit the car like you see those fishermen on TV...you know the ones...the ones who kill the seals by bashing them in the head. Is awful, really."

Ellis had a sick feeling in his stomach. Not over the seals. Over his baby. "But why? Why would they trash my car?"

"They didn't do anything to your car," Lothar said rather matter-of-factly.

The queasiness in Ellis' stomach was now matched by a throbbing in his head. He didn't know if it was his injury or if this sudden headache was being caused by the conversation. "Look," Ellis began, "you just said two guys came in here looking for my car. And that they smashed it up with baseball bats. Then you said they didn't do anything to my car. What the hell are you talking about?"

"No, no," Lothar countered. "You are not listening, my friend. I said that two men came in here looking for your car. Then I said two men smashed up a car. I did not say they smashed up your car."

"Let's just start by you showing me where my car is, okay?"

"Sure." Lothar said. Then he turned and walked over to the right side of the shed where a big white sheet was draped over a sporty looking lump. Without pausing for any dramatic flourishes, Lothar reached out and yanked the sheet from the automobile revealing Ellis's 1964 Mercedes 230 SL convertible looking exactly as it looked when he dropped it off on his way out of town.

Walking up swiftly and circling the car, the knot in Ellis' stomach started to untie itself. But his head was still giving him a hard time. "Okay, let me get this straight. Two guys come in here. They ask you about my car. Then what?"

"Well," Lothar replied, "I could tell by the way they asked...holding those baseball bats...that they were up to no good."

"Why didn't you just tell them that my car wasn't here?"

"You don't give bad news to men holding baseball bats."

Lothar said. "They came in here to do some damage. I could tell they were not going to leave until they did."

"So what did you do?" Ellis asked.

"I lied to them. I told them that your car was back here." As he reached the end of his sentence, Lothar was already on his way around to the back of his shed. Once Ellis turned the corner, he saw what his car might have been reduced to. There sat another white, late 60's SL. He wasn't sure of the model year. But he was sure it wasn't his and it definitely had the hell beaten out of it. The windshield was smashed from repeated blows from both the right and left. The side mirrors had been knocked off. Headlights and taillights were busted. There were various dents banged into the body on all sides. The dashboard, steering wheel and gearshift had been clubbed into mangled messes. Broken glass and chrome bumpers and door handles covered the ground surrounding the vehicle.

"Whose car was this?" Ellis asked.

"That asshole, Simpson," Lothar replied. "He's been screwing me for years. Getting me to fix his car and always making me wait, wait, wait. Sometimes not paying me at all. Well, I guess he won't be making a fool of me anymore, huh?"

"Let's get back to those guys," Ellis said. "What did they look like?"

"Both big. Both ugly."

"And they specifically asked for my car?"

"Yes. They asked where is Ellis's convertible? I knew I had the other convertible that was a lot like yours, so I told them it was in back. They found it and beat it."

"And they didn't say anything else? Didn't ask you to give me a message or anything?"

"I think the beating was the message," Lothar replied. "You don't know why?"

"I don't have any idea why, or any idea who they are."

"You should try to find out," Lothar said.

German humor is very dry, Ellis thought to himself.

"Oh yeah," Lothar remembered, "I changed the spark plugs and altered the timing. You owe me a hundred and twenty dollars."

"I owe you a lot more than that, Lothar. Thanks for what you did for me."

"No problem, Mr. Ellis. You are a good customer. You pay your bills on time."

"A practice I intend to continue," Ellis said.

After he put the top down and drove away from Deutschland, Ellis thought about how good it felt to be behind the wheel of a real car again. The sun on his face and the wind whipping by made him forget for a moment how strange things had been for the last few days. An elevator accident that was beginning to seem less and less like an accident. Two mugs trying to trash his ride. Somebody was trying to tell him something. But he didn't know what and he didn't know who. And he didn't know if it had anything to do with the Whitfield siblings and murder in Mexico. That's what it was, Ellis said to himself. Murder. That elderly couple was just as dead as if someone had walked up behind them and pulled a trigger. Sure, some revolutionary apologists would chalk it up to collateral damage. The unfortunate side effects of the people's struggle. Rena Whitfield might even see it that way. Though he hoped not. Ellis hoped she was still naive enough to believe that only the police station would be damaged. That only corrupt policemen who had been selling out their own people would be victims. Ellis knew that once you start accepting the death of innocents, that's when you start seeing more and more death. He also knew, even in the fog that clouded his head moments after the explosion, that he saw only Rena and her two silent pals rounding the corner of the cathedral. The other fellow who had been with them before they split up either lit out on his own or was picked up by the authorities after the fact. Or maybe he was picked up with a shovel when they started cleaning up the building. Martyrdom hadn't been a tactic of the Zapatistas prior to San Miguel. If that was the beginning, Ellis knew things would only get worse.

CHAPTER 16

After picking up Osgood, who was now sitting in the passenger seat, strapped in via the special harness Lothar had created for the pugnacious pooch, Ellis pushed in the clutch and pulled the gear shift back into second. Then he eased off the accelerator as he slowed to make the turn onto the coast highway. He opened it up a bit once he was sure there was no traffic to negotiate. It sounded good and it responded even better. Lothar had obviously worked his German magic yet again. As he got closer to Benny's his thoughts turned to the less complicated, less gruesome loose ends he had left behind before he left for Mexico. He assumed by now that Grif would have heard from Laney's insurance company and he'd be feeling less agitated than he had before Ellis said he'd help. He couldn't have been more wrong

Knotting Osgood's leash to a pole on the front deck, Ellis entered and saw Grif pouring himself a shot from the Cutty Sark behind the cash register. "*Jesus*, Grif, kinda' early for that, isn't it?"

"Yeah, well, life ain't always no bed of roses, you know," Grif said turning around to face Ellis. Upon seeing his wound, Grif blurted out, "What the fuck happened to you, man?" Is that some kind of head badge of courage, or what?"

Ignoring Grif's literary pun, Ellis responded, "Things got a little out of control." Then he went on to relate what had transpired. The whole time Ellis was filling Grif in however, he got the distinct impression the bar owner was getting only about every tenth word. When Grif started to pour himself another shot Ellis said, "Hey, if you're gonna swill down your own profits you might as well not do it alone. Fix me a Bloody Mary, okay?"

Grif said, "Sure. Sure." Then he turned around, reached for the vodka and started fixing the drink. Ellis noticed the place was virtually empty. Nobody at the tables and just one rummy at the end of the bar. It was still a good half hour before most started showing up for lunch, but in the past the place would have a few more early starters than this. When Grif set the drink down on the bar Ellis looked at it in disbelief. Tall mug with a big piece of celery sticking out of it. Just the way the tourists liked it, Ellis thought, but unlike any Bloody Mary Grif had fixed for him.

"What's on your mind, man?" Ellis said, pushing the drink

back toward Grif.

Grif looked down at it, then reality seemed to find its way to the front of his mind.

"Oh shit," Grif said, "did I do that? What a dumb ass!" He pulled the celery stalk out and tossed it in the Rubbermaid behind the bar. Then he quickly poured half the contents into a short glass and gave it back to Ellis.

"What's bugging you?" Ellis asked again.

"Oh, just lots of stuff, man. Nunez quit. Well, he didn't quit really. But anyway he's gone and I got somebody new and there's just things happening. It's no big deal."

"Did you hear from that insurance company...about your accident?"

"Yeah, I think so. I haven't actually talked to them yet. I think they called."

"You think they called. That was number one on our agenda when I left. What's the holdup?"

"Look, there's just been a lot going on, okay," Grif began. "Business stinks. People aren't drinking as much and they seem to be eating somewhere else too."

Just then a group of four women, obviously taking an early break from their office jobs, came in and asked if they could sit by the window.

"Yeah, go ahead," Grif answered. "Be there in a minute."

Downing his drink, Ellis said, "Well look, the lunch crowd's going to be starting any minute now. I'll let you get to it. Just call those insurance people back, okay?"

"Yeah, man. I will. Sorry about the drink."

"Don't give it another thought. Just keep your mind on your work, all right?"

"Sure," Grif's mouth said. But the look in his eyes said something entirely different.

Ellis never actually saw the look. He had already stepped outside, untied Osgood who had been catching a catnap in the sun, and started out to his car where his cell phone was in his glove box and a call to Laney Wilson was only moments away. The phone rang twice before it was answered.

"Hello."

"Laney?" He asked even though he recognized her voice.

And she recognized his. "Well, Mr. Ellis. So, what tall tale do you have in mind this time?"

"No tales. Just wanted to see how you were and how things went with Riley."

"Oh, things went fine with Riley, once he realized I was serious about handling the accident as an accident and not a windfall opportunity. I think it helped when I mentioned that you had volunteered to talk to him directly about it. He wasn't too keen on that idea. As for your first question, how am I, well...why don't you come over and see for yourself."

There was obvious pleasure in Ellis's voice when he answered. "Excellent idea. But there is one appointment I have to take care of this afternoon."

"No problem. Why don't you just plan on coming over this evening. If you bring the wine, I'll do the cooking."

"That sounds great. What time?"

"Eight would be good," Laney replied.

"I'll be there."

"See you tonight then, bye."

When he heard the phone click, he realized he hadn't asked what she planned on cooking. So he wasn't exactly sure what kind of wine to bring. Then he thought to himself she didn't really seem the type to be particularly snobbish about wine etiquette. Turning to Osgood, he said, "But just to keep my bases covered I'll pick up a white and a red after I drop you off at home and stop at the hospital to deliver my report to Terrance Whitfield." Osgood's mammoth tongue swept across his snub-nose face from jowl to flopping jowl, which Ellis decoded as placid agreement.

CHAPTER 17

As he walked down the hall to the room where he had spoken with Whitfield before leaving for Mexico, Ellis was struck with a familiar feeling. That old visceral loathing of hospitals. There never seemed to be a good reason to be in one. Sure, they helped people and if it wasn't for them everyone would be in a pretty sorry state, but he couldn't get it out of his head that they were always connected to sickness or pain. Even if you were getting patched up, you had to suffer a bit more so you wouldn't wind up infected or worse. Just coming in for a checkup you got poked and prodded and were made to suffer all sorts of indignities. As he walked by the nurses' station he found it hard to understand how anyone could enjoy working in a hospital. It takes a special kind of person he thought to himself. Someone who could look at the good they were doing and not get bogged down in the daily routine of crying children and needy patients and demanding relatives and the fear that was probably the cause of it all. No, Ellis said silently to himself, hospitals were not for him. The less time spent in one, the better. But now he was outside Whitfield's room and those thoughts left his mind as he opened the door slowly and let himself in.

Terrance Whitfield looked reasonably well for a man who had recently had his throat cut.

Bandages still completely encircled his neck but he seemed to sit up much more easily and was infinitely more alert than he had been when last they talked. Ellis began slowly and chronologically revealed the events of the previous days in Mexico. Even though he tried to be as gentle as he was honest, he couldn't help but notice a tear form in Whitfield's eye and run slowly down his cheek as the impact of what Rena had gotten involved in became more clear.

"But you don't know, right?" Whitfield began. "You don't know for sure if Rena knew what was going to happen."

The question caught Ellis by surprise. In point of fact, he did not know for sure that Rena was aware of what her comrades had in mind. He had assumed she did. He remembered she seemed to be in a hurry, and that the two men with her kept acting nervously.

"Look, I can't be a hundred percent positive," Ellis said, "but it's hard for me to believe that she didn't have knowledge of what was going down."

"I just can't believe she would knowingly be part of anything like that. She's the gentlest person I know," Whitfield countered. "You said there were men with her. Maybe she was being forced to take part. Maybe she didn't know what was going to happen. Maybe they told her one thing and did another. I think we should assume that's the case. I think we should believe she's being kept against her will and this is all some sort of elaborate kidnapping scheme to get funds for their organization. Like that Patty Hearst thing, you know?"

"Patty Hearst wound up going to jail," Ellis reminded Whitfield. "She got out, but she spent some time behind bars."

"I don't want to think about that," Whitfield blurted out. "I can't think about that. It's just unimaginable. This can't be happening to Rena. We've got to get her out of there. We've got to get her away from those people. Once she's back here, I'm sure she'll be okay. Anyway, there's no reason for the authorities to be involved, right? You told me she said she'd come back. She said she'd come back if we delivered the money, right? So it's like a ransom, then. It is a ransom. It's a kidnapping and a ransom. And once it's paid, she'll be back and she'll be safe. You can't be prosecuted for something your kidnappers did. She's the victim, see...she's the real victim here." Whitfield had become so agitated and moved his head so much when he talked, that a small, wet, red line had started to seep through the bandages around his neck.

"Take it easy," Ellis said. "You're moving around too much. I think I should get the nurse."

"Not just yet...I'll be quieter. Don't call her yet. Look, Mr. Ellis, can't we just treat this like a kidnapping? Can't we just take them the money, get Rena back and put the whole thing behind us?"

"Two million dollars is a lot of money. Do you have that kind of money available? Rena said you'd know where to get it."

"Rena knew what she was talking about. No, I don't have that kind of money, Mr. Ellis. But our father does. Our father has that kind of money and more."

"Well, does he know about all this? Have you kept him appraised of what's been going on?"

"No, I haven't spoken to my father in almost ten years. Or I guess it's more correct to say he hasn't spoken to me. In my father's eyes, Mr. Ellis, I no longer exist. Our mother is dead. She passed away when Rena and I were both children. So there is only Rena and me. And our father, the great Warren Whitfield, architect extraordinaire. But from my father's perspective, there is only Rena and him. He no longer admits to having a son. He hasn't admitted it for some time. Once I was, as he would say "of legal age," I've been out of his house and out of his life as well. Homosexuality was not what he had in mind for his offspring. And it certainly wasn't what he had in mind for the public image of his oldest heir. I was an anathema to him and his vision of his lineage. Think of me as the proverbial black sheep. So black in my father's eyes that I've been virtually erased from the family. But he loves Rena. He wouldn't let anything happen to her. I'm convinced of that. You must go seen him. You must show him the necklace that Rena gave you. That will prove to him you've spoken with her. He'll provide the money, I know he will. He loves her very much. He'll want her back here, safe again. In his eyes, she's the only child he has left."

Ellis continued talking with Whitfield. But as he talked he also pushed the nurse call button. That red line around the bandages was starting to get darker. As was the afternoon light that spilled into the room. Whitfield confided that while he couldn't speak to his father directly, he did have access to his parent's secretary. He said that he would call her and arrange an appointment for Ellis to meet with his father. He wouldn't tell the secretary everything. He thought it made more sense to keep as few people as necessary knowledgeable about the specifics regarding Rena. The secretary would arrange the meeting, then it would be up to Ellis to secure the father's involvement and hopefully the two million dollars.

Even though Terrance Whitfield had put a seed of doubt in Ellis's head about Rena's complicity in the San Miguel bombing, she still seemed like a convert to him. But he also knew it would be best for her if she were out of that situation and back in the states. Anyway, that's what he was getting paid for. Guilt or innocence was for someone else to worry about.

CHAPTER 18

Knock, knock, knock. Three always seemed right to Ellis. Less might not be heard. More might seem menacing. Three seemed firm, decisive, appropriate. He had his fist raised and was about to deliver three more when Laney opened the door. She smiled. He smiled back and said, "I forgot to ask what you were cooking. So I got red and white."

"Hedging your bet, huh Ellis? Smart move. Of course, I guess I should expect as much from you. Come on in."

As he walked in, Laney saw the abrasion on the side of his forehead. "Ooh," she said, reaching up and touching it gently with the tips of her fingers, "does it hurt? Should I ask how you got it?"

"It doesn't hurt as much as it did a couple of days ago. And I'm afraid how I got it falls into one of those Confidential Matters my business card refers to."

"Then I won't pry. I'm not one of those people who has to know everything. If it's none of my business, fine," she said as she crossed her living room and headed into the kitchen.

Ellis followed behind her and set the bottles of wine on the kitchen counter saying, "It looks worse than it actually is. Hopefully it won't look that way for long. That way I won't have to keep answering questions about it."

"You could have just made something up. Like you bumped it on the car door or something."

"I'd rather not lie to you," Ellis said

"Oh really," Laney countered with an upturned eyebrow, "It didn't seem to bother you when you called me on the phone and convinced me you were a policeman."

"That was before I knew you. Now that I do, I won't be lying to you anymore."

"Is that a promise?" Laney questioned, turning away and reaching up to pull a couple of wine glasses from the cupboard. When she turned back, Ellis was right behind her. He put his hands on the counter, one on each side of her so she had no way to do anything other than look directly into his eyes.

"What can I do to convince you?" he asked softly.

Laney made no move to extricate herself. "Whatever you think is appropriate," she said just as quietly.

He bent down and kissed her. Softly at first. Then when he felt her respond, he pressed his lips more firmly into hers. They lingered that way for a moment. Then he moved both his head and hands away and said, "Was that convincing?"

She blinked once and answered, "You know, I can't say that I'm totally convinced just yet."

"I was hoping you'd say that," Ellis said, as he wrapped his arms under hers and pulled her against him, kissing her slowly and this time, longer than before.

Laney stayed in his caress, both arms extended, a wine glass in each hand as she accepted and returned his kiss. This time when they parted she said, "Okay, let's say I'm convinced...at least for the moment. Why don't you open that Cabernet. I'll put this White Burgundy on to chill. We'll have dinner and we can see how long lasting this conviction really is."

They ate dinner slowly, laughed a lot, drank both bottles of wine and had each other for dessert. Ellis explored every curve of Laney's hourglass form. He stood naked behind her, reached around and cupped her soft breasts in both hands. His fingers running over her hardened nipples made him grow firm against the center of her round bottom. He bent down and kissed her shoulder. Then his lips and tongue made their way slowly up her neck, around her ear, across her jaw line and she turned so their lips could find each other. As she pressed against him, he felt the cushion of her breasts warm him. She felt his desire against her belly as they sank down on the foot of the bed and rolled to the center where they sealed their lovers' union once and then again before drifting asleep.

Later, when he opened his eyes she was staring at his face and tracing the line of the abrasion. "Do you get hurt often?"

"I'm usually able to avoid it," he replied, "this was really more of an accident than anything else."

"Now, Mr. Ellis," she said, "what was that about no lies?"

"And what was that about no prying?"

"Touché" Laney replied.

There was the usual conversation about the hour being late. Ellis was cautious. He didn't want to seem presumptive. He had been invited over for the evening. An invitation to stay the night had not been extended. At least not yet. So he felt he had to balance not appearing to be in a hurry to leave, with not appearing to be planning on leaving at all. Laney kept him from performing a prolonged balancing act by saying, "Will you call me? Or, can I call you?"

Ellis recognized an invitation to leave when he heard one. Even one delivered so demurely. "How about yes, and yes."

"Those are the answers I was hoping for," Laney said. She slid over and kissed his lips.

"Just press the button before you close the door. It will lock automatically. I'm tired and just want to sleep. It's all your fault."

"Guilty as charged," Ellis quipped, "and a happier man for it." He kissed her, then rose and began to get dressed.

As he drove through the warm night breeze, top down, on the way to his place, Sinatra intoned, "No, no, they can't take that away from me."

Ellis wasn't exactly sure how to feel. As far as he was concerned it had been a wonderful evening. The meal was good. The sex was great. But he didn't know for sure if Laney Wilson felt the same. And he had a sneaking suspicion she was in no hurry to let him know.

CHAPTER 19

Warren Whitfield sat working at his desk. Not the desk in his office, the desk in his bedroom. The desk was the biggest thing in his bedroom. A big, sprawling multilevel maple and glass, modern desk that held a computer, books, drawings and plans with everything precisely in it's place. Everything close at hand, ready to be used, but nothing just lying about as most things are on most peoples' desks. In fact, there was nothing just lying about anywhere in Warren Whitfield's bedroom. Or in Warren Whitfield's house for that matter. Particularly Warren. He had been working at his desk for three quarters of an hour. And the time was four forty-five a.m. This was not unusual for Warren. In fact, it was the reason Warren had a desk in his bedroom. He would frequently rise early, sometimes even in the middle of the night, when struck with a design idea that he simply had to get out of his head and onto a piece of paper or a memory chip. He would work for a while put his things away and return to bed if it was early enough. If the sun was anywhere near rising however, Warren would stay up, make himself coffee and return to his bedroom to witness the beginning of another day. This was why Warren had built a terrace just off his bedroom. So he could watch the sun come up whenever he wanted. He seldom, if ever, watched the sun go down. He was far too busy for that. Having a drink at sunset and enjoying the end of the day was something someone might do on vacation or with clients when finalizing a project. But the idea of not working until it was dark every day was an anathema to Warren. It was something slackers did. People just too lazy or too ignorant to realize how very important each and every minute of each and every day was.

It often astounded Warren that people, frequently educated people, talked about the need for a life beyond their work. Life is work thought Warren. Work is why we're here. It's why we're not fish or animals or birds. Work is what lets us know we have value. That we're not just taking up space. That we're not just using things up. That we're leaving something behind. Leaving things behind was very important to Warren. It was why he chose architecture in the first place. As he saw it, God left the most things behind. The mountains, the rivers, the deserts, the oceans. And while there was no competing with God, there were, in virtually every culture and every land, things left behind created by man. The edifices. The Pyramids, the Coliseum, Machu Pichu, the Flatiron Building. When it came to inspiration Warren was particularly eclectic. That's why his principles of design were rigid, but his designs themselves defied categorization. Warren Whitfield's first and foremost principle of design was to create for the centuries. Not just the centuries on either side of his. But also for the countless centuries to come. It was his duty to do this. He had been blessed with talent and vision and energy. He should therefore put that triumvirate to the task of creating edifices that would last as long as Versailles, Trevi Fountain, the Taj Mahal and San Simeon, assuming of course that the latter continues to last. Such devotion to his work had earned Warren Whitfield an enormous amount of money. Money that he poured into the things he built for himself; his school, his design studio, his home. Though they served three different purposes, they were all part of one vast compound that Warren had christened Eden's Edge.

Draped across a southern California hillside just north of San Diego, Eden's Edge was Warren's homage to himself. A single story maze of connecting buildings, each with staggeringly beautiful views of the Pacific. One end housed the school where ten resident students lived, learned from and worked for Warren Whitfield. All were graduate students who had received invitations in their final semester. Invitations to put off their own careers for two years while they learned at the hand of the master. Many had already received lucrative offers from prospective employers before they received their invitations. But none had ever turned down the chance to postpone their initial adventures in capitalism, realizing that their individual earning potential would skyrocket with the addition of Eden's Edge to their resumes. And while they were at the school, though they received no monetary compensation, each was fed well, worked hard and schooled not only in Warren Whitfield's particularly esoteric brand of architecture, but also in his personal appreciation of art, wine, music, and literature. Warren knew that if grand edifices were going to continue to be left behind, there would come a time when younger Warren Whitfield devotees would be needed to succeed him. And there was no better way to secure architectural immortality than by creating a cadre of Whitfield clones who would continue to pass on his particular brand of creation from generation to generation.

Between the school and the home was the octagonal design studio. Here, he, his employees and occasionally the students would work on commissions in progress. The studio was a two-level structure resembling a windowed amphitheater. Since Warren felt that a two-story design would have seemed a blight on the rolling hillside, the lower level was actually below ground. Warren's work area was on the upper level but raised above the multiple desks, drafting tables and files. It was accessible by stairs on either side of it, which gave the not unintended impression of a bishop's pulpit. From this vantage point, Warren could oversee everyone working below him. And each of those would in turn, have to ascend to enter Warren's space. There was a continuing joke at the school that whoever entered that space was not required to give a centurion salute, but neither was one ever chastised for doing so. The top level served as a light source from the outside and a viewing area for students and those rare clients or guests who were granted admission to what Warren always felt was the working heart of Eden's Edge.

North of the studio and connected by a glass-walled tunnel was Warren Whitfield's home. The tunnel itself served as mood modifier between one place and the other. A long, wooden bridge, raised in the middle, ran the length of the tunnel. Beneath it, a hundred Japanese koi swam silently in the enclosed pond. All had been individually chosen by Warren for their size and markings and the way their color shone beneath the surface of the water. Crossing from home to studio or studio to home, the tunnel served as a reminder to Warren that a change in his demeanor was appropriate for either the start or the end of his day.

Warren Whitfield's living quarters were expansive, expensive and empty. He liked the drama of vast rooms with little or no furniture. Floor to ceiling windows in the living and dining area made sure that the ocean was always the center of attention. Minimal adornment forced one to appreciate the dwelling rather than the artifacts in it. To be sure, there were chairs and tables and objects d'art to compliment the surroundings, but mostly there were the surroundings. Warren was fond of emptiness.

After watching the morning sunrise, Warren shaved and showered and selected one of his many French cuffed tailored shirts with WW monogrammed on the collar. After putting on the jacket of his summer-weight double-breasted suit, he took one last look at himself in the mirror. Raising his right hand to his temple, he brushed the hair back just over his ear. He knew that his barber would be coming tomorrow. Everyone came to Warren Whitfield. When Warren left Eden's Edge it would be to go to an event, or business function. Never to see anyone. People who wanted to see Warren came to him. And later that morning the man coming to see him would be Brig Ellis.

Ellis had gotten a phone call from Terrance Whitfield telling him that the appointment had been arranged. He followed the directions he had received and turned off the main thoroughfare and onto the private road that would take him to the main gate leading to Eden's Edge. The gate was manned by a security guard who asked to see Ellis' I D. After checking the I D against his list, the guard opened the gate and motioned for Ellis to drive through. As the weathered, but still classic Mercedes convertible made its way slowly up the hill and over the winding drive that lead to the compound, Ellis found it easy to believe that whomever lived here could definitely put together two million dollars in cash if the occasion called for it. He had seen other grand private residences in places like Columbia and Panama. But there he wasn't driving in. He was on foot, usually in the dead of night. And he wasn't there to converse with a world famous architect. He was there to eradicate world-class drug lords or corrupt officials who had made too many payments to too many inappropriate alliances. This morning, ironically, he was here in search of such a payment. Funny how the world goes around, thought Ellis, as he slowed down and parked in the rectangular driveway that fronted the home.

The butler, or a man Ellis assumed was the butler, greeted him at the front door. The man was older, late sixties or early seventies Ellis guessed. He wore a dark black suit with a white shirt and black tie. His gaunt face was deeply lined yet unexpressive. After Ellis gave the man his name, he was led him to a foyer where he was told to wait.

The first thing that struck Ellis about the home was the seeming openness of it all. He could see the ocean on the far side of the house. He could see different rooms branching off in different directions. The area where he had been asked to wait wasn't really enclosed. It was simply a holding space for visitors to take stock of the surrounding residence. Although, from his vantage point, Ellis could only get glimpses of what the rest of the building looked like. In what seemed less than a minute, the man who had originally greeted him returned and asked Ellis to follow. Doing so, he soon found himself in what he took to be the study. It was a room surrounded on three sides by bookshelves that were filled from floor to ceiling. The fourth side had a waist-high wall with a built in desktop. Above it, glass climbed to the ceiling, framing a view of the hill running down to the sea. As he walked toward the glass to get a closer look at the view, he heard the door close behind him. Turning, he saw someone he didn't know standing by the door. The man made no immediate move to come deeper into the room. He simply stood there in his tailored suit, hands clasped behind his back. His bearing led Ellis to believe this was the man he had come to see.

"Mr. Whitfield?" Ellis asked.

The man's right arm moved from behind his back and came up as he grasped his glasses with two fingers and pushed them slightly higher on his nose. "Yes, I'm Warren Whitfield," the man said still studying the visitor before him. "Your name is Ellis, I believe. My secretary seemed insistent that I meet with you, though she was not precise about the reason. Something regarding my daughter, is it?"

Ellis had already decided not to be coy with someone he was hoping to get two million dollars from. "Actually, it pertains to your daughter and your son, Mr. Whitfield."

Warren Whitfield blinked once, but his stony facade never changed. "I'm not the least bit interested in anything that has to do with my son, sir. You will refrain from mentioning him again. And as for my daughter, please be quick about why you're here. I have a number of things to accomplish today."

It was evident to Ellis that few if any particulars had been shared with the secretary or with Warren Whitfield. "Mr. Whitfield, give me five uninterrupted minutes of your time. You'll know precisely why I'm here and then if you wish to continue, I'll answer any questions you might have."

"Are you going to be vague?" Whitfield asked, not trying to hide his condescention.

"No. I'll be very direct," Ellis answered earnestly.

"Then I shan't have any questions." With his right hand, he

pushed back the cuff on his left arm and glanced at his wrist. "You now have four minutes and forty-five seconds."

That was enough for Ellis. He thought to himself, okay, if you want to do it this way, we'll do it this way. Then he said, "Your son showed me a letter from your daughter, who is now in Mexico. The letter indicated she had gotten involved with the Zapatista rebels. Your son hired me to go to Mexico and see if I could convince her to come back to the states. Then your son had his throat cut. He's still alive. He's in a hospital in San Diego. I went to Mexico. I met with your daughter. She was accompanied by men whom I took to be Zapatistas. Your daughter told me that if I brought two million dollars back to Mexico for her to give to the Zapatistas, she would return to the states. Then the police station in San Miguel de Allende, where we were, was blown up. As best I could tell, your daughter was unharmed. But at least two people were killed. I returned to San Diego and gave this information to your son. He asked that I tell you what had happened. He felt that you would want to provide the money your daughter was asking for. I came here today to tell you this and see what you wanted to do."

Ellis then looked down at his own watch. When he looked back up at Warren Whitfield, he said, "Now, I think that only took about two minutes. So I guess we have another two minutes and forty-five seconds to kill."

Whitfield had been returning Ellis's stare throughout the unvarnished monologue. He stepped forward and again raised his hand to his glasses to adjust them as he slowly lowered himself into one of the two chairs on either end of the study. Motioning to the other chair across the room, he said, "Have a seat Mr. Ellis."

There was a pregnant pause while both men sat at either end of the room staring across the floor at each other. Ellis gave him the time he needed. Then Whitfield spoke. The questions started slowly. What proof did he have of this wild story he was telling? Ellis walked across the room and gave Whitfield the letter that Rena had written to her brother. He went back to his seat as Whitfield read it. How could he be sure that Ellis actually talked with his daughter? Again Ellis rose, walked over and handed Whitfield the necklace that Rena had given him in San Miguel. Was she all right? Did she look to be in good health? Did Ellis think any harm had come to her? Had she been coerced into doing what she was doing or had she become one of them? What did the authorities know? Particularly the American authorities. Question after question after question. All questions about Rena. Not one single inquiry from Warren Whitfield about his son.

Ellis answered every interrogative with the truth, as he knew it. Just as he had with Rena's brother, he indicated that in his best judgment, she was not a hostage, but a helper. When Whitfield asked, "Do you think she's telling the truth, Mr. Ellis? Do you think she'll come out of Mexico with you if you give them the money?"

Ellis answered, "I can't know for sure. But I think she will."

There was another extended pause in their conversation. Whitfield seemed to be mulling things over in his mind. He rose from his chair, walked to the center of the room and said, "I have numerous contacts in Mexico and Latin America. I will make some inquiries. San Miguel is not unknown to me. In fact, did you know Mr. Ellis, that the sometime writer, Neal Cassidy, traveling companion to Allen Ginsberg, Jack Kerouac and other of the so-called "beat" generation writers, came to his end in San Miguel. Expired of exposure on a frosty evening on the railroad tracks outside of town. Does it surprise you that I would have knowledge of such gadabouts and perpetrators of dubious literary distinction?" Not waiting for an answer Whitfield continued, "The study of structure, Mr. Ellis, takes many forms. Architecture. Music. Art. Literature. It is all about structure. The things that last are built on a foundation of strength. A foundation of order and discipline. Example? Abstraction in painting is a fad. A multigenerational fad, I grant you, but a fad nevertheless. It will pass. As will the beats free verse. It was always a distraction at best. A blip on the radar of time. In days to come, few if any, will remember it at all." As quickly as he had seemed to drift away, Whitfield came back to the heart of the matter. "I will do some checking, Mr. Ellis. With my contacts in Mexico and my contacts here. I will be checking on you as well. It will not take long. I will get back to you quickly. How can I get in touch with you?"

Ellis reached into his breast pocket and handed him his card.

"Anderson will see you out. Good day, Mr. Ellis." With that, Whitfield turned and left Ellis alone in the room. Moments later, Anderson, the man Ellis had taken to be the butler, returned and escorted him back outside to the driveway. As Ellis stood there beside his car grasping the door handle, he didn't think about whether or not he'd get the money, or how long it might take Whitfield to get back to him, or even how incredibly beautiful this place called Eden's Edge was. He stood there thinking that he had just told a man that his only son's throat had been slashed and the man never asked one word about it.

CHAPTER 20

On his way back to the city Ellis used his cell phone to call the hospital. He brought the younger Whitfield up to speed regarding the conversation with his father. Terrance Whitfield suggested to Ellis that he wouldn't have to wait long to hear back. "If he said he'd get back to you quickly, believe me, he will. And, if he said he'd check you out, count on the fact he'll do that too." The son went on to ask if Ellis thought his father would come up with the money.

"Well, while he didn't come right out and say he would, he definitely didn't say he wouldn't."

"That's a good sign," Terrance Whitfield said with an audible sigh. "My guess is you'll hear from him in the next day or two. Call me as soon as you know anything."

It was mid afternoon when Ellis got back and wheeled into the parking lot. He thought he'd spend some time in his office before heading to his apartment. There was a momentary pause as he stepped into the elevator. No, he thought. Lightning seldom strikes twice in the same place. And he could hardly stay out of elevators for the rest of his life. So he pushed the button and up he went. Stepping out into the hallway, he turned and started toward his office. But a few feet away he stopped. The door was ajar. Not good, Ellis thought. He knew he hadn't left it unlocked. Ellis walked toward the half open door slowly, stepping as lightly as he could on the uncarpeted floor. He was listening for voices or sounds. Listening with one hand inside his suit on the handle of his Glock. But he heard neither sounds nor voices. So he used his right foot to slowly push the door all the way open. "Well, I'll be damned," Ellis said out loud. Followed by an annoyed, "Fuck me."

The cause of his chagrin was evident. Ransacked was a word he didn't normally use. But it came to mind immediately. Chairs, desk, and files overturned. Drawers pulled out and dumped. Papers, notes and various other junk he had rat-holed in his desk was now sprayed all over the floor. And in the middle of it all was his computer. His computer with the monitor kicked in, the keyboard snapped in half, the wires ripped out and dangling from overturned furniture. Walking through the chaos of what was normally a relatively organized office, Ellis began looking for what wasn't there. Surely they must have taken something, he said to himself. They must have been after something. But the more he looked, the more he found. And the more he came to realize that apparently nothing was missing. Lots of things destroyed. But nothing gone. This hadn't been about taking something, Ellis reasoned. It had been about leaving something. Another message apparently. From those same oafs who took a Louisville slugger to the car of that poor schmuck who didn't pay Lothar on time.

He could have called the cops. But until he knew why these goons were going off on him, he didn't want to get the police involved. He could have gone downstairs and checked with Harley to see if the well meaning but ineffectual security guard knew anything about the perpetrators of this crash and bash party. But there was always time for that later. He could have left the whole mess for the night cleaning crew to deal with. But he knew that would probably make it even harder for him to put things back where they ought to be. So he picked up the wooden coat rack, took off his jacket, draped it across one of the limbs and set about putting the place back together as best he could.

About a half hour into his reorganization the phone rang. Apparently the demolition duo hadn't seen fit to spend as much quality time with it as they had with his computer. Picking it up after the first ring, he said (not particularly amicably) "This is Ellis."

"So is that your professional response? I guess gruff is good in your line of work, but you might want to tone it down just a bit."

He recognized Laney's voice immediately. "Laney...hey, sorry. Been less than a stellar day so far."

"Well, why don't we try to change that. Want to meet me for a drink at the Del Coronado?"

"Hey listen. I thought your place was just fine. No need to get an expensive hotel room on my account."

"I said a drink, big shot," Laney fired back with a smile. "I've got a hostess gig there later this evening. Some sort of jewelry show, marketing convention thing. For some reason they seem to think the jewels look better if they're around the necks of real, live women."

"Well, if all the real, live women look like you, then I think they have a point. Maybe I should take a look at this show."

"Sorry, it's invitation only. For industry types and big wigs.

But I thought maybe you'd have time for a drink before the whole thing gets started."

"I like the way you think. A drink is definitely in order. Is about an hour from now good?"

"Yeah, that'll be perfect," Laney said. "Meet me at the poolside bar. We can have a drink and look at the ocean before I join the rest of the harem."

"See you there," Ellis said hanging up the phone. He could still devote another half hour to putting things back together before he left for the hotel. And he could always catch up with Harley tomorrow and see if he could get more of a line on who the hell had it in for him. And perhaps even more importantly, why.

CHAPTER 21

With Sinatra on the tape singing She gets too hungry for dinner at eight...Ellis reflected that of the many small pleasures in life, surely one of them is driving an open-top car across the Coronado bridge on a sunny California afternoon. With the bay on one side and an island on the other and a lovely woman waiting to have a drink with him at one of the world's more beautiful Victorian resort hotels, he could almost forget about his office being mugged and his car's narrow escape and his elevator thrill ride. Not to mention the mayhem at Benny's, the bombing in Mexico and a family called Whitfield seemingly in the midst of being drawn and quartered. Funny, Ellis thought, how everything else at the moment was sort of taking second place to the memory of Laney lying naked in his arms. The round curve of her hips. The soft, sweet scent of her neck. The way her head rested in the small of his shoulder. That's what was on Ellis's mind as he left his car with the valet at the entrance to the sprawling, white wooden framed wonder most locals simply called The Del.

He held that thought as he walked through the main lobby. Glancing over to his right he could see the Crown Room was already being prepared for the evening's festivities. He wondered how much time he'd have with Laney. Well, he thought, whether it's a lot or a little, it's a good sign she called and wanted to see him. And he was certainly looking forward to seeing her.

Ellis walked though the hotel, onto the patio and was almost to the pool when he heard, "Hey, handsome, buy a girl a drink?"

Odd, Ellis thought. The voice was coming from behind him. When he turned he saw Laney sitting at a patio table. He knew immediately why he had walked right by her. She was dressed for an evening out. Black, strapless evening gown. Hair pulled back tight. Silver high heels that matched the choker around her neck. He had never seen her looking so formal. But he didn't miss a beat. "Well, I would but I'm here to meet someone I know and she might not be thrilled about me spending time with such a beautiful distraction."

"Pretty good comeback Ellis. I just assumed you had work on your mind."

As Ellis pulled out the chair next to hers and began to sit he said, "The truth is I was thinking entirely of you, but not in this particular attire. Excuse me, have I said yet how stunning you look. Let me say that. You look stunning."

"That's very sweet of you. And if I didn't have to worry about mussing myself up, I'd give you a big kiss."

"Well if I had my way you'd definitely get mussed up, but why the big concern? When do you have to go to work?"

"I'm working right now. This is known as the pre-show entertainment. We sit around outside showing off the merchandise and getting buyers used to looking at us. So when they see us later inside they can all start a conversation with...I saw you earlier this evening by the pool...or something like that. The main objective is to keep them feeling friendly and talkative. Take a look around Ellis. You think all these women out here dressed in evening gowns and expensive baubles is just coincidental. And what about those big lugs near the door. You think they're just enjoying the sunset. I thought you were supposed to be some sort of super sleuth."

"Okay," Ellis replied, "now I see there are a number of beautiful women around here dressed to the nines. But with you on my mind, how could I have noticed them before?"

"Damn, Ellis, you're good. I'm gonna kiss you anyway." And with that they both moved forward and pressed their lips together softly.

"Is that part of the show too?" Ellis asked, hoping that the answer was no.

"No, that was for real. Didn't it feel real to you?"

"Yes. It did. It really did."

Their eyes held on each other for a moment, then Laney reached out and took Ellis' hand with both of hers. "But I am working, believe it or not. So let's just have that drink, okay?"

"Hey, that's what I'm here for. Let me get the waiter's attention."

Their next forty minutes together went much like those minutes do between lovers who are having a hard time keeping their hands off each other, but because of circumstance, find themselves immersed in each other's words not locked in each other's arms.

"I'm going to have to go in." Laney said, "We all have to be in before seven for a costume change."

"Well, look, why don't I swing by when you're finished. Is

your car here, did you drive?"

"Oh no, it's going to be much too late. And I will have been on my feet for four or five hours. Believe me, I'll be dead by then."

"That's why I should pick you up. You shouldn't be driving home when you're that tired."

"I won't have to drive. All the girls came together in a van. It's the agency's way of making sure they get all the jewelry, dresses and other merchandise back. They also like to say it's their way of making sure we don't have to deal with drunken buyers or conventioneers. But if you ask me, I think it's just their way of making sure they don't wind up with a missing bracelet or ring or a really terrific pair of shoes. But it takes a long time to take inventory before we all leave the hotel. So it will just be too late. Anyway, didn't you say, the other night, that you'd call me. I haven't actually received a call yet."

"As you could probably tell earlier...on the phone...I had a pretty full day."

"Even another reason to make it another time. But do call me, like you said you would."

"Will do," said Ellis. Then Laney leaned over, kissed him again, got up and joined the other knockouts that were all now making their way back into the hotel.

Ellis watched her as she and the other models, who had started to chat, moved inside. No doubt about it, even though she may have been a few years older than her cohorts, she definitely held her own. She brought a symmetry to that tight black evening gown that made Ellis say to himself, yeah, I hate to see you go...but I love to watch you walk away.

CHAPTER 22

A soft pink glow, slowly burning yellow, was ushering in the sun's arrival. A predawn overture that silhouetted Cubilete, the 2500 meter peak that is the center of Mexico. Rena Whitfield gazed at the enormous figure of Christ atop the summit and wondered if his eyes saw the same sorrow and suffering that weighed so heavily upon her soul. Surely he had seen it longer? Maybe he had become immune to it. Perhaps it no longer obsessed him as it did her. Otherwise he would have done something about it by now. But he had done nothing. Nothing but stand there, rigid and unmoving. Accepting the adoration of those poor souls who made their way to him, climbed up inside his cement entrails until they reached the platform that would give them access to the same awe-inspiring view that he had of a land once bursting with a belly full of silver. Silver that brought wealth and luxury to so few, while it brought poverty and misery to so many. Where was the justice in that? Where was the fairness? Perhaps gods are content to do nothing amid such injustice. But not mortals. At least not her. And not Diego.

Diego Marquez was awakening slowly. His eyes beginning to focus on the rumpled blankets beside him. There was no form to give them shape. They lay virtually flat. The top of one flipped back revealing its occupant was already up. This was odd, Diego thought. He usually rose before Rena. She liked to stay in her warm cocoon until he had gotten up, relieved himself, and started the fire that would warm their morning.

He rolled slowly to his other side and saw Rena standing a few yards away. Her back to him, arms folded, staring toward the first streaks of light bursting from the oncoming sun. Diego took his arm from beneath the blanket and pulled it aside so he too could rise. Walking softly he came up behind her and put both hands on her shoulders.

"Don't think I didn't hear you," she said.

"I was not trying to surprise you. I purposely stepped on three twigs so you could hear me coming." Still holding her from behind he said, "Why are you up so early? Could you not sleep?"

Her gaze still transfixed on the upcoming sun and Cubeleti, she said, "I slept fine. I just wanted to see the sunrise on this beautiful day when we will do something good for the people."

Diego turned her around slowly so that she was no longer looking at the sun breaking over the mountain. She was looking up into his dark brown eyes, which were as penetrating as the first time she saw them. Two fierce yet kind doorways to the soul of a man who had chosen to stand up for what he believed in. "You say the people...not our people. Do we still remain objects of your conscience rather than your heart?"

"My heart is filled with love for you. Your struggle is my struggle. Your people...mine. You make too much of one three-letter word versus another."

Smiling, Diego replied, "I know. It is simply my sly way of hearing you say you love me."

"You needn't be sly. I'll tell you anytime you want to hear," Rena said as she put her head back and rose slightly to meet his lips. As Diego released her from his embrace, Rena, now in a more playful mood, went on to say, "In fact, I'll tell anyone who wants to hear." Her voice rising with each word, *"I love Diego Marquez!"*

Diego put his hand across her mouth muffling the shout of his elongated name. He wrestled her lovingly to him but her fun had its effect. The rest of the camp began to stir and come to life with the dawn of the new day.

As breakfasts were made and bladders emptied and daily greetings exchanged, Rena found herself reflecting on how she had come to feel part of this gypsy band of both male and female soldados. She knew she was a pampered California princess who never really had to work for much of anything in her life. But she seemed to always have a soft spot for those less fortunate than her. The cook's children. The underprivileged ghetto kids her school used to have parties for at Christmas. The men with vacant eyes and unshaved faces who mumbled "spare change" as you passed them on downtown streets on your way to the theater or cafe. She had always noticed them. Always cared about them. Or at least she assumed she had. But the more she turned it over in her mind the more she knew she really must not have cared for them at all. For if she had, why did she only give the cook toys and clothes she no longer wanted? Why did she play Santa for the children who were bussed to her school for a one-hour Christmas party but never did another single thing for them during the other three hundred and sixty four days of the year? Why did she walk through city streets dropping a few pieces of silver into outstretched palms but always making sure never to actually touch one of those hands?

Somehow that had all changed in Mexico. Perhaps the change began when she saw the children in the streets. Children who buzzed round you like flies. Swarming each time you left the hotel or restaurant or the taxicab. Children with dirt on their angelic faces. Faces with sorrow etched into their down-turned mouths. Mouths that seldom uttered a word. And you wondered if the silence was from the shame of having nothing or from having to ask you for what you had. You thought the children in the cities were poor, until you went into the country. Before Mexico, poverty was only a word. A placeholder in clever phrases at the end of public service announcements. But it wasn't just a word, was it? It was a living, breathing disease that was turning children into old men and women before they became teenagers. You should be old in this life before you experience the pain and hunger you saw on the faces of those children, Rena thought. Children hungry not just for food, but for kindness, and perhaps most of all, hungry for even the smallest vestige of hope.

Or perhaps it was the corruption that made Rena see things differently. Corruption from those who stopped her from helping those who needed help the most. The ones who took their food and medicine and supplies that would have gone so far and done so much. How could they do such things? They were the lucky ones. The ones who had lived and found employment and conveniently forgot about the places and the people they had come from. The one's who had not only turned their backs on their brothers and sisters, but gave the back of their hands to those who were the weakest among them. They were bastardos only out for themselves. They sickened her.

Or perhaps Rena's change began the first time she saw Diego's eyes. Eyes visible only between the bill of a fatigue cap and the opening of a ski mask. But eyes that seemed to stare into her soul. It felt as if the eyes of all humanity were asking her questions she had never dared asked herself. How can you see what you see and not be moved? How can you profess to help and then turn back at the slightest obstacle? How can you say these people's lives have worth if you are not willing to count their lives as important as your own? He had never uttered those words. His eyes had. And from that moment Rena knew her life would never be the same.

Can you fall in love with a pair of eyes? Eyes that reflect the emptiness of your own life. Eyes that remind you there is more to live for than wealth and comfort and the scraps of paper that are supposed to give meaning to what you've done. The diplomas and the commendations and the certifications of hours spent memorizing facts and dogma and doctrine tend to pale when compared to the respect these men were given by people who had nothing else to give. Rena had received appreciation from those who received the remaining trinkets the corrupt ones had not confiscated. But she had not received the genuine devotion and affection that was given to these fatigue-clad comrades in their collective struggle. Especially to the one called Diego. The one with the eyes.

An hour before they finished clearing camp, Diego sent a scout ahead to Comanjila. Entering a town or city without reconnoitering it first just wasn't done. Even when the mission was one like this morning's. That's what had Rena in such a good mood. The morning, in fact the whole day, was to be a public celebration. It wasn't the first time they had done this. Especially in small villages. A cadre of Zapatistas would come into locales and participate in festivities that sometimes went on even more than a day. Outsiders hearing of the event would come as well. Tents and tarps and hammocks would be set up everywhere to help shelter the people and the people's fighters. It was not uncommon to see the public address announcer at the basketball game wearing a ski mask to shield his identity. Even the players themselves would adorn bandanas. As would the ice cream vendors and the marimba band. In town halls and public squares, speeches would be made. Signs were set up around the community to let people know that they were now entering territory of the Zapatistas in rebellion. Street vendors would offer plums, watermelons, boiled corn-on-the-cob and tamales to the milling visitors. The federal authorities stayed away believing that violent opposition to the Zapatistas only made the local citizenry even more loyal to the masked militia. They were willing to play a wait-and-see game. In hopes that eventually all this rebellion would simply go away. As long as it did not reach the major cities, the government saw it as a boil on the backside of the nation that would eventually lance itself.

But this morning, as Rena and Diego and the eight other

soldados approached the outskirts of the city, they could quickly tell that something was wrong. Usually the festivities would have already begun before their arrival. But there was no music, no gaiety, no games being played or speeches being made. Diego had the group fan out as they reached the railroad tracks that bordered the north end of the village. With his right arm he reached out and moved Rena to a position behind him. Crossing the tracks they continued on their way. Then, just before entering the alleys between the wood and adobe houses and shops, he saw Miguel coming toward him with an old woman by his side.

Rena listened as Diego and Miguel and the old woman spoke in Spanish. She was able to pick up most of the conversation. The police had been there three days before. Not the village police, but police from somewhere else. The old woman wasn't sure. They went from house to house looking for young ones. Not babies, but children from ten to fifteen years of age. Boys only. They told the parents they had work for the boys and that they would be treated well and each would be returned to his home in a matter of weeks. Then they gave the parents money. An advance on the boys' wages they said. Two hundred pesos per boy. Most of these villagers had never received so many pesos at one time. Many did not want their sons to go. But the police were firm while all the time saying each would be returned safely in a few weeks. By the time they left most of the village's young boys were packed in the beds of trucks. Some of the younger ones were crying. And the parents told the older boys to comfort and watch over their younger hermanos. The police came without any warning. They said this was a great opportunity for each family and for the village itself. But they were in a big hurry. There was no time for one family to talk to another about it. No time for a community meeting. There were some holdouts. One or two fathers and mothers did not want their sons to go. No matter how much was being paid. They saw what was happening in the houses next to them so they hid their children until the police had gone.

Diego asked the old woman if she could take him to one of the fathers whose boys were taken. She said she could. So Rena stayed with Miguel and the rest of the group as Diego accompanied the old woman back to the village.

About half an hour later Diego returned alone and spoke to the group as one. He recounted to all of them what the old woman had told him.   Of course Miguel had shared most of the same information while Diego was away.   He said the villagers were frightened. They were remorseful about what they had done. In the house of the man Diego spoke to, the pesos are still on the kitchen table. The man can't believe he let his two boys go without knowing more about precisely when they would return. He had never seen that much money at one time before. Now he could not touch it. Even to move it from his sight. Diego instructed the others to go from house to house and find out what more they could from other villagers. They would regroup in an hour.

Once the others left, Rena said, "What does it mean, Diego? Where have they been taken? How could the parents do this?"

"They wanted to believe the police," Diego replied. "They wanted to see this as an opportunity. And the police seemed very organized."

"What do you mean?" Rena asked.

"The police had one of those instant cameras with them. A Polaroid or something like it. They would take two pictures of each boy. Then they would give one to the parents, and on the back of the other they would write the boy's name and house number. They told the parents that the boys would be working on a farm...a collective. Easy work they said, that would allow each boy to come back in a few weeks with more money than most of these people can make in months."

"Do you believe that, Diego?"

"I believe that if I had a son...I would have hidden him too."

Rena started to reply, paused, then quickly said only "What will we do?"

"I will take the platoon and we will see if we can find where the boys have been taken. You and Miguel and Benito will go to Guanajuato. You have work to do there. Do you think he will come? Do you think he will come with the money?"

Rena didn't hesitate. "Yes, I believe he will come with my father's money. And he will expect me to go back with him."

Diego reached out and held her arm. "And you will go back with him. You will go back to your life in the states just as we decided."

"As *you* decided," Rena snapped back. "Not me."

Now, with his other arm, Diego held her by the shoulders and looked into her eyes as he spoke. "It must be this way. With this act...with this money...you will have done more for the cause than anyone before you. This money will keep the cause alive for years to come. But if you stay, you know what will happen. More men will be sent to find you. The governments of both your and my country will be forced to find the American girl who is with the rebels. We will be called villains and kidnappers in the press of Mexico and the United States. You will become bigger than the cause. Such things happen in this world today. The story of one American girl becomes more important than the lives of thousands of Mexicanos. But you have the power to keep that from happening. You have the power to help so many. You can help them by simply going back to your home."

A tear had already begun to slide slowly down her cheek as Rena said, "I had hoped my home was here with you."

"Your home will always be with me. No matter where you are. No matter where I am. And someday, we may be together again. But for now, it is best that you fight for us in America with the press and others who can contribute to our cause. While I fight for us here...in my own way. You know this. You know all this. We have talked about it over and over."

"I know," Rena replied, "but that doesn't make it any easier."

"Nor for me," Diego responded, as he crushed her against him and kissed her.

She kissed him back, her hands pressed against his temples, holding him to her mouth. Rena was afraid to let him go. She feared the parting of their breath would pull the words from her throat, *Diego my love, I carry our child.*

CHAPTER 23

Decisions had been made. Warren Whitfield had checked on Ellis as he said he would. He then summoned Ellis back to Eden's Edge. Once again they met in the study. Whitfield spoke first, foregoing anything remotely resembling a greeting.

"I've looked into your credentials. They seem to be in order. How exactly do you plan to carry out this..."

"Assignment?" Ellis volunteered.

"Yes. Assignment. How precisely do you plan to bring my daughter home?"

"I prefer to keep the specifics to myself, Mr. Whitfield. The fewer people who know about how I plan to get in and out of Mexico, the less chance there is of something going wrong."

"Yes, well this type of cloak and dagger thing may be acceptable to vengeful wives trying to root out the whereabouts of their husbands' assignations, but we're talking about two million dollars of my money, Mr. Ellis, not to mention my daughter."

"I understand your concern, Mr. Whitfield, but I'm afraid I'll have to insist on this being done my way. Yes, it's your money and your daughter, but it's...pardon the expression...my ass on the line. The individuals your daughter is involved with have already taken lives. Granted, we can't be positive that they did so on purpose. But whether by design or incompetence, some people are still pretty damn dead."

Whitfield adjusted his glasses. He wasn't used to being talked to so directly. But neither was he used to having his daughter around such danger. And somehow, he felt a modicum of assurance in what he perceived as this fellow's arrogant confidence.

"All right, Mr. Ellis, I'll revise my request. You need not provide me the precise details. But I would like some idea as to how you plan to bring Rena home safely."

Ellis kept his response to a minimum. Leaving out what he thought of as operational logistics and yet still trying to be as straightforward as he could. "It's really up to your daughter, sir. Or the people she either is or isn't working with. It's probably occurred to you that there are numerous similarities between this meet and the one in San Miguel. Public place. Quick exchange. Nighttime. That can all be good if their intentions are good. It can be deadly if their intentions are bad. If they've come only for the money and the exchange, things should be fine. Your daughter and I will be back in the states the following day. If they've come for the money and something similar to what happened before...well, I'll just have to play that by ear."

Whitfield came back quickly, "If there's any danger, Mr. Ellis, please take care of Rena. They can have the money. Just do everything possible to bring Rena back safely."

Ellis felt the need to offer more encouragement. "If you've checked into me as you say you have, Mr. Whitfield, you'll know that I do have experience in these sorts of operations, both in and out of the military. I'll do everything I possibly can to make sure both your daughter and I return just as quickly and safely as possible."

"But?" Whitfield asked. Sensing there was a but coming.

"But...it will really be up to them."

The rest of their conversation did involve a specific. Ellis didn't want that much cash going through airport security procedures. And it would take too long to drive from San Diego to the middle of Mexico. So he asked that the money be put in an account in Mexico City. An account he could empty once he was there. Even though it would take longer to drive from Mexico City to Guanajuato than if he flew into Leon, Ellis knew such a large transaction would attract much less attention in the sprawling capital city than in a smaller town. And he had another reason for wanting to go through the oldest capital in the New World. He had contacts there where he could arrange to pick up additional firepower he had not had with him in San Miguel. If trouble was on the menu, Ellis wanted to be able to give his own compliments to the chef.

Preparations were in order. There was much to do before leaving for Mexico. He would contact Terry Whitfield and let him know that everything was moving ahead. He would make flight and hotel reservations. Multiple reservations in multiple cities since he couldn't be sure exactly what circumstances would be surrounding his, and, he hoped, his quarry's departure. He would give Grif a call to see if things were copacetic with the insurance company. He would not take the time to check back with Harley or the cops about the vandalizing of his office just yet because he wanted to make sure he would have time to look in on Laney before heading south of the border again. And it would be another kennel stay for Osgood.

CHAPTER 24

The next night, lying together in Laney's bed, he waited until after they made love to say,

"I have to go out of town for a few days again. Can't say exactly when I'll be back. Probably somewhere around May seven or eight.

"More of that confidential work that is simply too hush-hush to talk about?"

"Yeah. I'm afraid so."

"Well, as it turns out, I'm going to be out of town as well. So we'll probably be gone around the same time."

"And is your trip confidential too?" Ellis asked.

"I should tell you it is," Laney kidded, "but the fact is, it's kind of an extension of the jewelry gig the other night. This time it's going to be in New York. The last one was such a success, they wanted to keep some of the same girls that were at the Del."

"Only some of the same girls?"

"Yeah," Laney continued, enjoying the momentary limelight, "only the real babes, you know?"

"Do I ever," Ellis responded, as he pulled her close and threw his leg over hers, "they certainly made the right choice."

This time there was no talk of things to do on the way out. Laney asked if he could stay and he jokingly replied, "I thought you'd never ask." Then it was a very long time before they actually went to sleep.

CHAPTER 25

The flight to Mexico City was uneventful. Something Ellis was always thankful for. But the plane had been virtually full. Ellis assumed it was due to the upcoming holiday, Cinco de Mayo, the fifth of May. In 1862 the invading French were turned back at the battle of Puebla de los Angeles and Mexicans have been celebrating the victory ever since. Fiestas, music, dancing and food would go on long into the night. The night that he was supposed to be swapping two million dollars for an American do-gooder who had almost gotten him killed once already. He hoped all the hoopla wouldn't make his job even harder but he had the feeling it probably would. As for now, there was the unenviable task of sharing the streets and roadways with twenty-five million inhabitants of one of the world's most populated cities.

Ellis didn't want to spend any more time in the Mexican megalopolis than was absolutely necessary. He had already arranged to meet with a concealed-carry supplier he had used before. A man with reliable equipment but somewhat excessive prices. Ellis wasn't overly concerned about the cost of equipment on this job though. Terrance Whitfield was paying him well and Warren Whitfield had ended their meeting with the promise of a sizable bonus on top of whatever the younger Whitfield was paying if Rena was returned to San Diego unharmed.

After renting a car, again a rather nondescript Japanese model in reasonable working order, Ellis began the half hour trip from the airport to the Grand Melia Mexico Reforma Hotel where his contact had already rented a room in which to do business. Driving in Mexico City, Ellis thought, is a bit like swimming against a current surrounded by jellyfish. Progress is inordinately slow and the imminent likelihood of immediate disaster is avoided only by the intricate balance of individual bravado and extremely skillful defensive driving. While the miles are few from the airport to the inner city, the desperation is continual. As Ellis passed through a succession of dreary, dusty, smog ridden streets in bumper to bumper claustrophobic conditions, he stayed focused on getting to the red-jacketed valet at the Gran Melia who would take his car off his hands and direct him through the towering granite and glass of one of Mexico City's most modern Euro-Mexican designed hotels.

Upon arrival he entered the cavernous lobby following the valet's directions to the house phones located near the elongated check-in counter. "Alphonso Velasco," Ellis said to the operator.

There was a slight pause as she found the appropriate room number and replied, "I will connect you, senor."

On the third ring a man's voice answered with. "Hola."

"Velasco?" Ellis questioned.

"Si. Senor Ellis?"

"Yes. This is Ellis."

"Room six two five," Velasco said. Then hung up the phone.

Ellis put his receiver down and looked around the lobby until he saw the elevator bank. After pushing the button and starting to ascend, his mind flashed back quickly to his earlier elevator incident. But it was only momentary and it was immediately replaced with a focus on what he was there for. He stepped onto the sixth floor and immediately saw the small sign at eye level on the wall in front of him that indicated rooms six hundred to six twenty would be found on his left and rooms six twenty one to six forty would be found on his right. Making sure no one was in the hallways, he turned right and moved slowly down the corridor. Heading for his destination he noticed that odd numbered rooms were on one side of the hallway and even numbered rooms on the other. So, just before reaching room six twenty-five, he stepped to the opposite side of the hallway, put his back against the wall, reached out with his left arm and knocked on the door of room six twenty-four and said "Domesticos."

There was no response from inside, then after a momentary pause, the door opened. A head with slick black hair combed straight back emerged just enough for Ellis to grab it by the shirt collar and pull it and the body that was attached to it swiftly to the floor. Ellis dropped down with it so his knee would rest on the chest of Alphonso Velasco.

The Mexican, flat on his back and still in the grip of the American smiled and said, "Senor Ellis. So good to see you again."

Ellis, loosening his grip on Velasco's shirt, but keeping his weight on the prostrate body said, "I believe you gave me the wrong room number."

"Si, an old trick, I admit. But I wanted to be able to look through the key hole and make sure it was you."

Ellis took his knee off Velasco's chest, pulled the smaller

Mexican up with him and straightened out his shirt front as he said, "Admirable caution, but don't you remember that it was me who taught you that trick."

"Ah yes. So it was. So it was," Velasco replied smiling. "I forget. Please, come in before some German tourist calls downstairs and complains about the noise in the hall."

Ellis walked into a room he quickly realized only well-heeled travelers, expense-account businessmen or successful gun-dealers like Velasco could afford. The walls were papered in gold brocade. A lush black and brown striped carpet was underfoot. A dark mahogany desk was just to the left with a computer keyboard and a fax machine atop it. Floor to ceiling windows ran the length of one side of the room and the light from the hot Mexican afternoon was spilling in. A cushioned chair and ottoman upholstered in gold and brown stripes somewhat wider than those on the floor sat near the sun splashed windows. The bed itself was covered in a downy soft comforter reprising the gold and brown stripes, only wider, bolder, even more audacious. And above, an enormous mirror ran vertically from the headboard to the ceiling and horizontally from one side of the bed to the other. If this were someplace other than one of the largest, most well-known hotels in Mexico City, Ellis would have made sure there was actually a wall behind that mirror and not a camera on the other side of it. But here, he didn't feel it was necessary.

"Do you mind if I use your bathroom?" Ellis asked. "It's been a long trip."

"Of course not, mi amigo. But do you really need to...or are you just checking to see if I have a compatriot hiding in there?"

"Actually, both." said Ellis as he walked past Velasco and stepped slowly through the already open bathroom door.

While Ellis relieved himself, Velasco opened the closet doors and retrieved two full-sized ostrich-covered suitcases. He put each of them on the bed so that when they were opened, both sides could lay flat exposing their lethal content. But he didn't open them yet. He was never one to pass up an opportunity for dramatic impact.

Ellis stepped back into the room a moment later and Velasco said, "Would you like some coffee, my friend? I have some here. Or we could order something more from room service. Something stronger perhaps? Even something to eat if you like."

"No thanks. I'd just as soon we get to it. I assume those cases on the bed are what we're here to discuss," Ellis remarked.

"Yes. They are lovely aren't they?"

"Oh yeah, they're lovely if you want to attract lots of attention. But I would have thought in your line of work, Alphonso, attention would be the last thing you'd want."

"Of course you are right, Senor Ellis. But sometimes I just can't help myself. I love beautiful things. And if you think these are beautiful...wait until you see what's inside."

With that, Velasco popped two snaps on one suitcase, followed by the other. Then, at the same time, in something approaching a flourish, he threw open both cases and pirouetted to face Ellis saying, "My little shrine to the day of the dead."

It was impressive. Ellis had to admit. Both cases contained precisely cut foam that cradled the various weaponry nestled within it. Plus there was an added touch. Each case also contained a carved Mexican death mask in the shape of a skull. The white mask was highlighted with red, black, and green icons, and its oversized teeth were stretched into a hideous smile. But the inclusion guaranteed to start every conversation were the tiny candles that stood upright in the skull's eye sockets.

"Okay, I'll ask," Ellis began, "what are the candles for?"

"When I sell an instrument of death, I always light a candle. Others go to church and light candles for the dead. I light them in my little church of the soon-to-be-departed. Just because I deal in violence doesn't mean I can't be religious."

"You can be whatever you want to be," Ellis said. "Lets just conduct our business."

"Excellent idea," Velasco began, "of course I have no way of knowing what kind of operation you are on...and rest assured the last thing I would do is ask about such a private matter...because I am nothing if not discreet... but allow me to highlight a few items of interest you may want to consider."

Without even looking at it, Velasco reached down and pulled out the pistol that was nearest him in the case. Extending it toward Ellis like a waiter would show the wine selection, Velasco intoned, "The Kimber Tactical Custom II. Because dangerous combat can call for precision with either the right or left hand. Sometimes both. That's the beauty of this particular pistola. It has extended...how you say...ambidextrous...thumb safety levers on either side of the frame. And such a beautiful frame it is. Constructed of the same alloy they make aircraft frames with, it is light as a feather compared to many of the standard steel frames. And yet it is still very rugged and balances perfectly in the hand. Here, hold it. See for yourself."

Ellis wasn't really interested. But he held it nonetheless. While Velasco continued his spiel. "And of course, as a connoisseur of a weapon's appearance...note the macho battleship gray color which is achieved using a patented technique known only to the manufacturer."

"Thanks Alphonso, it's not really what I had in mind," Ellis said handing the gun back.

Velasco accepted it and tossed it on the bed in one motion while retrieving another from the case. This was far from the first time he had done this.

"Of course, I understand completely," Velasco said, as he pulled another gun from the same suitcase. "You are Americano. Red, white and blue, yes? You don't like to be without something from your homeland. I have it right here. The Smith & Wesson 329 PD Airlite. The newest thing in 44 Magnums. Dirty Harry, si? Make my day, right? What could be better?"

"It kicks too hard and weighs too much, my friend. Why don't you let me just do a little browsing," Ellis suggested.

"But of course," Velasco came back. Stepping aside with the battered pride of a salesman unwilling to admit that his inventory could likely do a better job of selling than he could.

It only took a moment for Ellis to find what he wanted. "Alphonso, what are you asking for this Glock 19?"

"Such a weapon provides defense senor Ellis, but it lacks charisma. It does little to express the real you."

"Look Alphonso, let me tell you what this weapon expresses. You can drop this thing in the sand, the dirt or the mud and it will still come up firing. You can hide it under water, retrieve it an hour later and it will fire first time, every time. You can run over it with a car, a truck...you can have a horse, a camel or an ox stomp on it, even shit on it, and you can still pick it up and blow somebody away with it. That's the only expression I'm looking for."

The best salesmen are nothing if not flexible. "And I have the perfect carrier for it," Velasco replied without missing a beat.

"Tito's Revenge." He pulled it from underneath a closed section of one of the cases. "It is a cross draw holster that can be worn without detection no matter how you are dressed. You can set it low inside the trousers, belt high. Wear your shirt on the outside, as I am doing and it will ride tight against your body so that no one can tell your are armed. I can also provide you with a mount for an illuminator which will provide you with a laser and white light which can prove very beneficial should night fighting be called for."

"At the moment, Alphonso, my friend...I wouldn't rule anything out."

"Senor Ellis, you have come to the right man."

"I hope so, Alphonso. I certainly hope so."

They concluded their negotiations with Ellis also selecting a combat knife with four inch folding blade and a leather ankle holster to keep it in. On a hunch, Ellis asked if the dealer had any smoke grenades and Velasco produced a couple from hidden compartments inside one of the cases. The entire transaction set Ellis back two thousand dollars.

"Damn pricey, even for you, Alphonso."

"There are no retirement plans in my line of work. No pensions. No 401K's. I must provide for my old age."

"I would think someone in your line of work never reaches old age," Ellis offered.

Velasco looked up and replied, "Nor in yours, my friend. Nor in yours."

CHAPTER 26

After leaving the hotel, Ellis went directly to the Banco de Mexico. Warren Whitfield had made arrangements in advance for the bank to call him when Ellis arrived. After providing the bank with identification, Whitfield was telephoned. Following a short exchange in which Ellis reiterated to Whitfield that all was in order and that things were proceeding as they had discussed, the bank manager got back on the line. Five minutes later Ellis walked out of one of Mexico's oldest financial institutions with two million U. S. dollars.

It took more than an hour for Ellis to slog his way through honking horns and crushing traffic and an endless flow of cars that seemed to start and stop for no perceptible reason. At one point, traffic was halted dead in its tracks on what appeared to be a four-lane highway leading out of the city. In any other part of the world, on a road such as this, cars would be breezing along at fifty or sixty miles per hour. But here, the creeping was so slow and the movement so infrequent that vendors were actually walking in and out between the cars offering water for the radiators or the driver's temperature, whichever reached the boiling point first.

Finally, outside the city, beyond the traffic, on one of the major highways that seemed to stretch on forever, Ellis took a few moments on the side of the road to drag, rake, kick and dustup a couple of brand new canvas carrying bags he had purchased before leaving the hotel. Since no one was coming down the highway, either in front or behind him, he even took the time to relieve himself, being sure to splatter a bit on the bags as well. Then opening the trunk of the car, he proceeded to empty the contents of the leather covered brief cases he had received from the bank, into the freshly weathered bags he had just created. The bank's cases he left in the ditch for the next road repair crew or sharp-eyed traveler. It had been Ellis' experience that nosy types were far more attracted to rich Corinthian leather than they were to dirty, piss-stained canvas. And where he was going, the less nosy types he attracted, the better.

To those who see it today, it looks like a European medieval city dropped right into the middle of Mexico. To the original human inhabitants it seemed appropriate to name it for those who were there ahead of them. They called it quanax-juato, the place of the frogs. To Ellis it was simply Guanajuato, a place to which he had been summoned by a young woman who seemed to be ransoming herself to help the oppressed.

There had certainly been plenty of those among the crooked, cobblestone callejones, or alleyways of this aged city. Five hundred years ago Cortez's armies came looking for gold. They left famine and disease and death in their wake. By the eighteenth century Guanajuato's Valencia mine was supplying two thirds of the world's silver production. Hundreds were amassing fortunes as hundreds of thousands were laboring from dawn to dusk with barely enough to sustain them from one day to the next. After another hundred years of inequity a ragtag group of revolutionaries entered the city determined to throw off the yoke of oppression. Among them was Juan Jose de los Reyes Martinez who strapped a paving stone to his back to shield himself from Spanish bullets as he made his way to a granary door that he set afire enabling his brethren to enter. A colossal statue of him still stands high above the city. Ellis had noticed it as he drove into town. And he wondered if that was what Rena Whitfield was really after. Recognition. Recognition if not by others, then by herself that her life had meaning and purpose. Ellis remembered others who had asked that question. Others he had fought with. All young. All dead.

The rightful place for such questions is the classroom or the union hall or the parade ground. Not the battlefield, Ellis thought. On the battlefield, the people who ask such questions never seem to live long enough to find the answers.

Ellis had booked a room at the Parador San Javier. This time he didn't have a young entrepreneur to help him. But he muddled his way in and around town until he found the hotel. There was a valet at the front to greet him. He showed Ellis where he could park his car in a gated area in the back. Ellis accepted the offer of help with his bags. To have not done so might have attracted more speculation about his personal items than he wanted. Ellis' roadside weatherizing must have been worthwhile as he noticed the valet seemed to keep his bags as much at arm's length as possible.

Walking by old stonewalls with brilliantly colored bougainvillea tumbling over the sides, Ellis paid more attention to the route to and from his car than he paid to the central courtyard with its huge shade trees, tropical plants and fountains. In his room, after the valet left, the first thing that Ellis looked at was a map he found in the desk. It showed the area surrounding the hotel and Ellis noticed it was only a few blocks to the El Jardin de la Union where his meeting with Rena Whitfield was to take place. Just as he had in San Miguel, Ellis had selected a hotel that was close enough to be convenient, but not so close that it would make him easy to find if he didn't want to be found. And after his last experience with Ms. Whitfield's friends he was not about to stay closer than he had too.

Once again he had arrived a day before the meeting was to take place. So there would be time enough tomorrow to check out the area. It had been a long and tiring day of travel. And even though his hacienda room had shiny wood floors, a fireplace and extensive tile work in the bathroom, the thing that looked the most appealing to him was the bed he couldn't wait to fall into.

The next morning Ellis woke early and had breakfast in the hotel. Coffee, juice, fresh baked bread and fruit. Strawberries, peaches, and guanabananas. He was feeling rested and revived and the seventy-five degree temperature made for a perfect day to explore the surrounding area. Before he left the hotel, he took his two canvas bags and locked them in the trunk of his car. Better there he thought than in the way of some overly curious housekeeper.

Map in hand, Ellis walked toward the center of the city. Guanajuato was a bit like his breakfast, he thought. A big bowl of fruit surrounded by mountains and hills, it sits in the bottom of a valley. And just as the milk runs over and under and around the fruit in the bowl, rain and river water used to rush down from the mountains flooding the city. According to the concierge at the hotel he had stopped to chat with, before he began his walk, floods used to cover the city so often that today's Guanajuato is actually built on top of the cities that came before it. "Long ago it was indeed a place for frogs," the garrulous concierge had said. He went on to tell Ellis that eventually a dam was built to contain and reroute the Guanajuato River, which now runs beneath the city for over three miles. "And we have great subterranean streets...you know, tunnels...dip down and take you under the city. But you will get lost for sure. You should walk, senor. Walking is the best way to see the real Guanajuato." Which was exactly what Ellis had in mind. For reasons the concierge could never have imagined.

When Ellis reached El Jardin de la Union he immediately knew why Rena Whitfield, or the people Rena was working for, had chosen it as their meeting place. A relatively small, triangular flat area, in the middle of countless streets that zigzag in and out of it, it seemed the perfect place to do lots of damage and have lots of alternate escape routes. You couldn't get above it, or slightly beyond it as he hand done in San Miguel, because here the shady, garden area was covered almost entirely by a thick canopy of trees. It was a gathering place. A people-watching place. The kind of place that draws people like picnics draw ants. And if he was going to find Rena again, or if Rena was going to find him, he'd have to be right there in the middle, among both the ants and picnickers.

Of course Ellis couldn't be sure that Rena and her Zapatista friends had the same thing planned for Guanajuato that happened in San Miguel. Hell, he thought to himself, he didn't even know for sure if they were her friends or her captors. Maybe she really was planning to go back to the states. Maybe she was totally innocent. Yeah, he thought, and maybe the frogs they talk so much about here have wings and don't bump their butts on the ground. Ellis had never been one to leave things to chance. He wasn't about to start doing so now.

CHAPTER 27

The celebrations started early on May 5th. Parades seemed to be the order of the day. There were makeshift bands, children's groups, politicians waving and smiling. Puppet shows sprung up on corners. Along with groups of strolling players strumming guitars and serenading the tourists and locals alike. Food, festivities and fun seemed to be part of almost every street and alley in and around the central part of the city.

Ellis spent the majority of the day going over the different routes from his hotel to the Jardin. As well as determining how to get to the one major street leading out of downtown that cars could take to the outskirts of the city. By eight that evening he was already seated at the Cafe Valdez sipping cappuccino and this time, waiting to be found. The area was teeming with people walking, sitting, laughing, enjoying the evening. Ellis didn't have to wait the full hour. At a quarter of nine he saw Rena Whitfield and two men emerge from the crowd just to his right. As they walked toward him he stood to greet them.

"Ms. Whitfield, it's good to see you again. Please have a seat. We can pull a couple of chairs up for your friends."

"Is my brother with you?" Rena asked, looking around

"No. He still didn't feel quite up to traveling. I'm afraid it is still just me."

The two men with her had chosen to stand. One on either side of her.

"Please, have the gentlemen take a seat," Ellis reiterated.

"We're not going to be here that long," Rena answered curtly. "Did you bring it with you?"

"Well, yes and no. I did bring it, but it's not with me."

"Why not?" Rena said. Ellis sensed concern in her voice.

"You could hardly expect me to bring that amount into a crowd like this...and considering what happened last time, well I think even you'll agree a bit of caution is in order."

"Last time was a mistake. An accident. No one was supposed to get hurt. Just the building. The police building. To let them know they can't keep taking children. Do you know what child labor is like in this country? And why it's getting worse?"

Ellis started to answer but Rena cut him off.

"Listen, it doesn't matter. Let's just get on with it. Where did you leave it? Let's go get it."

Ellis answered with a question, "And as you said before, once I deliver the money, you'll return with me to the states?"

Rena opened her mouth to reply but before the words could come out, Benito, who had been on her left, fell across the table knocking the cappuccino cup and saucer to the floor with a clatter. Rena brought a hand to her mouth and stifled a cry as she and Ellis saw the bullet hole at the same time. Just as Ellis realized he had not heard a shot, Miguel, who had started to grab Rena by the shoulders to pull her away, was hit in the base of the neck. Rena felt him grip her like a vice with both hands for a second, then he suddenly went limp and fell over, pinning her beneath him. As other diners began to see the blood, people started yelling and trying to get up and away as quickly as they could. Rena struggled to get out from under her dead protector. Ellis however reached under the table and jerked free the smoke grenade he had taped to his left ankle. Pulling the pin, he rolled it a few feet away, then swung around the side of the table and tossed Miguel's body off Rena.

"They're hurt. They're hurt," Rena kept saying as Ellis was pulling her away. "We've got to help them."

"They're dead," Ellis replied. "Both of them. We can't help them now. Stay close to me."

By now the smoke had curled around them. People were scurrying wildly to get away, bumping into tables and chairs and each other. Ellis's mind was racing. He realized quickly that since he hadn't heard any shots, a silencer was being used. There had been too much activity and the restaurant was too crowded for both kills to have been long distance. So the shooter, or the shooters, must still be close. With both hands on Rena's shoulders he guided her into and along with the crowd that was spilling out toward the street. Trying to stay surrounded by as many people as possible, he couldn't be sure he wasn't standing right next to whoever just dropped Rena's comrades. But he was sure this tactic was safer than separating from the crowd too quickly and becoming an even easier target.

As the crowd's surge went beneath the outdoor awnings that led directly to the open street, Ellis knew he only had seconds. Then he spotted a godsend. "In just a moment we're going to run," he said to Rena. "So hold on and stay with me." As the family in front of them started to turn to the right, Ellis jerked Rena abruptly to the left and said, "Now, let's go."

Directly across the street, the doors of the elegant Theater Juarez had opened and a throng of concertgoers was just starting to emerge. Dashing across the street with Rena firmly in tow, Ellis began to wade into the middle of the oncoming mob. Like salmon swimming upstream, Ellis and Rena bumped and elbowed their way to the top of the stairs, then slid to one side behind one of the huge marble pillars that had been a gateway to Guanajuato society for over a hundred and twenty five years. From that vantage point Ellis began to scan the street and the scene below them.

Rena, still winded, said in short, puffy breaths, "What...or who...are you looking for?"

Ellis replied quickly, "Whoever's looking for us." He continued to keep his eyes on the street as he asked Rena, "How many people knew you were coming here tonight...and how many people knew why?"

"Well," she started to answer, then realized why he was asking, "no...it's impossible...these people are not like that. Miguel and Benito back there, they were our brothers. Our brothers in the struggle."

"Two million dollars can start a lot of family feuds."

"You are crazy. These people are Zapatistas. They are Soldados. They would never..."

Whatever the rest of Rena's sentence was, Ellis didn't hear it. He had caught sight of two men standing beneath one of the giant Indian laurel trees that ran down the center of the street. Unlike virtually everyone else in El Jardin who was fascinated by the smoke and the people still spilling out of Cafe Galeria, these two were turned the other way. Their searching eyes and their attention was focused on the theater and the crowd that was continuing to pour out of it. They were not about to look away.

Pulling Rena up close to him, Ellis said, "Look. Over there. Under that tree. Those two men who are looking this way. Do you know them?"

When Rena looked she saw a short, bald man on the right. He was wearing white slacks and a white shirt over them. The man on the left was somewhat taller and younger. The t-shirt he wore revealed that he worked out. It was as tight as the jeans he was wearing. Both were Mexican.

"No, I don't know them. Do you think they are the ones? The ones who murdered Miguel and Benito?"

"I take the short guy for the shooter," Ellis said, "easy to hide a piece under that shirt. The other guy's the muscle. Look, we're going to join the crowd that's leaving here. We're going to stay right with them until they start to disperse. Then if I move quickly, you do too, okay? The last thing we want is to get separated. If we're lucky, they may not see us."

They weren't lucky. As they swung round the pillar to blend in with the crowd, the bald man spotted them. He quickly grabbed his partner and pointed out where Ellis and Rena had fallen in with the mass of bodies descending the stairs. Then he shoved the younger man off to the right as he started walking swiftly to get on the opposite side of the crowd.

Ellis and Rena had their heads down as they milled in with the others. When Ellis brought his eyes up to check again, he saw only tree trunk. "Damn," he said involuntarily.

"What's the matter?" Rena asked.

"They've moved," Ellis said, trying to look above the crowd to find them again. He spotted the bald man on the right. "Let's go this way," he said as he turned Rena swiftly to the left. They cut in front of and jostled a couple moving next to them. "Lo Siento," Rena apologized out of habit, but Ellis hustled her past them before they had time to respond.

Weaving in and out of other pedestrians strolling down the street, Ellis saw the taller man watching him and Rena. He was about sixty feet away walking parallel to them. Ellis could tell he wasn't sure what to do. The man kept looking nervously at the couple as he continued to steal glances back to the left trying to find his partner. It was obvious to Ellis the guy didn't want to lose them but he didn't want to act on his own either.

A few yards up the street another opportunity presented itself. They were getting close to one of Guanajuato's most popular though macabre attractions, the Museo de las Momias. A bizarre museum that houses over a hundred dried up cadavers displayed in glass cases. Tourists were always milling in and out of it at all hours. Pausing, just a second, to make sure the tall man saw them,

Ellis then quickly turned Rena into the entrance. Once inside he pulled her against the wall and peered out just in time to catch sight of the taller man running back to get his partner. A gaggle of about a dozen senior citizens were on their way out the door. Ellis took them to be some tour group who weren't all that thrilled about having spent the last half hour with baby mummies, pregnant mummies, and all sorts of leathery, naturally mummified corpses who had been disinterred by the locals and put on display for profit.

"Crouch down," he said to Rena, then he pulled her into the middle of the elderly group who were heading back into the street. Once outside the visitors started to voice their real feelings about their recent experience not even taking note of the two younger people among them.

"Wasn't that just dreadful!" I couldn't believe they would take us there," a blue haired matron was saying to apparently anyone near enough to hear her.

A weathered little guy, himself not too far from mummy bait, commented. "It's the chemical mix of the soil...that and the dry mountain air. That's why some of 'em decompose but some don't."

Shielded from view by the clattering septuagenarians, Ellis saw both men running back to the entrance of the mummy museum. The bald one did the talking and sent the taller one inside. If Rena weren't with him, Ellis thought, this would be the right time to deal with the chrome dome in white. But he wasn't sure how the guy would react and he didn't want to take a chance of Rena or one of the old folks getting hurt. So he pulled Rena slowly to the opposite edge of the crowd from where the bald man stood. Then, just as they were about to slip further away, a young street vendor, no more than twelve at most, ran up to Ellis and Rena shouting, "Senor, senor! A flower for the pretty lady. It is only twenty pesos. Buy one for the pretty lady, senor!"

The bald man turned and saw them.

Ellis grabbed Rena's hand and took off swiftly down the street. There were still plenty of people milling about, but Ellis knew that had yet to deter their hunters. So he decided to change the venue. Just up the street, less than fifteen yards in front of them, one of the hundreds of alleyways that crisscrossed the city jutted diagonally off to the left. Upon reaching it, he jerked Rena violently to his side and ran her down the alley that was far less crowded and well lit than the street they had been on. He didn't have to look back to know that the bald man would be following. Sprinting now, he and Rena sped down the cobblestones that formed a narrow pathway between the brick and stucco buildings that rose on either side of them. Ahead, the alley took another turn to the right, but just before that corner there was a doorway barely wide enough for both of them to stand in. Without looking back, hoping he had judged their lead correctly, Ellis swung Rena into the doorway. Her back hit the door. "Don't talk," he whispered. For an instant there was silence. Then the sound of heels hitting cobblestones. Coming fast. But only for a moment. Then the sound stopped.

The hunter now had to decide if he had become the hunted. Ahead of him was the corner. They could have turned that corner, running fast and breathing heavy, and trying to get away. Or, had he been lured into this place of darkness? Was he now being watched, just as earlier, he had watched them. No, the gringo was not that smart, the bald man said to himself. And he wouldn't take a chance like that with the girl. He would want to get away. He would want to get her to safety. All of these things were in his mind as he slowly walked toward the corner. Then he saw what might be a doorway. And as a thought was beginning to form in his head that such a doorway could partially hide a man or a woman, his intellectual process was interrupted by the bullet that ripped into his thigh. He went down hard as his leg jerked out from under him, blown back by Ellis's Glock. Lying prostrate on the cobblestones, the pain felt as if someone had set fire to his leg from the inside. He began to squeal in pain.

Still in the doorway, Ellis said to Rena, "Stay here. I mean it. No matter what happens. Stay right here until I come back. Okay?"

Rena, shaking and holding her hands to her mouth didn't answer. But she nodded yes.

Ellis approached slowly. Even though the man was on the ground writhing in pain, Ellis hadn't seen the gun fall from his hand when he went down. As he got closer, he could see the dark red and black stain on the bald man's white trousers getting bigger. In the middle of his pain, the man saw Ellis coming toward him, gun at the ready in the firing position. Now he had to quickly decide whether the gringo was coming to finish him off or merely to relieve him of his gun. Having made the wrong decision just moments ago by

128

following the pair into the alley, he followed it with another. Summoning all his strength, he tried to rise and shoot simultaneously. Ellis saw the appendage and the gun at the end of it coming up. He quickly put another round into the bald man's armpit. This time the gun flopped from his hand like a trout breaking free of the line. His pain was so intense the bald man began to quiver and wet himself. Ellis picked up the weapon that had just been dropped and holstered his Glock.

He walked over to the bald man who was still shaking but too weak to scream. "Who sent you?" Ellis asked. "Tell me who sent you and I'll get you some help."

"No...habla...Englese." The bald man managed to squeeze the words out one by one.

Ellis wasn't buying it. He took the muzzle of the silencer and pressed it hard into the thigh wound. Then he said again, "Who sent you?"

The bald man convulsed with unimaginable pain. Ellis removed the muzzle and asked again, "Who sent you?"

Through tears that had now started to run down his face and into his mouth, the answer came back. "La arana. La arana."

The sound of boot heels on cobblestone streets intensifies with speed. And the sound was definitely getting louder and louder as Ellis looked up to see a male form, silhouetted by the lights, racing straight for him. He wasn't close enough yet for Ellis to be sure it was the bald man's partner he had seen a few minutes earlier. But the similarities were there. Tight shirt. Bulky torso. Longer hair. Jeans. And Ellis assumed it was possible this muscle bound machismo heading toward him might have been close enough to hear the second shot. He knew he didn't have time to switch weapons, so he quickly took up a kneeling position with the bald man's gun aimed at the oncoming shape. He would have to wait until the man was almost on him to know for sure if it was the second of the pair. And if it was, he could only hope that the barrel-chested assistant hadn't come up with a piece somewhere between the mummy museum and the alley.

As he got closer, a slow roar started to rumble up from the running man's diaphragm. It climbed into his throat and when it left his mouth it sounded like blind rage played in a base key. He did have some kind of weapon in his hand, and as he ran he lifted it high above his head, immediately telling Ellis it was a knife, not a gun. Could this guy be as dumb as he was pissed off? A step or two more and Ellis would be able to see his face. But two strides after that and the man would be on him. Ellis waited less than a second.

Thump. Thump. The silenced Smith & Wesson propelled two slugs into the on-rusher's chest. Ellis had to roll to the side after firing to avoid being bowled over as the man's legs buckled beneath him but his momentum still carried him forward until he crashed face first into the dark cobblestones.

Ellis went back over to the bald man. He had stopped twitching. In fact he had stopped being conscious at all. Probably passed out from shock, Ellis thought. No way to tell how long he'd be out. Or whether or not he would wake up at all before he bled to death. So Ellis walked over to where the partner lay face down. He laid the Smith & Wesson in the small of the fallen man's back and then took him by the heels and dragged him back to where his partner was. As he dragged him, the man's face scraped along the cobblestones and tore bits of flesh. But the fallen attacker was beyond pain. He had been dead before he slid to a stop. Ellis retrieved the weapon and put it in the man's free hand. His other, still clutching the knife. Let the policia sort it all out, Ellis thought. It was time to get out of there.

He walked over to Rena who was balled up on the ground in the doorway. "Come on, we've got to get out of here, " he said. Then he lifted her up and they rounded the corner. The corner Ellis chose not to round earlier.

Snaking through winding streets and alleyways to get back to his hotel, Ellis asked Rena, "What does "la arana mean?"

"The spider," she answered.

"The spider. Does that mean anything to you?"

"No."

"No one in your group...the group you're with here in Mexico...is called the spider?"

"I told you, the Zapatistas had nothing to do with this."

"So you said," Ellis responded. "So you said."

CHAPTER 28

As they made their way back to his hotel, Ellis kept running things over in his mind. Maybe Rena was right. Maybe the Zapatistas did have nothing to do with it. But maybe she didn't realize the allure of so much money. Especially to people who have had nothing all their lives. But if it wasn't someone within the Zapatistas, who then? Maybe someone at the bank in Mexico City. Someone who knew about the transaction. Ellis didn't think he had been followed. But he couldn't be sure. That was a lot of cash for one man to carry out of a bank. It could be very tempting for some low level executive, even some bank security type who might have been alerted without Ellis' knowledge, that such a large sum was leaving the bank. They'd certainly want to avoid any incidents on bank property. Or even close by. Maybe it was someone in security at Banco de Mexico. In the states the only two people he told about the meeting time and place were the two Whitfields. Of course he couldn't be positive they hadn't passed along the information. But why would they? That didn't make any sense. But logical or not, there were three, maybe four dead bodies that didn't get that way accidentally. Someone started the chain of events that made it happen. And someone would eventually wind up paying for it. Ellis was determined that it wasn't going to be him.

About a hundred feet from his hotel, Ellis took Rena by the arm and said, " Look, that's where I'm staying, just across the street. Now, if someone knew where we were meeting tonight, that same someone might know which hotel I was in."

Rena opened her mouth to speak but before she could, Ellis said, "Don't ask me how, I don't know. But lets assume it's possible. So here's what I want you to do. You see that Cantina over there. The one where those people are sitting at the tables on the sidewalk?"

"Yes, I see it," she answered.

"I want you to go over there, take that small table for two right by the street and buy yourself something to drink. I'll wait here to make sure everything's okay while you're doing it. Then I'll go over to the hotel...get my things and the car...and I'll pull up right beside your table and pick you up."

"And you'll bring the money? You said you had it."

"I'll have the money with me. Don't worry."

"You have to bring it. Please. If not, then it's like Miguel and Benito died for nothing."

"I'll bring it," Ellis reassured her. But just as quickly, he had to take some of that assurance away. "Listen, you're wearing a watch, right?"

"You should know," she answered quickly, "you've been crushing it into my wrist since we left the cafe."

"Sorry," Ellis said. "But here's what I want you to do. If I'm not there to pick you up in twenty minutes, just go to the American consulate, okay?"

"Do you really think I would do that?" she asked. Do you really think I would do that after what happened?"

"Well, look, if I'm not there in twenty minutes, just go somewhere. But don't come to the hotel. The point I'm trying to make is that the only thing that will keep me from picking you up...well, lets just say that if I'm not there to pick you up, I'll be beyond caring where you go, okay? But for your own safety, don't come over to the hotel."

"But, maybe I could help you. I could..."

"Believe me, the best way you can help is just to wait for me. Right over there. You did the right thing in the alley. Now I'm going to have to ask you to do it again. I'll be there to get you. Don't worry. Now go, I'll stay here until you're seated."

Ellis had to give her a gentle shove to get her started, but once she began walking she didn't look back. She walked straight up to the hostess, motioned to the table they had discussed and took a seat there. Then Ellis headed across the street.

As he approached the entrance, he kept his eyes open for anything that didn't look quite right. But there were no telltale signs of trouble. Moving under the archway that marked the center of the hotel, he glanced to his left and saw the night man behind the counter. He didn't appear to be nervous. Nor was he avoiding Ellis's eyes. "Buenos noches," the night man said to Ellis, who simply smiled and nodded in response. Stepping into the open inner courtyard, Ellis could see the front of almost every room in the hotel, including his own. When he left earlier in the evening, he made a point of leaving the drapes open. They were closed now. Sure, he thought to himself, a maid might have closed them. But no maid came the night before. And Ellis saw no upside in assuming tonight was any different. Particularly since the money wasn't in his room. He didn't feel comfortable leaving the canvas bags there for any curious or prying employee to inspect. So he had kept them locked in the trunk of his car. And if anyone had looked on his registration card to see what kind of car he was driving, they'd be directed to the white LTD he saw in the lot when he pulled in. A precautionary tactic he had used more than once. No. There was nothing in his room that was worth the risk. The parking lot was another story.

As Ellis walked through the courtyard he made a point of staying in the shadows. Reaching the alcove that lead to the parking lot, he decided to take his weapon from its holster. He kept his arm down, with the gun behind him. When he arrived at the parking lot, that proved to have been the right thing to do. There, in the rock and gravel quadrant behind the hotel where the guests' cars were parked, two men were hard at work. One wore the uniform of the hotel staff. Ellis took him to be the night parking lot attendant who locked and unlocked the gate for guests. The other man had on khaki pants and a shirt that looked brown in the dimly lit lot. The latter had a crow bar and was using it to open the trunks of the cars that were parked there. The line of raised trunk lids made it obvious they weren't sure which car was his. But Ellis knew it was only two cars down from the Buick they were in the middle of breaking into.

Since they hadn't taken time to close the trunks they had already checked out, Ellis assumed they weren't concerned about being confronted. That meant they were either confident about their own abilities to handle any sort of interruption, or they were laboring under some protective authorization. Such as the hotel's, Ellis thought, or maybe even the local police. So Ellis stayed quiet and approached them from behind. The rubber souls of his shoes on the gravel were not perfectly silent, but the men were so wrapped up in what they were doing that Ellis was able to get within six feet without them being aware of his presence. As the Buick's trunk sprung up, Ellis bolted forward and rammed his shoulder into the back of the man holding the crowbar. He fell headlong into the trunk with a grunt and a thud as his companion wheeled around to see what just happened. As he did, Ellis brought a swooping backhand across the startled man's face. The barrel of the Glock caught him square on the bridge of the nose, knocking him to the ground by the back of the Buick. Ellis quickly took one step back and made sure they both saw he was holding a gun. The first man's legs were still dangling from the trunk as he tried to get out.

"Nobody move." Ellis said menacingly as he pointed the gun back and forth between one and then the other. He knew the bigger danger was the crowbar in the hand of the man half in and half out of the trunk. The other guy was on his ass leaning against the car with one hand and cupping his bloody nose with the other. Ellis kicked the legs that were dangling from the trunk and said "Get 'em inside," as he pointed with his gun for emphasis. The man responded by slowly pulling his legs over the edge of the bumper until he was fully inside the trunk. Then, with the Glock, Ellis pointed toward the crowbar and said, "Toss it out. Toss it out on the ground." When the trunk occupant didn't respond immediately, Ellis put his gun to the temple of the man squatting on the ground nursing his broken nose. "Toss it out now," Ellis reiterated. This time the man did as he was told and tossed it out near where Ellis was standing. In fact, Ellis had to step back so it didn't land on his left foot. When he did, the grounded man took his hand from his nose and made a quick grab for the crowbar. Ellis stepped forward quickly and drove his heel into the man's outstretched hand. The Mexican winced and draw back in pain. Then Ellis picked up the crowbar in his free hand and smacked it across the nose-bleeder's shoulder saying, "Get in the trunk."

The man struggled to his feet pleading in a thick accent," Pero Senor, there is no room."

"Make room," Ellis said as he whacked the hapless attendant across the butt with the crowbar again. The man crawled slowly into the car's trunk as his compatriot tried to scrunch toward the back to make room for both of them. Once he was completely inside, Ellis dropped the crowbar on the ground and in one motion reached up and grabbed the top of the trunk and slammed it shut. It held. Holstering his weapon, he took his car keys from his pocket, walked over to his Japanese rental, opened his truck just to make sure everything was as he left it, closed the trunk swiftly, got behind the wheel and started the car. He didn't know how long that Buick trunk lid would stay shut, or whether or not someone would wander into the parking lot, but he didn't want to hang around to find out. Turning on his lights and backing up quickly, he wheeled the car around and started for the gated entrance. Normally, there would be an attendant on duty to let guests in or out. But the attendant was sandwiched into the trunk of the Buick. And the gate was locked. Ellis thought about it for a few seconds. Then said half out loud, "What the hell, it's a rental." He threw the sedan into reverse, backed halfway down the chorus line of cars with trunks in full salute, moved the gearshift lever to neutral and gunned the engine. Then he pulled it down into D spinning rock and gravel behind his back tires as he bolted straight for the gate. The force of the impact tore the lock off, banged the gate open and put a hell of a crease in the front of the hood as Ellis then took a hard right and rounded the corner. He sped to the spot where Rena was sitting, squealed to a stop, threw open the passenger door and said, "Get in." She got up and started to move to the car immediately. Then she hesitated, pulled some coins from her pocket and stepped back to put them on the table.

"Can we move this along?" Ellis bristled.

"Sorry, forgot the tip," Rena responded as she opened the door and slid in.

Ellis was about to ask how in hell she could be thinking about the tip at a time like this, then realized different people react very differently to stress. So he simply gunned the engine.

CHAPTER 29

They left the city via Miguel Hidalgo Street, the subterranean road that follows the Guanajuato River. As they drove into the night, the questions kept bouncing around in Ellis's brain. Was there someone waiting for him in his room? Quite likely. But who? How exactly did they learn where he was staying? Hard to say. Should he just take Rena back to the states now? Probably. He had her and the money. But he knew she was far from willing to leave Mexico without leaving the money with the Zapatistas. If he went to an airport she'd probably make a scene he wasn't prepared to deal with. If he tried to drive back to the states she'd have too many chances to bolt somewhere along the way. And at the border he'd have a hard time explaining to customs officials why that much cash was coming back into the states in two piss-stained canvas bags. No. Like it or not, he believed his best play was to take the girl and the money where she wanted to go. Then, he hoped she'd keep her word and they could both head north of the border.

With Rena giving directions they headed northwest. Well, Ellis thought, at least wherever we're going we'll be heading toward the states. Not knowing precisely when or how he'd have to leave Guanajuato, Ellis had taken the precaution to fill the rental car's tank with gas the afternoon he was to meet Rena. So they were able to drive through the night without stopping. The idea of putting as much space between them and the two bodies in the alley, plus the two he left squirming in the trunk, seemed like the thing to do.

After telling Ellis which highway to take, Rena fell asleep and Ellis let her stay that way. He figured she could use the rest and he wasn't too worried about being spotted since he assumed whoever was after them didn't know what kind of car they were in. The sun came up just as they were reaching the outskirts of Durango. Ellis felt Rena had gotten plenty of sack time. He reached over and put his hand on her shoulder and said, "Good morning. Time to wake up."

She, moaned, stretched her arms up and out, then rubbed her eyes and said, "Where are we?

"Just outside Durango. We can stop and get some breakfast. And coffee, plenty of coffee."

"Good idea," Rena replied. "And el bano."

"Restroom, yes," Ellis chimed in "an excellent idea."

Later, in the cafe as they ate, Ellis said, "Well, are you going to tell me where we're headed or do I simply divine which way to go when we leave."

"We still have to go north, a long way I'm afraid. They've been on the move since I left them."

"Was there a preconceived meet for you and...and..."

Rena filled in the names Ellis had forgotten. "Miguel and Benito."

"Yes, right. So was there a preconceived meet for you and Miguel and Benito and the other members of your group after the exchange?"

"There wasn't for me. I was supposed to be going with you."

"But you knew where it would be?"

"No, I didn't. But I found out with this," Rena said as she reached into her jacket pocket and pulled out a cell phone. "I made a call when I was in the ladies' room."

"Modern technology," Ellis said, "wonderful thing isn't it?"

"Yes, it is." Rena replied. "It could be one of the things that helps the people in this country grow and prosper. But think how many people in Mexico, especially the indigenous peoples, don't even know what a phone is, much less a cell phone. And do you know why? It's not because they can't learn, or don't want to learn...believe me they do. It's because the aristocracy here and the authorities won't let them learn. They create an entire society where children can't get an education. They keep the Indian people so poor, so poverty stricken that the children are forced to work so the family can eat. Sometimes they're even conscripted into work. Literally taken from their homes and forced into labor. Eight out of ten Mexican children go to work before they are fourteen years old. Nearly two million school-age kids never get to school because they have to work to help their families survive. There are children...little children pushing carts, washing dishes, picking fruit in the fields, unloading boats. Some as young as twelve or thirteen are operating machinery. Machinery that winds up taking their hands, or arms or legs. So that they can never do more than beg in the streets. Some children are forced to go out and beg everyday. Begging is work. Prostitution is work. You don't want to know how many children are forced into that here."

When she took a breath, Ellis cut in, "Well, I'd say you're

definitely awake now. But I'm not sure I'd have any more of that caffeine if I were you."

Rena smiled. "I'm sorry," she said, "I tend to get carried away at times. I guess I'm a bit passionate about it all."

"There are worse things in life than passionate people, " Ellis replied. "It's what you do, or don't do with that passion that really matters. Perhaps we should wrap things up and be on our way."

"Yes. Let's do that. Do you have enough for the meal, or should I help?"

"Oh I think I can swing it," Ellis said. "If not, I can always get some extra cash out of the trunk."

"Very funny." Rena said. "Very funny."

After their breakfast, they filled the car with gas again. Once they had gotten through Durango, Rena kept navigating north. They were heading for Hidalgo del Parral. But Ellis didn't know that yet. And Rena was in no hurry to tell him. She wasn't sure why. He seemed okay, she thought. He certainly seemed to know what he was doing back in Guanajuato. She had never seen anyone shot before. Much less killed. Last night she didn't have time to think much about that. She was too frightened. All she could think about was getting away. Now, on this long drive north, she had plenty of time to think. Time to think about how heavy Benito felt when he tumbled on top of her. Time to think about the blood on Miguel and Benito and the bald man in the white pants. Blood that seemed to grow and expand around his middle and then on his shirt. Blood that seemed to be everywhere.

"Can you pull over for a minute?" Rena asked Ellis, rolling down the window.

"What? Are you okay?"

"Just pull over," Rena shouted, "now!"

Ellis cut the wheels to the right and pressed the brake down smoothly but firmly. He came to a stop quickly on the side of the highway.

Rena threw open the door and hurriedly stepped out. She was doubled over at the waist and made no attempt to stand upright. She could feel the muscles in her stomach grip and roll like a towel being twisted. She heaved once, then again. But nothing came up. The tightness didn't let up however. And again she thought she was going to vomit, but nothing was on the way out except leftover fear.

Ellis had already gotten out of the car and come around to her side. He was putting his hands on her shoulders to steady her as he said, "It's okay. You're going to be okay. Just try to walk a little bit and take in some air."

Rena raised up slowly and awkwardly, testing herself. Her stomach was still tight but the more she breathed and the more she walked, the more she seemed to feel better. There was sweat on her brow and rubber in her legs and she appreciated the steady hands of Ellis as they walked.

"It's a little too soon for breakfast to have done that to you. My guess...it's probably a delayed reaction to last night. Don't worry about it. It happens to lots of people. I've seen guys a lot bigger and a lot meaner than you react a lot worse. You'll be okay in a second."

Moments later she did feel better. The gripping in her stomach went away. Along with the nausea. But she kept to herself that the cause wasn't only a delayed reaction to fear. Eventually she said, "Okay...I'm okay. We can go now."

"You sure?" Ellis questioned.

"I'm sure," Rena replied.

"Good," Ellis said. "Then you drive. Sometimes hanging on to something, even if it's a steering wheel, can help too."

Once they were back on the road and had gone a couple of miles in silence, Rena said, "You've seen a lot of this sort of thing, haven't you? People dying I mean."

"I was in the military," Ellis answered. "Combat does different things to different people. Especially the first time."

"You're not going to tell me it's something one gets used to...are you?"

"You never get used to people dying," Ellis said. "Not if you're lucky. And you never get used to people trying to kill you. Not if you have any sense at all."

"Then why do you do this kind of thing?" Rena asked, keeping her eyes on the road as she spoke.

"You take the things that you're taught and you apply them," Ellis responded. "That's what anybody does. Teachers. Lawyers. Mechanics."

"Teachers, lawyers, and mechanics don't go looking for trouble. They don't seek it out."

"I wasn't looking for trouble either. I was looking for you."

"But you were ready for trouble, weren't you," Rena came back quickly. "Tell me...I'm curious...what did you do in the military? What kind of jobs did you work on before you met my brother? Why did you take this job?"

"I tell you what," Ellis said, "it's obvious you're feeling better now. So I'm just going to put my head back and catch a few winks. Like you did last night."

"Don't like to talk about yourself? The strong, silent type?"

There was no response from the passenger side of the car. By now Rena knew enough about Ellis to know that was a response in itself.

CHAPTER 30

It was late in the afternoon when they reached the outskirts of Hidalgo de Parral. Once known for its mining output, the small town now held the historic distinction of being the place where fabled revolutionary leader, Pancho Villa met his end at the hands of rifled assassins while he cruised through the village behind the wheel of his automobile. The dirt roads Villa traversed had long since been paved, but the potholes were still jarring enough to wake Ellis.

"Where are we?" he asked, while rising in his seat and rubbing his eyes.

"Hidalgo de Parral," Rena answered.

She told Ellis they were going to the Cafe Excelsior' to meet with the man to whom they would turn over the money. His name is Diego Marquez. He's the head of the platoon I was with. And he has the confidence of Subcomandante Marcos, head of all the Zapatista units. He will see to it that the money is used as it should be used."

"You seem to be putting a lot of trust into this particular individual," Ellis replied. "Two million dollars is an awful lot of money. Are you sure you can count on this guy?"

"I'm sure," Rena answered quickly. "I'm very sure."

Rena drove down narrow back alleys and eventually made her way to Gambino Barrera, a street of pock marked pavement with painted benches and shops on both sides. As they turned onto it, Ellis could see a four-corner intersection about a hundred feet ahead. To his left, at the end of the block, he noted blue calligraphy on a sandy stucco building that read, Cafe Excelsior'. Beneath that moniker a young Mexican stood smoking a cigarette. He wore fatigue pants, a T-shirt and a straw cowboy hat with the brim pulled down low in front and back while the sides curled up. Rena recognized him immediately.

"That's Juan," she said. Then she pulled the car over to the side of the street so that the passenger side tires were actually on the sidewalk. Turning the ignition off, she pulled the keys out and started to open her door.

"Are you sure it's okay?" Ellis asked.

"Yes. Let's go." Rena said as she pushed the door closed and started walking toward the young man she called Juan. Ellis followed a few steps behind. His eyes scanned both sides of the street as they moved forward.

Juan recognized Rena as they approached and walked over to meet her. For a few minutes they conversed in Spanish. Ellis picked up some words here and there but he didn't get the crux of it until Rena turned to him and said "Marquez is not here. But Juan can take us to him. We should go now."

"Listen, Rena....," Ellis began.

But she jumped in before he could finish. "Juan says we should go now. I'll keep my word. But you must keep yours."

Ellis answered with a question. "Does Juan need a ride or are we following him?"

"He'll come with us," Rena said.

This time Ellis took the wheel, Rena the passenger seat, and Juan got in the back then slid to the middle of the seat and said "Derecho."

Rena started to translate, but Ellis cut in, "I got it...straight ahead. But I'm sure I'll need help later."

The midday sun was up and their windows were down as they started their ascent into the high desert. All around them, the land began to look more barren, drier. There were fewer and fewer trees. Ravines cut along the sides of the road and prickly pear cacti dotted the hillsides. This was a lonely place, Ellis thought, an unforgiving land that asked no quarter and gave none in return. A hard land for hard people. Like Juan. Ellis would occasionally glance at the rear view mirror to make sure the boy was keeping them on course. There was no cause for concern. Juan kept his eyes straight ahead. Intently watching. His was a face old beyond his years, Ellis noted. Skin browned deep by the sun. Lined in the forehead and cheekbones. His dark eyes misty and red-rimmed. It was a face far more weathered than the teens north of the border. Such are the vicissitudes of fate, Ellis reflected. Some young people are preoccupied with proms and prep schools, while others are focused on struggle and survival. The difference between a life of ease and privilege versus a hardscrabble existence is sometimes simply a matter of geography. But Ellis's philosophical musings were quickly snapped back to matters more practical when Juan leaned forward and said, "El camino."

Rena said, "He wants us to take that trail up there."

Ellis could see a one-lane dirt path etched into the landscape off to the right. It looked like it led to a set of hills that appeared to be a few miles from the main road. He turned and started down the narrow strip of earth, a plume of dust trailing behind him. For over half an hour the trio endured a rib-rattling ride over rocky terrain that brought them to the foothills Ellis had seen earlier in the distance. Then they began to climb. Taking a slow, serpentine route up the mountain, there was little or no conversation except for the occasional "Precaucion" Juan would offer just prior to coming upon nasty, narrow, non-railed turns whose hillsides dropped precipitously away for hundreds of feet. Ellis was surprised that the shopworn sedan seemed to be taking the journey in stride. Well, he joked to himself, if it can knock down a wrought iron gate, I guess climbing a mountain is not a big deal. Grinning as he thought about it, Rena saw his smile and said, "Don't tell me you're enjoying this?"

"Hey, I'm just happy we're still here after that last turn. And I bet there are even more of them to come."

"Thanks," Rena said, "that's very reassuring."

"Glad I could help," Ellis quipped.

Juan, of course, understood none of what they said and would have had little interest in it even if he had, because as their climb continued, he knew the next twist in the road they were following would take them to their destination.

"Aqui. Parada!" Juan said.

Rena understood immediately, "Stop here," she said.

Ellis slowly applied the break, then kept his foot pressed down as they were still on a steep incline. Juan got out of the back seat, slammed the door shut and walked to the front of the car. He looked back at Ellis and Rena and raised his arm with his palm upright toward them.

"He wants us to stay here," Rena said.

"Well, that's up to the brakes," Ellis replied, "but they seem to be cooperating."

After they had sat there a for a few moments, Rena said, "He didn't say where he was going."

"Either he needs to take a leak or he's checking with someone your cohorts left behind to watch the road."

"You think so?"

Ellis didn't have to answer. Just as Rena finished asking the question, Juan came back around the bend and he wasn't alone. Beside him was a soldier even smaller than Juan. The soldado was carrying a rifle and was dressed in traditional Zapatista gear. Jeans, bulky sweater, a ski mask with a cap over it. As the pair walked toward the car, the soldier removed the cap and ski mask and a cascade of long black curls dropped down.

"It's Dolores," Rena said as she stepped out of the car to greet them. The three spoke for a moment in front of the vehicle, then Rena went back around to the passenger side and Juan and Dolores climbed into the back seat.

"It's just ahead," Rena said. "You'll see the campsite."

Ellis moved his right leg so that the ball of his foot actually pressed on the accelerator before he removed his heel from the brake. The car jerked forward and up the hill they went. Rounding the turn Ellis saw they were coming up on a huge plateau. Camp had been made far enough from the turn so that it couldn't be seen by an approaching car. The plateau itself was so immense and there were so many alligator juniper and ponderosa pine trees atop it that one couldn't see how far across it actually stretched. Ellis pulled the car to a stop and got out. As the other three talked to one another, Ellis retired to the cover of the nearest lechuguilla and baptized the scrub brush surrounding it. After he finished, he walked over and joined the others who were already sharing coffee. Juan passed a cup to him as Rena's cell phone rang.

"Hello", she said, then smiled as she heard the reply and answered, "it's good to hear your voice too."

Ellis could tell by her tone that whoever was on the other end of the call was more than just an acquaintance.

"Oh, all right. Yes. No. He won't be trouble. He doesn't want trouble," Rena said as she glanced at Ellis. "Here...Dolores, he wants to talk to you," she said, handing the phone to the girl whose hair was as dark as her own. Then Rena turned and addressed Ellis. "He wants us to come to him. Dolores will show us the way."

"Apurarse!" Dolores said, rising with her rifle as she handed Rena's phone back to her.

"Juan will stay here," Rena said, "Dolores will lead us."

No one seemed to be waiting for Ellis to agree or disagree. Both Rena and Dolores had started moving from the camp just after they spoke. So Ellis fell in behind them, eager to see who changed

Rena's mood with just the sound of his...or her...voice.

The three hikers made their way through the juniper and pine as they headed west. Ellis had taken a look at his watch as they left and now noted it was just about twenty minutes into their walk as they cleared the grove of trees and saw a group of Zapatistas lying in the high grass near the western cliff of the plateau. Immediately upon seeing them Dolores crouched low and motioned for Rena and Ellis to do likewise. Bent over at the waist, they continued to make their way toward the group. A couple of soldiers, hearing them approach, turned and looked at the three for a moment. Then they returned their gaze to whatever was holding their attention. Ellis was convinced it wasn't just the scenery.

Within twenty feet of the group, Dolores dropped to her knees and crawled the rest of the way. Rena and Ellis quickly followed suit. Rena went directly to the man in the center and whispered something in his ear. He acknowledged her, then looked back at Ellis. "Come forward, senor," he said, keeping his voice just above a whisper.

With Rena on the man's right, Ellis dropped to his elbows and crawled forward to his left so that the man was now flanked by Rena on one side and Ellis on the other.

"My name is Diego Marquez. I want to think you for taking care of Rena. When we talked on the phone this morning she told me how you protected her."

"That's one of the things I was sent here to do. The other was to bring her home."

Avoiding Ellis pregnant point, Marquez said, "Look senor, have you ever seen anything like it?" Then turned his eyes back to the valley below.

Ellis looked down. And the next few seconds passed in silence. There, in a lush, green valley that was the antithesis of the baked and bone-dry mountain they had snaked up less than an hour ago, was something beyond words. Beyond definitions. Ellis wasn't sure what it was. But he was sure he had never seen anything to equal it.

Its beauty was as stark as it was original. The overall shape and design was impossible to categorize. It appeared to be exotic, but of indeterminate origin. The central core seemed to be some sort of huge, sculpted, steel-reinforced concrete blocks that produced dramatically gigantic cantilevers. Was it a fortress, Ellis wondered. Surely not. Though it was massive enough, or one day would be as it was obviously still in mid construction. But it was too ornate to house soldiers and weapons. The front, virtually windowless, was elevated and seemingly anchored by a colossal Moorish styled, diamond-shaped centerpiece of slate gray stone that appeared to interlock the entire structure. Stretching, Ellis estimated, almost a quarter of a mile behind it, was a courtyard open in the center but flanked on both sides by contiguous one-story rooms with ceilings and walls of beveled glass. Running the length of that center courtyard was a glorious blue water pool surrounded by green velvet grass and boulders that looked as if each had been put in place by the hand of God. Was it a hotel or resort, Ellis asked himself. Unlikely. Too far from any reasonable expectation of surrounding amenities. And if it was to eventually be filled with people, where was the parking lot? There was none in any direction. In fact, there appeared to be only one road winding its way to the enormous structure and it ended right at the front gates. Immense gates of brushed steel with stylized palm and banana leaves that spilled forward forming a protective canopy. Finally, Ellis decided to answer Marquez's question with a question.

"What the hell is it?" He said.

Before Marquez could answer, Rena spoke.

"It's a house. My god...it's his house."

Then she quickly turned and crawled back from the ledge of the cliff. "Diego, I'm going back to camp. When we get back, I have to tell you something." Then she took off in the direction of the grove.

"We will all go back for now," Marquez said, motioning to his men as they pulled away from the precipice. "Senor Ellis, walk with me."

As they headed back to camp Rena's pace grew quicker and quicker. She put distance between herself and the rest. She obviously wanted time alone. Marquez wanted just the opposite. He needed a sounding board for what was on his mind.

"Did you see the outer buildings...away from the main one?" Marquez asked Ellis.

"You mean the temporary structures? The wooden building and all the tents?" Even though they were at least a half-mile from

146

the main building, Ellis had spotted them. Old reconnoitering habits are not like old soldiers. They never fade away.

"Si, that is where they keep the children. The children being used like the Egyptian Pharaoh used the Jews to work and die building their monuments. Like the Spanish used our people as slave labor to mine the silver and the gold. It is happening again Senor. Only more subtle this time."

"How do you mean?" Ellis asked.

"No longer do they come as conquerors," Marquez began. "Today they come with their papers and their promises. They tell mothers and fathers that their sons will have light work...easy work...and that they will be paid for it. They are paid all right. Sometimes a peso a day. A peso a day, Senor. Slave wages. And the work is not children's work. They are not used as houseboys. They do not help in the kitchens. The do the work of men. Carrying stone. Mixing cement. Climbing and working on roofs and ceilings. If they are injured, if they get hurt, nothing. No compensation. They are robbed of both their childhood and their future. All so traitors can line their pockets."

"What you're saying," Ellis said, "is that the builders...the contractors or the subcontractors use a hundred or so kids instead of twenty or thirty guys to complete a job. They'll keep enough adults around to direct things...show the boys what to do. Then they pay all the kids even less than they'd pay fewer guys and pocket what they save. Is that it?"

"That is indeed it, senor. But the numbers are more like two hundred or three hundred boys, depending on the project. The one we just saw is close to completion. There are probably no more than a hundred or a hundred and fifty boys still working there. Perhaps less than a dozen men to direct them. We cannot help all those who labored on this project before today. But we can liberate the ones who are still here."

"What's your plan?" Ellis asked.

For the remainder of the walk back to camp, Marquez explained how he had already sent for trucks that would help expedite the boys' removal. He planned to take his soldados down the side of the cliff after midnight. There was a path unknown to those in charge at the structure. They would overrun the adult quarters. Marquez was certain he could catch them by surprise.

"How can you be sure?" Ellis questioned.

"We have been here for two nights. They have posted no sentries. They believe the isolation keeps the boys in and preying eyes out."

"What do you plan to do with the men?"

"We will keep them here for a day or two. Until enough time has passed so that it will be difficult for them to gather the boys again. Perhaps we will even let their employers know what we have done. And obtain proper wages which can be distributed to the families later."

"There are some who might call that extortion...even kidnapping," Ellis said.

"Yes." Marquez replied. "And there are others who might call it justice."

The bulk of Marquez's soldiers were just starting out of the grove when shots shattered the stillness. Two went down. One was Dolores. Marquez and Ellis, who were a hundred feet behind the others, immediately sprinted forward. As he ran, Marquez called for his men to get down. Reaching the tree line, he could see that two of his people had been hit. Both were at least thirty feet beyond the trees in the high grass. One was lying face down, motionless. The other, Dolores, was on her back moaning and writhing in pain as she clasped her bloody shoulder. Marquez motioned for the rest of his men to come up. Positioning them along a horizontal line, still in the cover of the grove, he spoke to each one in Spanish but Ellis had a pretty good idea of what he was planning. When Marquez pulled his rifle strap over his shoulder and set the weapon on the ground, Ellis was sure of it. He went up to him and spoke.

"Don't go out there standing up. Even with cover fire you'll likely be hit."

"We can not leave her there. I must bring her here to give her aid," Marquez said. "And I will not have the strength to pull her back if I do not stand up.

"You won't. But we will." Ellis replied. He was unbuttoning and pulling off his shirt as he talked. "We'll crawl out, each on opposite sides of her, staying on our bellies. When we get there, spin around so you're facing back this way. Then grab her just above the ankle. I'll do the same. We'll pull ourselves with one arm and her with the other. And once we start back, don't stop. No matter how much she yells." Now, down to just a t-shirt covering his torso, Ellis added, "And she will yell."

"I understand." Marquez said.

"Make sure when your men start firing that they don't stop until we get back."

"You give orders easily, Senor."

"Sorry. Reflex reaction."

Marquez barked the orders to his men in Spanish, paused for a moment, then shouted, "Tirar!"

Ellis and Marquez hit the ground flat. Their arms bent in front, they started pulling with them and pushing with their feet. Moving through the tall grass as quickly as they could, they heard the popping of their compatriots' gunfire over their heads. Ellis reached Dolores first. He spun around on his stomach and grabbed her by the ankle. Marquez arrived on the other side. He rotated, took hold of her other ankle and as they simultaneously started to move, Dolores started to scream. On the backside of her shoulder, where the bullet had exited, it had taken shards of bone with it. She was being dragged across her wound and the pain was unbearable. Her shrieks were louder than the gunfire overhead. Half way back to the grove, Ellis and Marquez started hearing the whiz of rounds cutting the grass and kicking up the sod around them. There was nothing to do but keep going. Only inches from the safety of the trees, a bullet ripped by Ellis's left ear spraying dirt and pine needles into his face as the round burrowed into the earth. But moments later they were back in the safety of the grove and Marquez gave the order for his men to stop firing. Then two of the soldiers came back to administer to Dolores.

"You realize Rena is not here," Marquez said.

"It was the first thing I realized," Ellis replied.

Marquez went on, "She was upset. In a hurry to leave the cliff. It is possible she reached the camp before the others came out of the grove."

"Very possible," Ellis answered, "in fact, it's probably why they fired just as your people cleared the tree line. They want to keep us here. It will give them more time to get Rena away."

"They want to take her away? That is what you were here for. That is why you came. You believe that is what this is about?"

"This is about the money. The money you wanted. The

money someone else in Guanajuato wanted."

Marquez bristled. "The money is for the cause. Not for us."

"Well, right now," Ellis said, "the money's for the taking. And so is Rena."

A stifled cry came from Dolores. Her face was contorted with pain as her two comrades tore her shirt away and poured water from a canteen over the wound. She tried to weep silently as they applied bandages to her shoulder.

Marquez, hearing Dolores, turned his head toward her. Ellis reached out and grabbed him by the arm trying to refocus his attention. He said, "Listen, I think we should move quickly. The longer we wait, the further away they get with Rena."

"But they have the advantage," Marquez countered, "There is too much open ground to cross."

"My guess is we have the advantage," Ellis said. "There should have been more rounds fired at us. I bet they only left a man or two behind to keep us pinned down here."

"What would you recommend, Senor? You seem to have experience in such tactics."

Glancing over at Dolores, Ellis said, "Leave one man with her. Have the rest fan out. When we're in position, have them all fire three rounds. Then everyone moves out together. Just like we did. If they return fire, we return it. If not, we keep going."

"It could take a long time to crawl back to camp, Senor."

"You stay in the center. I'll be on the far left. Tell your men to watch you. And you watch me. If I get up and go, then you do the same. If we all go, we go fast and low and ready to fire. Got it?"

"Si. I will tell the men. Do you want to take Dolores' rifle?"

Ellis crossed his stomach with his right hand and pulled his Glock from the holster that cradled it. "If I'm not close enough to use this, it won't matter anyway."

As Marquez called his men around to give them instructions, Ellis ejected his clip to make sure it was full. He knew the answer in advance, but habits are hard to break. Once the men were in position, Marquez gave the signal and the firing began. Then they started to move out. Ten men slithering through tall grass like snakes spilled from a burlap bag. Ellis listened for return fire. He didn't hear any. But it was still a long run to the edge of the campsite. He kept going. And as he did, he looked down the line of crawlers. They took orders well. Marquez was an able leader, he thought. They continued to move ahead. Elbows, knees, heels. All pushing them forward. Still no sound of fire from the camp. Ellis stopped. And Marquez signaled for the others to do the same. There was an eerie quiet. No sound at all except the light breeze that bent the grass in its path. Then Ellis heard a gasp of air suddenly released. Followed immediately by a pain-racked cry. Then a single shot. But it didn't come their way. Ellis sprang to his feet just in time to see a big man, a fat man struggling to his feet, rifle in hand, doing his best to beat a hasty retreat from his forward position.

"Let's go!" Ellis yelled as he started sprinting dead out for the camp. "And don't shoot at him."

Ellis didn't look back to see if Marquez had conveyed the message to the rest of the men. He was too intent on making up ground between him and the fat man. The portly figure in some sort of uniform was stumbling his way through the camp trying to get to the bend in the road that exited the plateau. With each step his heart beat stronger and his breath grew shorter and his pants fell further down his waist until the crack of his ass was exposed to Ellis rushing nearer and nearer. It took only a few more seconds for Ellis to reach him and with both hands, shove him violently forward. There was no chance of the obese one staying vertical. He slammed to the earth like an oak felled by a woodsman's ax, his rifle spilling from his hand. Ellis was on him in a moment. Knee in his back and pistol to his head, he said, "Stay!" Then he shoved the muzzle of the Glock into the chubby neck of the horizontal man for emphasis. Turning back toward Marquez and the approaching group he said, "Send one of your men over here to watch him."

Ellis, now breathing hard, though paling in comparison to the heaving whale he left in the care of Marquez's man, walked back to the group who were standing over two bodies. One was dressed in a uniform similar to the fat man's. The other was still wearing his cowboy hat. Ellis bent down beside Marquez who was on one knee next to Juan and said, "The knife is still in his hand. I heard him stab this one. Then the fat guy shot him."

"They must have thought Juan was already dead."

"Yep," Ellis replied, "this is an exit wound in the stomach. Handgun of some kind. They must have shot him from behind initially. The chest hole is from the big boy's rifle."

"His name was Juan Merida. He was a fine young man," Marquez said.

"He seemed that way to me," Ellis said. A moment passed. Then Ellis spoke again. "We've got to find out where's Rena's been taken."

"Oh we will find out, Senor," Marquez replied. "We will definitely find out."

They rose and returned to where the fat man was being held. Marquez spoke to them and his men turned him over and propped him up against a boulder that was just a few feet away.

"Habla Ingles?" Marquez asked.

"Muy poco," the stout one replied, still breathing heavy.

"I'm going to ask you three questions," Ellis said, holding his fingers up in front of the man as he spoke. "Three...do you understand?"

'Si. Tres."

Marquez drove his rifle butt deep into the man's soft belly as he said, "Speak English!"

The large one brought his knees up to his middle, groaned and said, "Yes...three."

Ellis began. "Who has the American girl?"

"Mi jeffe, Senor."

Marquez raised his rifle butt again and the big man quickly amended his answer.

"My boss...my boss has the American."

Ellis quickly asked, "Where is he taking her?"

"I don't know Senor...mi jeffe, he no tell me where--"

In one swift move Marquez pulled his hunting knife from under his cartridge belt and brought it down hard, lopping off two fingers on the right hand the fat man was leaning on. For an instant there was only silence. Then the seated bull raised his shaking hand and saw the two appendages stay on the bloody rock and pine needles beneath it. His eyes widened and he started to take big, gulping breaths as the pain and the reality set in simultaneously. Marquez 's men held him tight as he began to make guttural noises like a wounded boar rooting and snorting in the mud. Marquez stepped astride him, sat down on his legs and looked directly in his face. Then he reached down, jerked open the flabby one's belt, pulled down the zipper on his pants and grabbed the man's cock and balls together in one hand while he raised his knife in the other and said, "Answer the question."

The fat man's head was starting to quiver as he bleated, "Chihuahua. The train to Los Mochis...Chihuahua...The train to Los Mochis." He was crying as he kept repeating it again and again.

Ellis moved forward, grabbing a hunk of the flabby skin that hung beneath the man's chin and said, "Who is your boss? Who is el jeffe?"

"La arana," the crying man whimpered, "la arana."

Ellis got up and took a couple of steps away. Marquez did the same as his men continued to stand over the sobbing prisoner.

"That's the second time that name's come up. Do you know anyone called that?" Ellis asked Marquez.

"No. But I do know the train he spoke of. The Ferrocarriles Chihuahua el Pacifico. It goes north to Los Mochis and crosses the Sierra Madre Occidental...what Norte Americanos call the Copper Canyon. Once the train leaves Chihuahua it is a twelve hour journey to Los Mochis."

"They can't be that far ahead of us. If we go now, we might be able to get to Chihuahua before the train leaves."

"I can not go with you," Marquez replied. "There is unfinished work here that has already begun. When the trucks arrive tonight, we must be here also...to see that the young ones get out."

"But I got the feeling there was something between you and Rena," Ellis said.

"There is much between us, Senor. But first there is always the struggle. Rena knows that. Rena believes in that. Take Dolores with you. She knows Chihuahua. She can help guide you. And she can be seen by a doctor there."

"If I'm going to catch up with them, I won't have time to help her find medical help."

"She knows who to see, Senor. She knows where to go. We have many friends who are willing to help."

Ellis glanced over to where his rented sedan stood with its trunk door raised. He said, "You haven't said anything about the money."

"I know if you find them, you will do the right thing. Rena will help see to that."

Marquez then spoke to his men and had them help Dolores

who had been carried from the grove once the camp was retaken, to Ellis's car. While that was being done, he took a small note pad from his shirt pocket and with the stub of a pencil that was no longer than his little finger, wrote a name and an address on a piece of paper. Tearing it off and handing it to Ellis, Marquez said, "If you get to Los Mochis and you need anything, see this man. He can be trusted."

"Glancing at the paper he had just been handed, Ellis said, "Same last name as yours. Coincidence?"

"There are no coincidences, Senor Ellis. There is only fate. And please, tell Rena I love her."

"I've got a feeling she knows that. But I'll tell her anyway."

CHAPTER 31

As the battered rental snaked down the road it had come up earlier, Dolores rode with her head laid back against the seat. Ellis wouldn't need any help retracing his way down the mountain. It was only when they got back to the main highway that he asked Dolores, "Which way to Chihuahua?" She responded by pointing to the right with her good arm and they roared off down the highway.

Ellis kept the windows down as he drove. He thought the fresh air would make it easier on Dolores. The road was wide and open so he kept the pedal to the floor and pushed the Japanese model for all it could give. Barreling along the blacktop, the questions kept running in and out of his consciousness. Who was la arana? How did the spider know where they had gone? Or where they'd be? Had they been followed from Guanajuato? Why was Rena so upset? And what did she mean when she said, "It's his house." And of course the question that kept coming up over and over again...would he get there on time? Would he get to Chihuahua before the train left for Los Mochis? There was no point discussing any of this with Dolores. She kept slipping in and out of consciousness. He'd let her rest for now. He'd need all the attention she could muster when they reached the city, he thought, as he passed the sign along Mexico highway 24 that said Chihuahua 100 kilometers.

A little less than two hours later he was approaching the outskirts of the city. Ellis reached over, woke Dolores and said, "We're here. We're in Chihuahua. Train station...which way to the train station?"

With one hand Dolores rubbed her right eye and then her left. Wincing with pain, she sat up in the seat and looked around trying to get her bearings. Finally she said, "Derecho."

"Straight?" Ellis asked.

"Si. Straight. Derecho." Dolores answered, pointing forward and jabbing her finger in front of her.

And so it went for what seemed an eternity to Ellis. Dolores looking, pointing and gesturing. Ellis navigating his way through the tall buildings that cast dark shadows across streets filled with people and pigeons and pink quarry stone churches. They were getting deeper and deeper into the city. The buildings began to surround them. Then Dolores thrust her arm out the window and

155

shouted, "Chihuahua al Pacifico! Chihuahua al Pacifico!"

Ellis took an abrupt right in the direction Dolores was pointing. Then he stepped hard on the gas and sped down the street past old Volkswagen Beetles, ice cream vendors, shops and storefronts until they emerged at the end of the block seventy-five yards in front of the Chihuahua train station. He scanned the streets for someplace to park and a saw an old Cadillac Seville pulling away from the curb. Gunning the engine he roared right up behind it, then threw the car into reverse and quickly parallel parked. Ellis had barely turned the engine off as Dolores opened the passenger side door and stepped onto the sidewalk. He got out of the car and as he turned to face Dolores, she said, "Adios, Senor. Buena suerte!"

"Good bye, Dolores. And good luck to you," Ellis answered. Then he turned and started running down the street toward the train station. The old, Spanish mission style building had a tile covered portico over the entrance. A few people were milling about beneath it. Ellis dodged them as he ran through, but once inside something brought him to a full stop. Emptiness. His eyes swept the enormous hall taking in the heavy high-back wooden benches cemented to the floor. No one was sitting on them. Rays from the last light of sundown were streaming through the arched, latticework floor-to-ceiling windows. No one stood looking out of them. A huge mahogany desk and counter than ran half the length of one wall was thirty feet in front of him to his right. No one manned it. A sick feeling began to rise up in Ellis' stomach. "I'm too late," he said almost audibly. Then suddenly, a small head and the body that was attached to it rose from behind the counter. Ellis dashed over, shouting as he went.

"The train to Los Mochis...I need to get on it."

From behind the counter, the tiny man with deep-set eyes and wire-rimmed glasses responded, "Lo siento, senor. The train, she is soon to leave the station."

Immediately reaching into his pocket for cash, Ellis blurted out, "Quick then, give me a ticket. I have to get to Los Mochis."

"Lo siento...I am sorry, senor. I cannot sell you a ticket. This trip to Los Mochis has been purchased by a private party. We can sell no seats on this run, senor. Maybe manana."

Ellis stuffed the cash back in his pocket then quickly reached across and grabbed the little man by his waistcoat. Yanking him off his feet and onto the flat of the counter, Ellis demanded, "How many people in the party?"

"Quatro, senor. Only four. But they paid for all the seats."

Ellis shook the frightened station attendant as he continued, "Was there a woman with them...an American?"

The man's glasses had shaken loose and were now hanging lopsided over his nose as he responded, "Si, senor. Three men and one woman. American, I think."

Still holding the man atop the counter, Ellis looked over to his left at two massive double doors. "Is that the way to the train?"

"Si...but the train is leaving Senor. The train is..."

Ellis plopped the employee back on the floor in mid sentence and sprinted to the double doors. On the other side he came face to face with a wide wooden staircase that climbed about seven feet then branched off to the right and left. In the center of the staircase was a multicolored stained glass window depicting two Indians looking off into the distance at a mountain range. Ellis had to make an immediate decision. He went with the Indians. Bounding up the stairs he turned to the right, the direction the Indians were pointing, and then followed a second set of stairs that took him outside and onto the platform. As he emerged into the fading light of day, he caught sight of the train that had already started to pull away. A total of five cars were attached to the engine that was quickly picking up speed. Ellis had no way of knowing where Rena was being kept or even where on the train her captors were. The only thing he knew was that if he didn't get on it, he would have no chance at all of getting Rena or the money back.

He began sprinting at full speed toward the end of the platform, which was fifty yards away. As he got closer to the end of the platform, the train got further from it. Ellis realized the last car was going to pass the end of the platform just as he was reaching it. With no time left to contemplate the wisdom of such a move, Ellis called up all the speed and force and spring he could muster. Then he leapt off the end of the platform just as the final car was pulling beyond it. As his trajectory thrust him upward, he realized he wasn't going to be able to make the car feet first. So pushing the upper part of his body forward, he reached out his arms as far in front of him as he could. The force of his weight hurtling down sent bolts of pain through both his hands that clamped like vices onto the back handrail of the car. His lower body, now dangling from the back of the train, was starting to twist and turn as his feet were bounced around like pinballs on the gravel and rails. Summoning all his strength, he released his right hand and reached up higher on one of the two vertical bars that centered the handrail. Straining mightily to pull himself higher one hand at a time, he was able to bring his legs up on the floor and then step over the rail. Ellis then immediately turned his back to the back wall of the car and slid down. He didn't want to be seen by anyone who might have been in that last car. But he also desperately needed a few seconds to sit and catch his breath as the station he just left grew smaller and smaller in the gathering twilight.

CHAPTER 32

As Ellis sat there, numbers started running through his mind. Three men. Yes. Three passengers. But what about the engineer, the conductor, the cook, the servers? No way to be sure how many bystanders might be involved. Or whether they'd remain bystanders. One woman. Where would they be keeping her? Two moneybags. They wouldn't be unattended. Five rail cars. Passenger cars, a dining car, maybe a bar car too, he thought. Twelve hours to Los Mochis. Half of those hours in the dark. He hoped that might work to his advantage.

Since no one had burst through the back door yet, Ellis was prepared to assume no one had seen him make his desperate entrance. But as the train rolled into the oncoming evening and swayed, almost imperceptibly, from side to side, he realized he was in a vulnerable position if someone did decide to step out. So crawling below the pane of glass in the door, Ellis made his way to the port side of the train. Slowly he peered around and saw what he hoped to find, a ladder leading to the roof of the car. He realized he'd be taking a chance of being seen if he swung around and scurried up it. But he also knew it was dicey to stay put. Luckily, the train was approaching the first of eighty-six tunnels that had been cut along the four hundred mile journey from Chihuahua to Los Mochis. When his car entered the tunnel he made his move. And when the train emerged from the tunnel, Ellis was lying flat atop the end car in the cool Mexican night.

He hadn't been on the roof long when he heard a number of voices. Some sort of group was apparently crossing from the fourth to the fifth car. Separate conversations were going on in both Spanish and English. Ellis listened for a female voice but all he could make out was a somewhat subdued cacophony of male mumbling. No longer hearing anything below him, he turned and quietly crawled to the very back to see if anyone had gone outside. The shake and rattle of the train in motion obscured the sound of him moving overhead. But it also made it difficult for him to hear what sounded like two men who were now standing where Ellis had been sitting just a few minutes earlier. Even though there was a full moon, he felt it was dark enough to advance to the edge of the roof to try to hear them better. Once there, he slowly peered over and saw two men standing shoulder to shoulder, both leaning on the rail he had used as a lifeline, smoking cigarettes and staring off into the darkness. One wore the traditional black suit and hat that immediately identified him as the conductor. He was a larger, older man with a dark mustache. The other was a younger man in a short white jacket. Probably a waiter or bus boy, Ellis thought. The younger man spoke first.

"Que pasa?"

"Speak English, Eduardo. You need the practice."

"Why we have to stay back here? All in this one car. Why can we not do our jobs?"

"He said we should all stay here...so we stay here. When one buys a private trip it can be as private as he wants. Do you know what this must have cost him?"

"How can the policia afford such a thing? And did you see his face? Madre mia!"

"An injury, to be sure. But count your blessings, Eduardo. Your face is still in one piece. And your ass can take it easy all the way to Los Mochis. As long as we stay back here like he said. So enjoy your smoke. This trip, you are the tourista."

Ellis immediately started to break down the intel he was overhearing. Whoever took Rena has cordoned off the staff, he said to himself. Put them all in one place. He must have wanted to eliminate her ability to interact with them. Separating a hostage from potential friendlies is standard operating procedure, Ellis realized. And...the guy just referred to him as policia. Chances are he'll be using other military tactics. The station agent said there were three men and the girl. Bet one will be stationed in the next car, Ellis reasoned. To make sure the train staff stays away.

Ellis turned again and started proceeding quietly and carefully from the back car toward the next one in line. As his knees and elbows moved him along under the Mexican moonlight, he rehearsed different scenarios in his mind. He also made a mental note of his advantages. Surprise and time. He didn't have to rush into anything. It was a long way to Los Mochis. Plus, the ensuing night and the need for sleep could also work in his favor. He should rest now, he thought. Then later, when all on board would need the tranquility that only sleep can bring, he would make his move. So, after reaching the front of the last car on the train, Ellis checked his watch, then put his head down and closed his eyes. His rest would not be deep. It would be stolen on the thin edge of consciousness at best. But still, it was preparation for what was to come.

Had it been daylight rather than dark, and had Ellis been just another passenger, he would have been awed by the majesty that surrounded him. As he rested and waited, the train rolled along the Copper Canyon railway that climbed, rimmed, and cut through mountains that were seven, even eight thousand feet above sea level. But Ellis saw only darkness and shadows and felt the crisp coolness of the night. Passing out of the high plateau, past the cultivated oat fields and apple orchards, he continued to see only blackness, but he heard muted clacking sounds caused by the wind rustling tin cans and old compact disc cases the locals had strung in the trees to ward off hungry birds. Mile after mile the train rumbled. Past Cuauhtemoc, home to Mennonites who had arrived in the 1920s. Past Perdernales, where Pancho Villa had holed up with his Division del Norte. Past San Juanito, Mexico's coldest, highest-elevated town. Through it all Ellis slept a kind of half-sleep, embracing the gentle sway of the train from side to side yet not allowing himself to lose so much consciousness that he missed any sound or movement below or around him. When Ellis checked his watch again it was nearly two a. m. Time to begin, he told himself.

Moving to the edge of the car, he again peered over cautiously to make sure there was no one outside. Gauging the distance from the roof to the floor below, he felt he could slide himself over, hang from the top and drop silently to the floor. Swinging his legs around and holding tight to the rim of the roof, he let his body come down, then dropped the few remaining feet. Stealing a glance back into the car, he saw the train staff scattered in various forms of slumber. Some stretched across seats. Some leaning together for support. Others sitting upright with eyes closed and mouths open. They were seldom afforded such a luxury. And they were taking advantage of it.

Ellis turned and stepped across the walkway that linked one car to the next. Looking through the glass pane in the door he could see no one. But his view of the car's interior was limited. He reached across and pulled his Glock from its holster, then opened the door as quietly as he could. Stepping inside, the car still appeared empty. Ellis put his ear to the door of the restroom but heard no sound. Walking slowly down the isle he checked each pair of seats to his right and left. The car was indeed vacant. Which led Ellis to extrapolate that the next car would not be. One of the captors would be stationed between the staff and the rest of them. A perimeter guard was standard operating procedure.

Before opening the door to move from the fourth car to the third, Ellis tried in vain to see all the way through. But it was impossible. So once again he stepped outside into the night and onto the walkway that bridged the cars. Just as he was about to reach the door on the other side, he saw a figure move into the aisle. Ellis immediately dropped into a crouch and threw himself against the back wall. He hadn't had time to see the face of whoever was in the car. But he was hesitant to peek inside as he thought the figure had turned in his direction. It only took a moment before he realized he was correct. The back door opened and out staggered a small man clutching a very big bottle of Tequila in one hand and reaching for the zipper of his trousers with the other. Even though they were less than five feet apart, the man took no notice of Ellis as he turned his eyes to the stars and his dick down wind and began the task that his drunken stupor had taken him past the restroom and outside to complete.

This was too good an opportunity to pass up. Recognizing the same uniform that had been worn by the fat man he had interrogated earlier in the day, Ellis rose from his crouched position, turned slightly sideways and thrust his right leg out and up catching the unsuspecting pisser squarely between the shoulder blades. The force sent him tumbling headfirst over the side rail and into the darkness. There was no scream of surprise. No sound of impact. And no longer a little man peeing. One down, two to go, Ellis said to himself.

Again, entering slowly, Ellis checked out the car to make sure no one was there. Two thirds of the way through, he came across the rifle and the cartridge belt the little man had left sitting on the plush, upholstered seat when nature called. He checked the bolt-action rifle to make sure it was ready to fire. Then he put it and the cartridges in the overhead luggage rack. Taking it with him would be cumbersome, but if he had to make his way back through this car, extra firepower would be out of site but available should he need it.

Once again he tried, without results, to see into the next car before leaving the one he was in. Impossible. So, with Glock in hand, he kept moving forward. Outside, he stayed low crossing from the third to the second car. Stealing a peek inside, he realized the stakes had just been raised. This was the dining car. And while there were no apparent diners, there were impediments to knowing whether anyone was or wasn't in the car. Chin-high frosted, beveled glass cordoned off the dining area in the center of the car. It would be virtually impossible to see if anyone was beyond that glass until you were almost upon it. But, Ellis thought, that was a problem that worked both ways. If someone was on the other side, that someone wouldn't know Ellis was coming until he was almost upon them. And he still had surprise on his side. So as silently as possible, he opened the door and entered the car. He heard nothing. Slowly, he moved down the center aisle. Then he heard a voice. A voice that seemed to be coming from the air itself.

"Cesar. Cesar! Go check on Ramón. Make sure he es no ebrio. Cesar?"

It wasn't the air. It was an intercom. Ellis could hear someone rustling up ahead of him. Then he heard the mumbled response.

"Si. Si, mi Capitan."

Ellis quickly stepped up and just behind the first glass partition. He got low in the seat so the approaching guard wouldn't see his head. There were only seconds for Ellis to make a decision. He couldn't let the guard go by and not find his compatriot. He couldn't risk a shot or a tussle with the guard. Either noise would be heard over the open intercom. He quickly holstered his Glock, bent his knee and brought his right leg up closer to him. Pulling his pant leg up he slid the knife out of its sheath that was secured at his ankle. Just then the guard walked through the center aisle inches from Ellis' position. There was no thought in his mind that he might not be alone in the car. He was simply on his way to make sure his stupid friend wasn't drunk. Then, in an instant, he was dying.

Ellis had sprung just as he walked past. Simultaneously, he swung his left arm around the guard's middle to break his fall as his right hand came up fast and hard and drove the knife up to the hilt in the guard's right temple. The Mexican instantly became rigid, then started to jerk and convulse. Ellis hugged him tight and held the knife in place that had entered his brain. After only a few seconds the guard collapsed but Ellis supported his weight so he wouldn't drop to the floor. Then he eased the body face down into the aisle. Pulling his own arms out from under the dead man, he saw that his right arm and hand and the knife itself was covered in blood. Moving the silverware off the fine linen napkins on the table closest to him, he wiped the blood from himself and his blade. It took all four napkins to complete the cleanup. Then reaching toward the center of the dead man's back, he bunched up the guard's shirt and drug him down the center aisle back to the door he had come through minutes earlier. Propping the door open with his leg, he pulled and slid the body onto the outside platform. The less proof of what had gone on the better, he thought. It would be hard enough to explain away the blood, should it ever come to that. No point in making it even more difficult by leaving a body in the middle of it all. As he pulled the lifeless form up far enough to flip it over the side, he caught his first glimpse of the man's face. A grizzled, vacuous mug that wouldn't have given Ellis a second thought had it not been for the teeth. The green and mangled teeth, that for an instant, Ellis was sure he had seen before. But he shifted the weight over the side anyway. Over the side and into oblivion.

Walking back into the dinning car, Ellis again heard the intercom. But this time it was a sound Ellis hadn't heard since back at the camp. It was the sound of Rena's voice. Rena in conversation with her captor, who had no way of knowing he was now without support.

"Where are we? How long was I asleep?" Rena asked.

"You were very tired. You should continue to sleep."

I know that voice, Ellis said to himself.

Rena was in no mood to go back to sleep. "You can't keep me here. I want to get off at the next stop."

"On this trip, there is but one stop. The end of the line in Los Mochis. We have made arrangements to cancel the other stops."

The measured tones. The cadence. Damn, where do I know that voice, Ellis wondered.

"I'll tell the authorities you kidnapped me. I'll tell my father you stole his money."

"Senorita Whitfield, perhaps it has escaped your attention. We are the authorities."

Jesus, Ellis said under his breath. "I knew I recognized that voice. It's Morales. Captain Morales. Of course, la arana. The gangly fucker looks like a spider. Why didn't I realize that?"

"And as for your father, senorita, his money will be returned to him...less our expenses, of course. We are meeting his emissaries in Los Mochis."

"That money is for the people," Rena snapped. "Not the Zapatistas. They were going to distribute it to the Tarahumarans and others like them."

"It was going to the Zapatistas. To support more terror and insurrection. Your father does not support that."

"You talk of terror," Rena shot back, "it's you and your kind who terrorize the poor. You keep them in poverty. You keep them uneducated. My father can't be part of that."

"Your father is a practical man, senorita. You saw what he was building in the wilderness. He has many such projects in Mexico. They require time and land and labor. They will be here far beyond our lifetimes. He is leaving a legacy of beauty in our country."

"And you supply the labor for that beauty, right? Children, who can't fight for themselves...who'll do anything to help their parents. Don't you see, it's a cycle that just keeps repeating itself."

"Senorita, I am but a cog in the wheel. The wheel of progress. And it moves only one way, forward. The Zapatistas, the Tarahumarans, they are Mexico's past, not its future."

Realizing she was getting nowhere, Rena tried a different approach. "What about your future?"

How much is my father paying you to bring me and his money back? You've got the money right here. You could take a lot more than he's giving you and let me take the rest. Then just tell him you couldn't find me...or I got away...and you never got the money."

"I am not a greedy man, senorita. I am being well compensated. And I will continue to be. Your father knows many people in Mexico. People in high office. It would not do to make enemies of such people."

"No," Rena came back sarcastically, "you prefer enemies that are helpless and disadvantaged, don't you? You're disgusting."

Morales let the insult hang in the air for a moment. The he replied, "Such moral superiority is understandable from one as

165

young as yourself, senorita Whitfield. But it is hypocritical at best, is it not? Coming from one in league with the killers of a helpless elderly couple in San Miguel."

"That was an accident. It wasn't supposed to happen like that at all."

"Be that as it may, your stay in this country has come to an end. Were your father not so influential, you would be on your way to prison, in accommodations far less pleasant than these."

Rena shot back, "Prison is where you should be going. You shot Juan."

"A casualty in an ongoing war the rebels have chosen. Such things happen." Morales answered.

"The two men you left at the camp...they won't be able to hold off the others, you know."

"They held them long enough for us to make our train. If they were unable to hold them longer, it is unfortunate. But they were expendable."

"You bastard," Rena said.

"Si. But perhaps not so unlike the bastard you carry. Right senorita?"

"What? What are you talking about?"

"You talk in your sleep, senorita. You talk of this Diego, whose child you carry."

Ellis couldn't see it, but he felt what must have been the shock on Rena's face. If he could only get a fix on exactly where she was in the car. Was she restrained? Was she free to move around? Perhaps she was, Ellis thought. Morales probably figures she has nowhere to go. No place to escape to as long as the train keeps moving. But he'll keep her away from the money, Ellis reasoned. He's betting she'll be less likely to try something if she doesn't have quick access to what she's wanted all along, money for those she came to Mexico to help. Money that might even help her own child if she and the baby were to stay in this country that had somehow turned her from a girl to a woman.

Time is still on my side, Ellis thought. Morales doesn't know I'm here. He'll wait and listen. The captain's last revelation had silenced Rena. If she gives up, and goes back to sleep, Morales might allow himself to close at least one eye. And if he does, Capitan spider might just wake up with a surprise in his web.

Silence ensured. Ellis checked his watch. It was almost twenty minutes before he heard Morales's voice over the intercom again. But this time it was quieter. Ellis guessed that Rena was asleep and the captain was in no hurry to wake her and have to engage in the same argument they had probably been having since he abducted her from the plateau.

"Cesar. Cesar, answer me. Cesar. Imbecile."

Maybe he'll think his guard is sleeping, Ellis thought. Chances are he won't come looking for him. He won't want to separate himself from Rena or the money. But how long will he wait when there's no reply? And how long will the train's staff stay in the last car before wandering up to see if anything is needed? Soon it will be daybreak. Ellis didn't have all the information he wanted regarding Rena and the money's whereabouts, but he determined he wasn't likely to get more. He realized it was now time to move.

Taking the Glock from its holster and moving to the front of the dining car, Ellis checked to make sure there was no one there. He then went outside and crossed onto the platform that led to the front car. The first rays of morning sunlight were just starting to peek over the towering precipices. Crusty cliffs the color of copper were etched into the mountainside to his left. To his right an abyss plunged seven thousand feet to the canyon floor. But Ellis was too preoccupied to notice the spectacular scenery. He had decided it was too risky to simply rush Morales. He might grab Rena and use her as a shield. But maybe he could make the captain come to him. It was worth a try.

Crouching down, he reached up, turned the door latch, and let the door of the bar car swing open. Then, with his back to the wall beside the open door, he waited for Morales to attend to it.

The clacking sound of iron on iron entered the bar car as the door came open. Morales's head and eyes turned instinctively to the source of the noise. Then he looked over at Rena who was slumped in a seat across the aisle from him. She sighed and unconsciously rearranged herself to get more comfortable. Morales refocused his attention on the open door at the rear of the car. He had noticed no irregular movement that might have jarred the door open. As he waited to see if Cesar or anyone else was about to enter, he reached forward on the table in front of him and picked up his service revolver that had been lying there. Why had the door suddenly come open, he wondered. Why hadn't Cesar reported back to him? Why did he have a strange feeling something wasn't right? With his pistol pointed toward the door, he rose slowly and stepped into the aisle. Taking a step forward he paused. Surely nothing was wrong he thought, but why take a chance. So he reached out with his long left arm and wrapped tentacle-like fingers around Rena's bicep, pulling her across the seat and up next to him.

"What...what are you doing?" she mumbled, still half asleep.

Moving her in front of him, he raised his pistol to his lips indicating he wanted her quiet. Then he quickly moved his grip from her arm to around her shoulder. His wrist, palm and elongated fingers reaching up and closing around her mouth. Then, pulling her tighter against him, he started moving slowly toward the open door.

The wind whipping by and the rattle of the train on the tracks kept Ellis from hearing Rena's response. Still low, he had turned sideways and pointed the Glock toward the open door frame. Seconds went by. He thought he heard footsteps coming his way but the ambient noise made it impossible for him to be sure. Then, as his gaze was fixed on the doorway, he saw one foot slowly emerge. A foot wearing boots, but much smaller boots than he anticipated. Then Rena's body started to break the plane of the door. Her legs. Her chest. Her head with vine-like fingers covering her mouth. Rena's peripheral vision caught sight of someone to her right. Her head jerked instinctively in that direction. Morales felt her involuntary response the moment it happened and snatched her quickly back inside the car.

Ellis knew he no longer had the advantage of surprise. He couldn't give Morales time to regroup mentally. So he stood quickly and swung round in the center of the doorway, arms extended, his left hand bracing his right wrist that held the Glock.

Only feet apart, they stood looking at one another. Ellis with his weapon pointing straight at the contorted couple in front of him. Morales with his revolver pressed against Rena's temple. Though the lanky Mexican was doing his best to fold his thin frame behind his hostage, Ellis couldn't help but notice the cuts and scabs that streaked his head and cheek and the back of his hands. The explosion in San Miguel had charred the spider's flesh but not his ferocity. Ellis knew he was still deadly.

"Put down your weapon," Morales said as he moved

backward dragging Rena with him, and no harm will come to the senorita."

Walking forward, trying to keep the distance between them short, Ellis replied, "From what I've heard Captain, you're not likely to hurt her. Her father and his well-heeled friends would spare no expense in taking revenge on someone who harmed Warren Whitfield's daughter...and grandchild."

Continuing to move backwards, Morales said, "You have a point, Mr. Ellis. But it doesn't mean you have a victory. I can always kill her and tell everyone you accidentally shot her while trying to get to me."

"The minute you pull the trigger, Morales, you'll be as dead as her."

"Then we have, what is known as an impasse, yes?"

Ellis responded. "No. We don't. I'm thinking seriously about simply shooting you and her and taking the money for myself."

"Somehow I do not believe that. For someone who showed such empathy for that boy in the San Miguel station, I do not think you would do what you say."

"Willing to stake your life on it, Morales?"

The charred Captain paused for a just a moment before he replied. "Let me suggest an alternative. You return the girl to her father. I return the money. Everyone gets what they want. Her father. You. And I, Senor Ellis."

Rena squirmed and tried to break free. The captain's suggestion having nothing to do with what she wanted. But Morales's grip was too strong. He squeezed and held her tighter.

"Interesting offer," Ellis responded, moving at the same pace as his quarry, "but I have this nagging feeling that I can't really trust you."

Morales was almost back to the front of the car now. And Ellis could see why he wanted to get there. Sitting on the end of the curved bar were the two bags that had been in the trunk of his car.

"I am disappointed in you," Morales began. "I would have thought such a man as you would know when to...what is the term...cut your losses. Since you do not, you leave me no choice." Morales then cocked the hammer of the pistol that was still pressing into the side of Rena's head.

"Stop." Ellis broke in. "Don't you realize she's the only thing keeping me from wasting you. Kill her and you'll be dead before she hits the floor."

"But you Mr. Ellis, will have to live with the fact that you let a beautiful young woman and her unborn child die. Perhaps it is I who will be the fortunate one."

There was something in that grotesquely scarred face, something deep in his eyes and in the timber of his mincingly polite voice that made Ellis believe the freak was just crazy enough to believe what he said.

"Okay. Okay. "I'll put my gun on the bar," Ellis said, "Just don't shoot her, alright?"

"You do that. Then step away from…"

Ellis didn't give him time to finish his sentence. He put the Glock on the bar and immediately dove to the left. Morales threw Rena aside, brought his gun hand down and fired. The bullet tore through the leather-upholstered chair Ellis had jumped behind, burning the side of his cheek as it went by. Ellis then shoved the chair as hard as he could. It slid across the hardwood floor and banged into the captain's knees causing him to crumple into it. Ellis had to decide instantaneously whether to go for the captain or to go for his Glock. He instinctively leaped onto the bar, grabbed the weapon and let his momentum take him over it to the other side.

Rena, sensing this might be her only opportunity, grabbed the two bags and broke for the back of the car. Morales unwound his tangled limbs from the chair he had tumbled into, and fired a blind shot into the bar. The round splintered the walnut base and exploded a bottle of Smirnoff spraying shattered glass and vodka all over Ellis. Then the sound of heavy bootfalls told him that Morales was running toward the back of the car. He rose in a firing position and saw Rena reaching the open back door and the captain leaving his feet to stop her. Morales's bony arms seemed to stretch on forever in front of him as he dove for the girl and the money. His right hand caught Rena's heel just as it was leaving the floor, and while he couldn't hang on, he held it long enough to cause her to stagger, trip and then stumble forward through the open door and beyond Ellis's sight. He broke from behind the bar just as Morales was rolling over on his back. One man raised his gun to fire, the other lowered his. But Ellis was quicker and pumped two rounds into the center of the captain's chest as he ran past him toward the back of the car.

As he cleared the doorframe he saw the railing catch Rena squarely in the stomach. She hit it lunging forward and her momentum flipped her heels over head. Screaming and sprawling and trying to grab the rail as she went over, the bags she was clutching in each hand kept her from getting a grip. She released the bag in her left hand and it bounced off the rail and back onto the platform. Her right arm was the last thing to go over the side and as it did the bag caught the sharp, decorative tip of the rail puncturing the bag and leaving her hanging beneath it. Ellis dashed to the side to reach over and grab her, but the weight of Rena's flailing body caused the bag to rip and tear away. She fell from the train silently, her eyes staring up at the coach in seeming disbelief as her body plummeted toward the floor of the canyon seven thousand feet below. And as she fell, the bag released its contents and the crisp, green bills were caught in the wind and began a magnificent shower of free floating Ulysses S. Grants that rained like confetti behind her.

Ellis stood at the rail not wanting to believe what he had just seen. The remnants of the bag on the rail continued to flap in the wind though, reminding him it was all too real. He tore the tattered remains off and tossed them over the side.

Picking up the remaining bag from the platform, he turned and walked back into the bar car. Morales was lying in a pool of blood in the middle of the aisle. He was making weak, coughing sounds and trying to turn his head toward Ellis as he approached. Their eyes met and held for two seconds as Ellis stood over him. Then he pointed the Glock downward and fired point blank between the captain's eyes.

CHAPTER 33

It was another of those too perfect San Diego days. Just as the two before had been. But Ellis hadn't paid much attention to those days. Most of which he spent sleeping. Adrift in much needed rest after his return from Mexico.

He had performed a tuck-and-roll exit from the train, bag in hand, on the outskirts of Los Mochis well before the staff came forward to prepare for arrival. Hitching a ride in the back of a pickup truck, he rode past the sugar cane fields and into the city. There he took a cab to the home of the man whose name and address Marquez had scribbled on a piece of paper for him. After pocketing the money he was owed, he left the remainder with the man who said he'd make sure Marquez's people received it. For some reason Ellis believed him. And even if it didn't all get there, he sure as hell wasn't about to bring a dime of it back to Warren Whitfield.

After getting back to his apartment he crashed hard. Once he had showered, shaved, and torn through the Chinese food that he had ordered, he hit the sheets and slept. Slept right through the evening news and the morning papers and the minor item about the strange occurrence in Northern Mexico. The one about this ancient Indian tribe who lived apart from the majority of Mexicans in caves and cliff dwellings and stone shanties in some of the most rugged, uninhabitable regions of the Sierra Madre Occidental. Apparently there had been rumors of hundreds of thousands of dollars literally raining from the sky and dropping all around the villages of one of Mexico's poorest indigenous people, the Tarahumarans. There had been no solid confirmation however and so most were simply writing it off as a mystical event more appropriate for the supermarket tabloids than the international news.

After picking up Osgood from the kennel, Ellis had called the hospital trying to get in touch with Terrance Whitfield and found that he had been released. He then called the younger Whitfield's home number and got the answering machine. He left a message for Whitfield to meet him later that morning in the parking lot of the Balboa Park Zoo. Near the pole marked W1. If Whitfield couldn't make it, Ellis told him to just call his office number, which Ellis would check regularly, and they'd arrange another time to get together. On the message he left, Ellis said that Rena was not with him. He didn't want to say more than that until they were actually face to face.

This wasn't the first time Ellis had to deliver bad news. He had spoken to family members of guys in his unit who didn't come back from difficult missions. He had broken the news to heartsick relatives that the missing person they had sent him to find, wouldn't be coming home. It was never easy. And it never seemed to get any easier. One thing that did help, Ellis had found, was a big open place outdoors to deliver the message no one wanted to hear. In homes or apartments or hospitals, the walls seemed to just close in on people. Outside, in the fresh air and sunshine, somehow they didn't seem quite so alone.

Ellis had also called Laney that morning. Again, he had gotten a recorded message. Leaving word that he was back in town and wanted to see her, he said he'd try her again later in the day. Ellis drove over to the lot and parked under the tall W1 pole fifteen minutes in advance of the time he had asked Whitfield to meet him there. Using his cell phone, he had been periodically checking his office to see if Rena's brother had left any messages for him. He hadn't. So Ellis sat with the top down in his 230 SL and waited.

Ten minutes later Terrance Whitfield pulled up in a deep blue BMW sedan. As both men were getting out of their cars, Ellis noticed that Whitfield had one of those silky ascots tucked into the open collar of his shirt. It covered his neck completely. A new and permanent addition to his wardrobe, Ellis guessed.

"Where's Rena?" Whitfield asked.

"I'm afraid I've got some bad news," Ellis began.

It's best to get it out in a hurry, Ellis knew. Deal with the shock. Then go into the details. Terry, as Rena always called him, was devastated. For a moment he thought he was going to faint. The young man swooned when it initially sunk in. Ellis helped him over to the passenger seat of his open-topped car and had him sit down. Terry found it almost impossible to believe. He had expected to hear that perhaps Rena was coming back at a later time. Even worse, that she wasn't coming back. That she had decided to stay in Mexico. But dead? No. It had never occurred to him that death and Rena could be spoken of in the same sentence. She was so young, so vibrant, so filled with the fire of a life yet lived. It took a number of minutes for her brother to pull himself together.

Ellis let him take all the time he needed. Finally Whitfield asked Ellis to tell him everything. And Ellis did. Running down the events that unfolded, starting with his arrival in Guanajuato. Ellis held nothing back. Including the senior Whitfield's business involvement in the country and his collusion with Mexican officials to have both his daughter and his money returned to him. He also told Rena's brother that she had been pregnant.

That almost brought him some comfort for a moment. To know that Rena had known love and known the joy of having a life growing inside her. Then the crushing waste of it all hit him, and he sank down again and wept.

When he finally was able to speak again, he asked Ellis, "You said she recognized the structure, didn't you?"

"Yes," Ellis answered, "she called it his house."

"I'm not surprised," Whitfield said. "You have no idea how many times, as children, father told us about this magnificent house that he would one day build. He was constantly taking out the plans and showing them to us. He even had this incredible scale model of the thing that we were shown again and again, but never allowed to touch. Can you imagine that, Mr. Ellis? Being shown this wondrous miniature, only to be told we could never, ever touch it. Because it might break. Now he's built it. And we're broken. Rather ironic, wouldn't you say?"

Ellis let the question pass. He knew Whitfield didn't really want an answer.

"Do you think he knows yet? Father? Do you think he knows about Rena?"

"I'm sure he knows something went wrong. I heard Morales say your father's people would meet the train in Los Mochis and bring your sister and the money back to the states. Let's assume those men were there. All they met was a dead police captain, two missing guards, no girl and no money. There's no way he can know yet what happened. I'm the only one who can tell him. And I wanted you to know first. I'll go out to Eden's Edge in a day or so and fill him in."

"Odd, isn't it, Mr. Ellis? He abhors my lifestyle and yet it's his greed and his meddling that caused Rena's...and her child's death. Oh, I know...I know, he didn't make her stumble and fall. But he put the forces in play that lead to it. He couldn't just let you do what you went there to do. He had to control everything. The way he's always had to control everything. The money didn't mean that much to him. He could have made it back easily with another project, another assignment. But he wanted her to know that he would decide what she did with her life. Just like he's always decided what everyone should do. Everyone who has anything to do with the great Warren Whitfield."

Terry was silent for a moment. Then he went on. "Do you think there will be any reprisals? Do you think he'll try to do anything to you?"

"I doubt it," Ellis said. "Once he knows what happened, I think it will just be about damage control. I did what he sent me there to do. Deliver the money. As you say, everything that went down after that, he had a hand in. He won't be in a hurry for that kind of scandal. If there's anything that goes public at all...my guess is...the whole thing will be blamed on the Zapatistas."

"Fuck!" Terry Whitfield said.

"Fuck indeed," Ellis replied.

They parted shortly after that. Ellis watched young Whitfield get back in his car. After turning on the engine, the young man stopped for a moment, his head down, his eyes closed. Then he gunned the engine and peeled away from W1, back toward the street.

Before he left the parking lot, Ellis used his cell phone to call Laney again. This time a woman's voice answered, but he knew instantly it wasn't the woman he wanted it to be.

"I was trying to reach Laney Wilson," Ellis said.

"She's not here," the voice replied, "would you like to leave a message?"

"Could you tell her that Brig Ellis called. And ask her to call me back."

"Oh, Mr. Ellis. My name's Cindy. I'm a friend of Laney's and I'm housesitting for her while she's out of town. She said you might call."

"Oh." Ellis said. "When does she get back?"

"Well, I'm really not sure, exactly. But she calls and checks in pretty regularly. Like I said, she told me you might call. So, the next time she does, I'll let her know that you rang and that you'd like her to call you."

"Thanks. Thanks very much."

"So, are you as good looking as she said?"

"It's one of those eye-of-the-beholder things."

"What?" Cindy responded, clueless.

"Never mind," Ellis said. "Just tell her I called."

CHAPTER 34

It was almost noon and a beautiful day, Ellis finally noticed. So he decided to drive out to Benny's for some lunch before going into his office. He pulled out of the parking lot and wound his way slowly through Balboa Park, in no particular hurry. He decided to use West Broadway to take him down near the water so he could take the coast road. At the intersection of 12th Avenue and Broadway he stopped at the traffic light and checked his rear view mirror. Directly behind him was a black Caddy that he had first spotted following him out of the park. There were two guys in the front seat that seemed to fit the description his mechanic, Lothar, had given for the bozos who took baseball bats to the car they thought belonged to him. Both big. Both ugly. After making note of their license plate number, Ellis thought to himself, let's see how interested they really are.

The light was still red, but he dropped the gear shift down into first and squealed away from the light just barely squeezing between two cars that were crossing his path from both the right and left. The Caddy waited for an opening and then bore down on him. Ellis let them catch up. Then he came up on a light just turning yellow at 24th Street. Ellis hit his brakes hard to stop, causing the Caddy to dip its front grill to the pavement in order to stop without ramming him. Then, just as quickly, he floored it and sped through the light. The big car had to start and stop and honk and make its way through an intersection where it didn't have the right of way. In the time it took them to intimidate the other drivers and force their way through, a black and white had come up behind them, red lights flipping on and off. Ellis watched the Caddy pull over to the curb and knew that San Diego's finest would have them there for the next few minutes. He knew he could check with a buddy at motor vehicles and run down an address for that license plate number. So he decided to stick with his plan for lunch and get back with those two when he'd be the hunter rather than the prey.

When Ellis turned off Harbor Drive, he knew immediately something was wrong. There were no cars in Benny's parking lot. Except for Grif's Lincoln. And it was well past time for the early lunch crowd. He cruised right next to the entrance and saw one of those cheap CLOSED signs in the glass doorframe. But if the

Lincoln was there, maybe Grif was too, Ellis reasoned. Turning off the engine, he left his car where it was, got out, walked up the steps and tried the door. It opened.

The interior was as unoccupied as a Klan rally in Harlem. But seated at one of the tables near the window was Grif with a bottle of Glenfiddich, three fourths of which you could see through. He didn't notice Ellis walk in. The focus of his attention appeared to be directed at the portable video camera sitting on the table next to him and pointed directly at his face. Ellis approached slowly, looking around at the emptiness of what had seemed a thriving enterprise before he left for Mexico. He pulled up a chair and sat at the table with the camera. That's when he noticed Grif's eyes were closed.

"Hey," Ellis said loudly. Followed quickly with, "You aren't dead, are you?"

Grif raised his head, focused on who was speaking to him and said, "Mr. Ellis, what the hell are you doing here?"

"I thought I was gong to be having lunch. But it appears that's not the case."

"No...no'm lunch," Grif slurred. Then he composed himself a bit and said, "No lunch. No dinner. No drinks. No fuckin' nothin."

"Looks like you put a hell of a dent in that bottle of Scotch."

"Yes. Yes I did. Gonna' finish it too."

Ellis, nodding at the camera beside him, said, "What's with the video?"

The question caused Grif to cock his head and turn his eyes toward the beach as he responded. "I'm recording the end of an error."

"You mean era. The end of an era."

"Ha," Grif belched. "A fuckin' Freudian slip. For it's both the end of an era...as you say...and, the end of an error...as I said. Are you sure that's what I said?"

Ellis had never seen Grif so drunk. "Doesn't matter what you said. Why are you talking about endings anyway? What happened?"

"Did you know, my good man, that this was the way Mr. Benny, the original proprietor of Benny's, met his end? Sitting right here, drinking first class Scotch. Then, boom!"

Grif shouted, raising his arms and spilling half the contents of his glass. "Heart attack. Right here. I found him you know. And now...I've fucked up what he left me."

"Look," Ellis began, "concentrate for a minute. Tell me what's happened. Why are you closed in the middle of the day? Why are you sitting here shit-faced in front of a video camera?"

"I'm recording the end of an--"

Ellis cut him off. "Hey, we've been there already. Tell me what happened."

Grif took a sip from what remained in his glass and said, "I fucked up, man. I pissed it all away. I have this problem, you see."

"This doesn't have anything to do with the accident...the one we were looking into."

"Nope. This is another problem. A problem millions of people share. A problem..."

"Spare me the speech, okay? Just tell me what it is."

"I just gambled it all away, my man. Gambled and lost. Lost...and lost...and..."

"How much do you owe?" Ellis asked.

"Well, let's put it this way. If I sell this place...I might...might, mind you...get out from under."

"Can't you try something less extreme?"

"Oh, I've been trying things. Man have I been trying things. I tried laying off waitresses...then cooks. I tried robbing Peter to pay Paul. Then I had a great idea. I tried bettin' on ball games to pay off craps losses. I tried bettin' on the ponies to pay off the ball game losses. I even tried the newest thing, man...Internet gaming. And even when I won there...I lost. Those assholes are all set up somewhere offshore like Costa Rica, you know? They pay late. Or, they don't pay at all. And while I'm waiting for my winnings...I'm puttin' the difference down on soccer games in Amsterdam that ain't even legit. The damn things have already been played. The fuckin' spread's too good to pass up. So I take the spread and get screwed even more. They just got too many ways to screw you, man."

"Hang on a second," Ellis said. Then he got up, walked over to the bar and got himself a glass. Back at the table he picked up the Glenfiddich and poured himself a drink. "I'm not going to let you kill this whole thing by yourself." After taking a sip, Ellis said, "How'd you manage to keep it going so long? Why didn't they cut you off sooner if you kept losing all the time?"

Grif started to take a drink before he answered. He raised the glass to his lips, then pulled it away and said, "Oh, I found a way around that, man. A way that shows you just how fucked up I am."

"What do you mean?" Ellis asked.

"Well, I made 'em think I was someone I wasn't. So I could keep playin'. On the Internet, man. All you gotta' do is give 'em a name and a password and an e-mail address. Then you get one of them e-cash cards, you know? And you go to town. Only problem...I kept losin' there too."

There was something about the way Grif was looking at him. Something in those swollen, drunken, dog eyes that seemed to be asking for forgiveness. Then Ellis put it together.

"You son-of-a-bitch," Ellis said.

"I never meant it to get out of hand, this way. I never--"

"How'd you get information on me you could use?"

Grif answered, "You gave me your card, man. There's an office address, an e-mail address and a phone number on there."

"You must have needed more than that," Ellis countered.

"I remembered that you told me you were in the service, you know. Well, you probably don't know there are names and social security numbers on this U. S. military web site that's got retirees and shit like that on it. Hell, I didn't know 'til this computer geek mentioned it to me one night here in the bar."

"I can't believe you were going to let me take the heat from this." Ellis barked.

"I wasn't planning on you having a problem, man. Cause I wasn't planning on losin'. And I was desperate. I didn't know they were gonna' muscle you. I swear."

"How do you know about that?"

"That crazy Kraut mechanic of yours...the one that wears those stupid Elvis outfits. He was in here the other day. He told me what they tried to do to your car."

"Oh he did, did he? Well, you know what he didn't tell you? He didn't tell you that they tore up my office and were particularly unkind to my computer. He didn't tell you that they tried to turn the elevator in my building into a casket. He didn't tell you that they're following me around now...because he didn't know any of that."

Grif put his glass on the table while Ellis emptied his and

poured himself another.

"Look, Ellis, I had no idea, man. No idea. I was at my wit's end, you know. And when the German told me about your car...well I decided I just had to get the money to pay this thing off. I swear I didn't know they were trying to fuck you up."

Ellis sat there looking at Grif. A guy he had liked. A guy he had tried to help. A guy who had taken advantage of that. But he was also looking at a guy who was about to lose everything he had. Everything he had worked for. Damn, he thought. Why can't I be infuriated, instead of just sad.

"You got a buyer for this place?"

"Yeah," Grif replied. "There's a dude who's wanted to buy it for some time."

"And it will pay off everything?"

"Yeah. It will. It will. Of course, it won't leave me a pot to piss in."

"Tough shit," Ellis said. He turned away for a second and his eye caught the red light on the video recorder, reminding him the last few minutes had all been taped. He turned back to Grif.

"I'm going to take this tape with me. I know how to get hold of the goons who've been following up on your...not my...debt. I'm going to show them this tape and I'm going to tell them that you'll have their money by the end of the week. Can you do the deal by then?"

"Yes." Grif answered. "Look, Ellis, I know it's probably hard to believe, but once I realized I was screwing somebody else...somebody who had gone out of his way to help me...I knew I had to end it, man."

Ellis drained his glass, turned off the video camera, pulled the memory card out of the machine and said, "So, what will you do? Where will you go?"

"No place, man. I'll be back behind the bar when we open up again. The guy I'm selling to said he needed a good bartender. I know where he can find one. And hey, I'm sure as hell going to need the work."

"*Jesus*," Ellis sighed, as he turned and walked out.

CHAPTER 35

Later that night, Warren Whitfield was doing his best to concentrate on the architectural drawings spread across the desk in his bedroom. He had already gone to bed, then gotten up, slipped on his red and gold silk Chinese robe and spread the plans out so he could add a geometric cut-glass ornamentation to a room that even he found too Spartan. But try as he might, he couldn't keep his mind on what he was doing. Something had gone wrong in Mexico. Worse still, he didn't know what had actually happened. Or would happen next. Warren was not accustomed to being in the dark about anything that affected him. It kept him from sleeping. It kept him from focusing on his work. There was no greater irritant.

He rose and poured himself a glass of water from the stainless steel decanter on his desk. Then reaching over, he turned off the desk lamp. Sometimes it helped to be alone in the dark in his sanctuary. The moonlight spilling in from the windows comforted Warren. It renewed his appreciation of the cocoon he had constructed that combined the perfect balance of nature outside and nurture inside. The silence and the stillness helped create the feeling that time, at least for a moment, had virtually stopped to let Warren reflect on everything he had achieved and all that was still to be done. At such times, he would often wander from room to room seeing how the light, or the lack of it, played on the emptiness of each space. This night, as he walked from his bedroom, through the music chamber, past the dining cove to the grand living room, his thoughts were troubled but his spirit was as determined as ever to find answers to the questions that were plaguing him.

Often, when something happens that is incongruent with the natural order, it takes a moment to realize what's amiss. Such was the case with Warren and the faint red glow in the deep blue night. For just a second he smiled at the coming of morning, realizing he now had a reason to stay up and begin another day of work. Then, like an electric shock, it hit him. It was too early for morning. And that glow wasn't from the rising sun. It was from something burning at Eden's Edge.

The red sky was over the far end of the compound, near the garage and the utility buildings. Warren immediately went to the wall and turned on the overhead lights. Then he rushed across the room to the alcove on the opposite wall that been designed especially to hold the fully functional antique phone. Except now, it wasn't functioning. The line was dead. Warren tore out of the room and ran back through the rooms he had ambled through earlier. Racing to his desk, he picked up the phone. No dial tone. From his bedroom window the crimson sky seemed somehow closer. He unbolted the terrace doors and dashed outside to get a better look. Then wished he hadn't as his heart leapt into his throat. Not only was the entire west end of the compound on fire, but the flames were literally walking from wing to wing like a slow burning fuse. From seemingly nowhere he remembered his cell phone. He ran back into the bedroom. He knew it was somewhere. But where?

Bolting into his huge walk-in closet, he turned on the light as he entered. There, on the dresser with the other daily contents of his pockets, was the digital phone. He scooped it up and hurried back into the bedroom. His head was down, making sure the phone was on and being careful to press the 911 buttons as he walked. So he didn't see the figure standing beside his desk until he heard, "Put the phone down, father."

Looking up, Warren Whitfield saw a mirror image of himself thirty years earlier. He was momentarily confused. His mental focus seemed to wander. Then, just as quickly, it returned.

"Terrance? How dare you come here? I told you never to come here again." Warren was so distraught he never even noticed the Beretta that was being pointed at him.

"I said, put the phone down, father."

Warren Whitfield actually heard the bullet zip by his ear before he heard the crack of the shot and the crash of the glass panel in the terrace door as the round ripped through it. The rapid-fire cacophony brought him to his senses.

"What are you doing? Are you insane? I'm dialing 911. There's a fire. It's heading this way."

"I know about the fire, father. I set it. Now put the phone down," Terry said raising the pistol and pointing it at Warren's face.

"You what?" Warren said, dropping the phone on his bed. "You? What have you done?"

"It's not what I've done, father. It's what you've done. You've destroyed your own daughter. My sister."

"What are you talking about? "What do you mean?"

"She's dead, father. Dead because of your meddling. If you had let Ellis do his job, she'd be alive...and fine...and back here now. But you couldn't do that, could you? No. You had to have Rena and your money. You had to show her and everyone else that no Whitfield does anything that you don't control. Well, your control got your daughter killed. She isn't coming back, father. She's never coming back."

Listening to his son, the older man's strength seemed to ebb and he sunk slowly down on the side of his bed. "Dead? She's dead? But everything was arranged. Everything was set."

"You killed her, father. You did. Just as surely as if you had been there yourself." Terry's voice was rising. "And there's more. You killed your grandchild too. Maybe it was a boy. Maybe he would have been your heir. Another great architect like you. But you'll never know now. Will you father? You'll never know now!" He was talking louder to keep his words above the crackle of the flames and the popping of the timber that was now moving through the rooms Warren had been in just a few minutes earlier. "And for what? For what? To prove something to her? To everyone? To prove something to yourself?"

Completely befuddled now, Warren could only mumble, "What, what are you saying about some child?" Then he looked beyond Terry into the adjoining rooms and saw the flames entering.

"I was going to kill you father. For what you did. But then I thought better of it. Killing you would only let you off. Set you free. No. That's not enough penance for the master builder. Better for the master builder to see everything he's built destroyed. That will be your legacy, father. Not what you built, but what you destroyed. This enormous monument to your ego. Your daughter. Your grandchild. And me. In the end you destroyed it all, father. So live with that. Live with that legacy for the rest of your life."

Warren had never seen anyone shot before. It was as if ropes encircled his body and held him paralyzed on the edge of his bed. The last word had barely left Terry's lips when he swung the muzzle of the Beretta under his chin. Closing his eyes, he squeezed the trigger and sent the top of his skull skyward. It never reached the ceiling. Warren Whitfield was fond of massive rooms.

CHAPTER 36

During his run through the park that morning, Ellis thought about how he was going to handle his session with the elder Whitfield. He couldn't be sure the architect had given instructions to take him out. In all likelihood, that was probably Morales's idea. Ellis figured the master of Eden's Edge just wanted to keep his daughter and his money too. Maybe that's why the rich stay rich, Ellis said to himself.

After sharing a shower with Osgood and getting half dressed, Ellis fixed himself a cup of instant coffee. While he prepared to put on his socks and shoes, he turned on the television to keep him company. The picture emerged black and white and there was Alan Ladd grabbing some hood by his wide lapels and telling him what a "slimy no good" he really was. Ellis had fallen asleep the night before watching the classic movie station and he realized if he wanted the morning news he'd have to change the channel. Using the remote, he flipped through three or four programs before landing on a station that had one of those blood red bands on the bottom of the screen with scrolling white type giving you the opportunity to kill the sound if you thought the stuff at the bottom was a lot more interesting than what the anchor man was jawing about. Ellis was about to begin slipping on his socks and shoes when he began to hear a report obviously already in progress.

"...has been absolutely devastating. The entire facility, not to mention a good portion of the hillside, has simply been burned away. It took several fire departments working together to bring the blaze under control. This was actually the home, as well as the working offices and the school known as Eden's Edge."

Suddenly, Ellis's footwear was no longer the focus of his attention. He was glued to the TV set and the reporter walking in front of the scene of devastation he was describing.

"Renowned architect, Warren Whitfield's compound has been virtually leveled by this terrible conflagration. There are definitely casualties that occurred in the student dormitory area. According to authorities, neither the names nor the numbers of dead are going to be released until all identifications have been made and relatives contacted. Whitfield himself, the reclusive creator of what was an extraordinary facility that commanded a breathtaking view

of the Pacific, was found by the first firefighters on the scene before dawn came up. They said he was sitting on the hill about a hundred yards away, his back to the blaze, simply staring at the sea. Apparently in shock, he has been unable, or unwilling, to provide authorities with any information about what went on here last night. While there has been no official word as yet regarding what started this fire, there is apparently evidence of arson. At least that's what we at Channel Seven overheard being discussed between police and firemen on the scene. Although...again we caution that there has yet to be any official confirmation of that. And in another extremely bizarre twist to this terrible tragedy, there are rumors being reported...again unconfirmed by officials at this time...but there are rumors circulating on the scene here that a body was pulled from the central living quarters of the compound, and that body was said to have a gunshot wound to the head. Plus...and I know this is even harder to believe...but we've heard it from at least three sources on the scene...that the body apparently also showed signs of it's throat being cut. We're going to stay with this story as more and more information comes to light...but I'm getting word in my earpiece that we're going to go back to the studio and--"

Ellis flopped back in the chair still holding a sock in his left hand. Osgood began to tug at it. With his right hand, he picked up the remote and pushed the mute button.

As he sat there, he couldn't help but think of the photograph of Terry and Rena Whitfield. The one Terry had let him use so he'd be able to recognize Rena. They both looked so happy in that snapshot. So full of life. Then a discordant sound interrupted his thoughts. His phone was ringing. It rang four times before he eventually jerked the sock from Osgood's jaws, rose from his chair, walked over and picked it up.

"This is Ellis," he said.

"Gee. It's nicer than I hoped it would be to hear your voice."

"Laney?"

"Forgotten what I sound like already, huh?"

"No. It's just that I'm a bit distracted, I was watching television and…"

Laney interrupted him saying, "Look, if I don't just spit this out, I'm not sure I'm going to be able to say it."

"Pardon me?" Ellis said, not sure what she meant.

"I'm not coming back. I'm staying in New York."

"What? For how long?"

"For a long time, I think." Laney said. "Remember that jewelry show I was doing. Well, they want me full time now. They want me to be The Emerald Woman. There's going to be weeks of work here in New York, then a tour to lots of different cities around the world. Can you believe it? I thought I was done. But they said I was just what they needed. You know, someone not too young, but not too old either. They gave me a one-year contract with an option for another. But I've got to do all these things right away."

The silence wasn't all that long, but it was long enough.

"Aren't you going to say anything?" Laney asked.

"I'm...happy for you. You really deserve it. They couldn't have made a better choice."

"You bastard," Laney sighed. "I hoped you'd be a real creep about it. That way I wouldn't feel so lousy. Can I call you from time to time? Let you know where I am and what I'm doing. Hey, you might even wind up getting a gig that brings you to New York, huh? You seem to travel a lot in your business."

"Anything's possible," Ellis said softly. "If there's one thing I've learned, it's that."

There was an obvious pause, then Laney said, "I guess dragging this out is just going to make it harder. Isn't it?"

Ellis could tell she wasn't quite sure what to say. He simply responded, "You do what you need to do. Call me whenever you want."

"Really, that's great, cause I didn't want this to be like a good-bye, you know?"

"Yeah, I know. Take care, Laney."

He hung up the phone and looked out the window. The sky was as blue as a movie star's eyes. He looked down at Osgood and said, "Well, at least the fucking sun is shining, might as well go to the office." He knew there'd be no way to get into Eden's Edge with all the commotion up there. And now there was really no reason to go anyway.

"Yep, sport," he said, again addressing the white, short-haired anvil who was staring up at him with a look of heartfelt interest, "think I'll stop on the way and pick up a couple of coffees since this one's gone cold in the cup. Maybe even take a few minutes and let Harley know that all that trouble at the office hadn't been the work of terrorists. Yeah, I'll do that," Ellis told Osgood and himself. But then he just continued to stand there barefoot, staring out the window, holding a handful of sock.

About The Author

Joe Kilgore lives and writes in Austin, Texas. His wife, an accomplished artist, designed the cover of this book. Joe turned to writing fiction after a successful career in advertising where he created award-winning work for local, national and international clients on five continents.

Other novels by Joe Kilgore

The Blunder (2008)
The Golden Dancer (2013)

www.ingramcontent.com/pod-product-compliance
Lightning Source LLC
Chambersburg PA
CBHW050938120626
46552CB00001B/270

* 9 7 8 0 6 9 2 2 7 5 5 4 2 *